Praise fo… Kathryn Mackel'…

"In her new book *Outriders*, Kathryn Mackel takes us into a strange world of terrors and delights, a world in which science has merged with sorcery. Her writing crackles with energy and imagination, her characters are unforgettable, and she creates a world you'll want to visit again and again. Best of all, this futuristic parable is rich in life-changing spiritual truth. A wonderful and wonder-filled book!"

— Jim Denney, author of the Timebenders series

"Kathryn Mackel's *Outriders* is a fast-paced, fascinating journey into life on a bio-chemically terrorized Earth, where the forces of good and evil battle not only to survive, but for supremacy of the remaining lands and its inhabitants. God, however, hasn't forsaken His people, and Satan is still hard at work misleading struggling hearts and corrupting good intentions. Get ready for a spellbinding tale, memorable characters, and a well-drawn imaginary world. This series promises to grip teen-aged and older readers alike."

— Kathleen Morgan, author of the Guardians of Gadiel series

"Kathryn Mackel created a compelling fantasy world I didn't want to leave while tangling me in a web of adventure laced with spiritual truths. *Outriders* is not to be missed! This new series by master storyteller Mackel is going to be a classic."

— Colleen Coble, award-winning author of *Black Sands*

"A fabulous read! . . . *The Departed* gives riveting insight into the unsettling dangers of opening a door to the occult. I can't wait for her next endeavor!"

— Kelly Neutz, Namesake Entertainment

"As timely as today's *TV Guide*, Kathryn Mackel's *The Departed* offers both a chilling read and the brightness of divine truth."

— Angela Hunt, author of *Unspoken* and *The Awakening*

"*The Surrogate* is tightly woven and sharp, cutting to the marrow . . . You'll savor every page."

— Jerry B. Jenkins, author of the Left Behind series and the Soon trilogy

"*The Surrogate* is a fearless thriller that tackles uncharted territory with uncompromised skill and ease. It's a terrific and exciting read."

— Bill Myers, best-selling author of *Eli* and *Touch the Face of God*

"*The Surrogate* drives to the heart immediately and doesn't let go. I can't wait to see what it next!"

— Ralph Winter, producer, *X-Men, X2:X-Men United,* and *Planet of the Apes*; executive producer, *Star Trek V: Final Frontier*

OUTRIDERS

Also by Kathryn Mackel

The Surrogate

The Departed

OUTRIDERS

The Birthright Project: Book One

Kathryn Mackel

visit us at www.westbowpress.com

Published in Nashville, Tennessee, by WestBow Press, a division of Thomas Nelson, Inc.

Library of Congress Cataloging-in-Publication Data

Mackel, Kathryn, 1950–
Outriders / Kathryn Mackel.
p. cm.— (The birthright project ; bk. 1)
ISBN 1-59554-039-3 (trade paper)
I. Title. II. Series.
PS3613.A2734O96 2005
813'.6—dc22 2005011660

Printed in the United States of America

05 06 07 08 09 RRD 5 4 3 2 1

To Henry and Carol Norris,
with gratitude, admiration, and love.

I have been constantly on the move. I have been in danger from rivers, in danger from bandits, in danger from my own country-men, in danger from Gentiles; in danger in the city, in danger in the country, in danger at sea; and in danger from false brothers. I have labored and toiled and have often gone without sleep; I have known hunger and thirst and have often gone without food; I have been cold and naked.

2 CORINTHIANS 11:26–27

ONE

NIKI LEANED INTO THE WIND. STILL NO SIGN OF OPEN water. The endless stretch of ice was studded with boulders—not of stone but of frozen seawater, buckled and broken into a forbidding landscape.

The bone-rattling cold and shuddering winds made this arctic region a perfect pickup spot. So why the delay?

Maybe the terns were wrong. But Brady said they were never wrong, and the shelter waiting for her would be proof of that. She had arrived four days ago, stopping here because the terns swooped down and roosted on what looked like an ice boulder. On the far side, she had found a wind-carved cave, a perfect refuge for dogs and men alike.

Now the terns moved overhead in lazy circles. The dogs were quiet, content to eat or sleep until she needed them.

Niki pulled up her hood, checked the lacings of her boots, and tightened her crampons. Back home, in the forests and plains upground of Horesh, trees already budded and seedlings pushed up through moist ground. Here the only sign of spring was a sun that circled the horizon, no more than a fleck of gold straining to climb into full day.

When she picked up the dogs back in Chiungos, the weather had still been mild enough to keep her hood down and let the crisp air rush through her hair. She had forgotten how cold it could get this far north. She walked hard, her crampons biting the ice with an irritating *clip, clip, clip*. She was sick of frozen land and parched air and shy sun.

She was sick to death of trying to figure out why Brady had sent her here.

It had all come about those weeks ago, in the smithy of Horesh. Niki closed her eyes and saw the sparks flying from the grindstone as she laid her sword against the wheel. Even on this unrelenting prairie of ice, she could feel the fire of the forge. The smithy was a simple place where they sharpened swords, waxed bowstrings, notched arrows, and beat iron to fit their purpose.

Brady had bent over the anvil, hammering a horseshoe. He'd worn a heavy leather apron and gloves but no shirt—it was blazing hot between the forge and the anvil. His back was broad; his arms were heavy with muscle; his dark hair was twisted into a heavy braid and tied back to reveal silver streaks at his temples. *When had that happened?* Like Niki, he was only twenty-two.

Niki cringed at the scars lacing his back. The one on his left shoulder blade was ugly and jagged, proof that he was a warrior and not a surgeon or seamstress.

Brady looked up at her, his smile sudden and sweet.

Her blade slipped, showering sparks. "Youch!"

"Careful there, gal," Brady said.

"Careful is my middle name."

"There's some strong-arms that might dispute that." He pounded the glowing shoe.

"The ones that might dispute it, can't."

The unsaid hung between them: They can't dispute it because they're dead.

Niki fumbled to say the first thing that came to her mind. "I saw the terns come down this morning."

Brady dipped the shoe into the bucket, steam hissing around his arm. "Can you stop the wheel for a minute?"

She took her foot off the pedal, intent on the whir of the wheel as it slowed. "When are you leaving?"

"I'm not."

"I don't understand."

"I want you to take this transit, Nik."

"Me? But the transit is the leader's job."

"It's the leader's prerogative. His blessing. Which I am giving to you."

Niki shook her head. "I can't. I'm escorting Jayme's crew down to the Shoals. A monthlong mission, at least. Remember?"

"Bartoly will ride out with them. You will do this."

Her legs felt strange. Weak knees—something she had never experienced in battle. "Why would you send me away like this? I'm needed here to ride out with our people. I have a job to do."

Brady tossed his gloves aside so he could put his hand on her shoulder. "Nik, you are the bravest outrider in camp, probably the bravest in all the camps."

She lowered her gaze. "I do my duty."

"That you do. And you won't stop at anything to get it done."

He was close to her, so close she could smell his sweat and the mint leaves he loved to chew. His eyes were the color of a deep forest stream—sometimes green, sometimes brown. Always so clear, as if he had no secrets—but in this moment something secret had come between them. Though Brady's grip on her was firm, she felt him spin away.

"So why would you ask me to do something that isn't mine to do?" she said.

"Because you need time to think, Nik."

"About what?" She kept her voice light, the whirl of emotions buried deep.

A strange sorrow crept into his smile. "Let me ask you something, Nik. If you were asked, would you give up fighting?"

"I don't fight. I protect and defend. There's a difference." But he knew the difference. They had ridden out together for six years. So why did he search her face as if she were a stranger and not his second in command and comrade in arms?

"Let me ask you this," he said. "Would you give up being an outrider if God asked that of you?"

"Of course."

"Are you sure?"

"I don't understand. Why do you ask these questions? And why send me north on transit?" Her voice was a whisper, her hands tight on his.

"Because God speaks clearly over the ice. Listen, Niki." He touched her cheek, his eyes so clear she could not read them at all. "Listen well."

Since that night, she had ridden west to the Arojo range, then upriver to an outpost named Chiungos. From there she had taken the team of sled dogs further north over the snow—all the while trying to honor Brady's request that she *listen*.

As she paced, the vastness of the ice melded into the overcast sky—one hazy curtain, impenetrable and unforgiving. In four endless days of trying to listen, all she had heard were the dogs and her crampons biting into the ice.

A shiver seized Niki, shaking her from the inside out. The cold couldn't penetrate her garments, but the silence cut right through her.

All right, someone really messed up here.

Cooper was supposed to sleep through the transit. They all were.

Dr. Latham had given him, Kwesi, and Anastasia each a hefty shot of tranquilizer. He had felt drowsy and calm, barely noticing as his parents slobbered all over him and the husk molded around him. His last thought had been that he would wake up and, for the first time ever, see the sky. How jam-packin' that would be.

Sometimes it was hard to believe that a sky even existed. But Cooper knew this heaving darkness was not the sky. This was fright time, with one thought knocking at his ribs. *Not good. Not good at all.*

No one ever wakes in transit, they had told him. Ever. You go to sleep in the Ark and wake up in the world. That simple.

Leave it to Cooper to be the first. He knew he was special, but this wasn't exactly what he had programmed for himself. He'd been a little joe when the first birthrighters left the Ark, had just entered training when the first tales of valor came back. He had jammed with the other kids on stories of outriders fighting off evil stronghold princes and their frightening mogs. He had daydreamed for hours that he was a tracker, scaling cliffs, swimming rivers, crawling deep into the earth to find *originals* for Birthright.

Even with the old holovideos and the practice in simulated conditions, Cooper had trouble grasping what a river—water rushing hard and free—might feel like. One thing he did know was that he would grab the outside world by its transmogrified ears and shake it. Stories would come back to the Ark, and the name of Cooper would outshine Brady and Niki and the rest of them.

If he made it out of transit alive.

Why was he awake? Had the transit misfired? What if the three husks were to bounce and roll like this forever?

Cooper leaned left, feeling his husk pitch against what he hoped was another husk. "Stasia. Kwesi. You there?" The shroud material from which the husk was made swallowed his words just as it had swallowed him. No one would hear him. No one would know he was awake.

Another fear now—what if the husk broke open? Would he die immediately? Or would his skin be eaten through slowly while he gulped putrid air and prayed to somehow survive? They tranquilized rookies like him because transit was tough. To keep the Ark safe from discovery, they couldn't know the way back.

So why had his tranquilizer worn off? "Because you're so special, lump. Can't trank a good man to sleep when there's battles to be fought. So you woke up early. Just another notch in your reputation, Cooper."

He liked the feel of his voice coming out of his throat, even though he couldn't really hear himself. "Maybe this is just the beginning of your heroics. Staying awake in transit hasn't been done before, eya? They'll make up songs about you, the only birthrighter who had ever jammed through transit and lived to tell about it."

Assuming he did live to tell about it.

"So maybe this wasn't someone's mess-up—maybe it was meant to be. You know you're not just *no one*. You were born to be *someone*. You need to get into the world and show them what you're made of, what you think, what you can do, what you—"

He shut his mouth. What if there was only a limited amount of air? All his blabber could eat it up. He curled tight, trying to sleep. But sleep still wouldn't come. He counted seconds, then minutes.

Think jam-packin': How long would it be before he burst out of the husk and saw the sky? But the jam-punchin' bit back: How long would it be before he split through his skin with fear?

He remembered Mum's words as they sealed his husk: *The songs are given us for a reason, my son. When the time comes, sing through your fear.*

He hummed with the memory of his mother's voice, the words coming now, the music rising in him to fill the darkness:

You're one who heals the wounded.
You can calm the storm at sea . . .
Glorious! You are glorious . . .

Cooper sang it over and over, letting the music wrap him tighter than the husk, holding his praise like a lifeline, deciding he would hold it until he finally saw the sky.

Through the haze of shroud, he suddenly saw light.

"Oh, yeah." He felt a hard bounce, saw a round shadow pass over him as the first husk catapulted out. There was a flash of darkness, another rumble of air, and a second husk ejected. Cooper wrapped his arms across his chest and drew his knees up, waiting to be born again, because this is what they said it was like. Though he was supposed to sleep through this part, too, because no one could tolerate being coughed from under the ice into the cold, wide world.

Darkness closed in once more.

"No!" Cooper curled into a tight ball, feeling his heart pound into his knees. "Whatever it takes—I swear, I will do it," he said as he closed his eyes against the darkness. "Just get me out of here, please. Get me out."

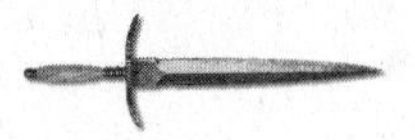

The ice sighed.

The dogs stirred, their leader growling. Niki signaled the dogs back down. "Relax. You've done this many more times than I have."

"Stay back and let it happen," Brady had said, but Niki's feet tap-danced, torn between running away from the rumbling ice or running right to it.

A white wall of ice crested upward, a mighty whack splitting the silence. The slab cracked and flipped onto itself, shattering in massive pieces. Just as it seemed the whole ice field would crack open, the slamming under the ice stopped. Dark, forbidding water lay beyond the newly formed devastation. The surface roiled, a huge bubble rising up, followed by a violent explosion of water that created an instant snow squall in the frigid air.

Niki knew what she would see next. She had made her own transit this way. Yet still she hardly dared believe it.

The back of the bowhead whale broke the surface, more massive and magnificent than anything she had collected or seen or even imagined. The creature's gray skin glistened and its tiny eye sought her out, making her want to cower. But she cowered before neither man nor creature.

The whale rolled, then arched its back. Niki's insides trembled with the ridiculous possibility that it would come right out of the water and crush her. But it held steady, riding on its tail flukes as it slowly opened its mouth. An irrational hope tugged at Niki's heart that maybe, somehow, they had gotten it wrong and this wasn't a transit off the Ark. Maybe this whale had come to take her back.

"Impossible," Niki muttered.

The bowhead rippled a fin as if to say, *Of course this is impossible.* Its jaw creaked, water and seaweed trickling out of its mouth. Its stomach erupted, shooting half-digested krill and one husk onto the ice. The bowhead gulped air and ejected the second husk. But then the creature slipped back into the water and circled, its fin sinking lower with each circle.

It was planning to dive.

"No, no, there's another one. Don't go! Stop! Don't go." Niki slipped in the freezing slime as she ran for the water. "There's supposed to be three! Don't you dare leave—not now!"

The bowhead slipped under the water, leaving silence in its wake.

Two rooks were safe in their husks, eyes closed, faces serene. Two rooks—but three terns had come to camp. Three terns had met Niki outside of Chiungos and brought her to this spot on the ice. One tern still circled, waiting for the third husk to be delivered. The whale had slipped under the water, hanging just below the surface as if to rest.

What should she make of all this? Maybe one of the rooks got too sick or scared to make the transit. Maybe the rook died in transit. But that never happened.

Did it?

Should Niki unshroud the two she had and ask them if she should be looking for a third rook? She had to do something—the water was already freezing over. She rolled the husks out of the stomach slime and onto the sled, gagging as acidified protein froze to her mittens. Behind her, she heard a tiny crinkle as the new ice cracked. The bowhead was up again.

She ran to where the gleaming eye could focus on her. "One more, you sorry sack of blubber. Give it up!"

The whale took a long draught of air, arched its back, diving this time for the deep. Niki knew all the way into her bones that it wasn't coming back.

She pulled off her jacket, her mask, mittens, tunic; kicked off her boots, but left on her pants and long shirt. She sprinted to the hole then skidded to a stop. A thin skin of ice already glazed over the water. Survival in there was a matter of a minute or less. It was insane even to consider what she was planning to do.

Niki took a huge breath and dove in.

The stillness hit her first, immense and final. The cold came next, convulsing her chest. She kicked and pulled in the whale's wake, with only seconds before her limbs numbed; a few more seconds before she slipped into a dull sleep, choking on water but not caring, too cold to fight back. Mere minutes before she died under the ice, closer to her parents than she had been in six years—they under the arctic ice, warm in the Ark, while she pressed up against the ice and eventually became the ice.

Black now, no blood, no vision, no feeling except silence and *Brady, why did you send me here? It's so silent . . .*

Niki bumped against the end of the world. But no, not the world—the bowhead. She dug her fingers into its blowhole, feeling pain as her knuckles warmed against the whale's skin.

The bowhead bucked, but she held on. The silence yielded to an explosion of noise: juices bubbling, baleen clicking, blood pounding as the whale opened its mouth.

She could let go now, go up to the surface and perhaps survive. But what if the whale felt her surrender and dove back down? She held on, kicking the whale's back with her feet, the last of her air seeping into her frozen muscles, the last of her sense slipping into darkness.

Come on, gal—just this once you could *let go.*

No. Not until the third husk was safe.

Something splintered against her back—the ice slick as the whale broke the surface. It reared back and, with a loud creak of its jaw, catapulted the husk onto the ice. Niki took in deep gulps of air, intending to jump off, but her arms and legs seemed to belong to the ice now and not to her body. She couldn't let go even if she wanted to, and so the whale would take her down into the depths and the husks would freeze onto the ice, the rooks never to see this world.

The whale tipped sideways and, with a blast of hot air from its blowhole, sent her flying off. Niki hit the ice with a thump that she could hear but couldn't feel because she was numb through and through. She skidded all the way to the sled, coming to rest against one of the husks.

"Get up," she told herself, but her limbs would not obey.

"Get up!" she yelled, and now she felt the pain as life returned to her legs. She struggled up, wrapping her coat around wet clothes that already stiffened in the wind. She slipped back into her boots, then moved clumsily to the three husks. She strapped them to the sled as best she could, grabbed the rope, and lumbered for the shelter of the cave.

Before ducking under the arch, Niki glanced back one last time at the open water.

The bowhead rose up on its flukes, blinked its eye once, and disappeared under the ice.

Two

THUNDER SHOOK BRADY OUT OF A DREAMLESS SLEEP.

He rolled out of his bunk, the ground cold under his feet. The whoosh of the river was not strong enough to dampen the thunder rumbling through the cliffs. As he yanked on his shirt and trousers, Brady muttered a quick prayer of thanks for seeing yet another day. He slipped into his boots, strapped on his short blade, and stepped outside.

Thunder rolled again, though there was not one cloud in the sky. The Blunt Cliffs towered on both sides of the river. The haze of shroud protecting Horesh stretched overhead like a colossal spider's web. A sprinkle of stars shone in the creeping dawn.

Brady ran upstream, bracing against the cold. Spring bloomed upground, but a winter chill lingered down here where the Grand River roared out of the Bashan Mountains and punched between the Blunts. He squeezed into the cleft they called the Hollow and hoisted himself onto the lookout ledge.

He slowly ducked under and up into the omniscope, a tunnel of cord and glass. The thunder rumbled through the cliffs, making the scope vibrate. Though dawn hadn't broken, Brady was in a tunnel of light. Kendo had woven a thousand curved mirrors into the cord, then suspended the top of his contraption high over the cliffs. The large mirrors aboveground passed images from one curved glass to another until coming to perfect resolution hundreds of feet below. It had taken Kendo a year to grind all the lenses, a month to silver them, and many more months to align each one so not one gleam of light would be lost.

Brady sighted north. The Bashans stood jagged and stern in the graying sky. To the west, watch fires still burned before the stronghold of Slade, but otherwise all seemed quiet. Mist rose to the south, where the Grand left the Narrows and broadened across the plains.

His throat tightened when he focused east. A hulking black mass moved out from Traxx, so immense it made the ground shake. It moved closer, and his stomach clenched in sickened realization. He had hoped—prayed—that the stronghold sorcerers would never been able to achieve such an outcome with their transmogrifications. And yet Brady had to believe his eyes.

Gargants. Men mogged by the sorcerer's potions to extreme sizes. A new weapon for Baron Alrod of Traxx in his battles against Slade.

Brady understood the strategy immediately. Gargants of this size could do what no soldiers could—leap the Narrows, the only unguarded boundary between Traxx and Slade.

Horesh had no stake in the Traxx-Slade wars, but even one gargant tumbling off the Blunts and onto the camp could bring disaster. Their living spaces, smithy, and stable would certainly be destroyed. And what of their people? Most of the birthrighters were out on mission, but two families were in camp, rescued from a mog lab and waiting for resettlement.

Brady rubbed his eyes. Perhaps this was all a dream and he could wake up from it. He stared up at the sky where the last stars winked out. No dream.

He jammed his fingers into his mouth and whistled. Canyon wrens flittered down from nesting places along the cliffs, hovering as they awaited his instructions. What course of action should he command?

"General Alarm! Ajoba is to take our deacons and children to the echo caves." Brady made each word distinct so the birds could mimic properly. "Birthrighters . . ."

Fight or flee?

The birds twittered, anxious to be off.

"Birthrighters to arms!" He whistled again, signaling the end of the messaging. The wrens flew off to rouse everyone in camp.

Fighting a horde of giants would be an impossible task.

But the birthrighters of Horesh did the impossible every day.

He knew that he had once made shoes. He knew that, once upon a lifetime, he'd had a name. He had been called by a quiet sound like the night wind in the trees, fitting because he had once been a quiet man.

Jasper. That was it—he had been Jasper, the cobbler. He had beat leather, cut it, pegged it, and made it shine. He had fit feet for marriages and funerals, for dancing and for fighting. Often those feet were no bigger than his hefty hands.

Had it been a hundred years ago or just yesterday that Jasper had been grabbed from his shop? Some dear woman had begged as he was dragged across the cobblestones: "No, not my husband. Please. Take someone else . . ."

Strong-arms had forced him to drink something that made him numb. A sorcerer had moved in on him, cloaked in shining purple, his eyes glowing like a wraith of the Narrows. He was no ghost but a man without mercy, sticking needles under Jasper's scalp, into his breastbone, even the calloused soles of his feet.

Long night followed, a darkness slashed by scarlet dreams. When Jasper reached the end of fear, his mind went numb too. As his skin split off his body, he could only stew in the mud and watch the moon shrink to nothing and fill with silver again. Many nights became one long nightmare . . . until this moment of waking.

He sat up, his head spinning. Someone shoved a bucket of ale that he gulped greedily. His eyes opened fully and saw that it was not a bucket he held but a barrel. In that moment Jasper knew that the sorcerer of Traxx had made him into what had been thought impossible. A gargant.

Jasper grabbed his own throat and tried to choke off his life. His neck was too thick with fat and bony tissue to dig his windpipe out from his skin.

A whip bit into his back. "Enough of that, drudge! Up with you, now."

Jasper shook his head, refusing. A chain slammed the side of his head. Let them scourge him to death. But their blows were no worse than a cuff. The strong-arms before whom he had once quaked were now entirely inadequate to kill him. Others like him sat or lay around nearby, a mass of gargants that could not be moved, despite threats and thrashings.

A hum arose, a steady drone that cut through the bellowing of the strong-arms and slapping of their whips. The sound deepened, a metal-hard buzz that made Jasper's teeth vibrate.

Hoornars!

Flooded with panic, Jasper wrapped his arms over his head. The hoornar came from above, stinging his back, igniting his skin. He pushed to his feet. He was willing to die, but he could not endure a death like the one a hoornar would deliver.

He had always been terrified of hornets and wasps, quaking when a mild honeybee merely brushed his hand. Once he had stepped in a hive hidden under a mound of feed hay. His foot had pulsed for days, but it was his sleep that suffered most as stinging creatures swarmed his every dream. And they had just been little insects, not like this mogged beast that hovered above him, its strong-arm rider clutching its reins, his jab-hand at the ready.

Jasper clenched his teeth, trying to find the will to unfold his arms and face the stinger head-on. If only he could offer his heart to be burst with venom, he could be done with this monstrous existence that had been forced on him. But he turned just as the stinger curled back toward him, his instinct to flee overruling his desire to die.

"Move forward," the strong-arm rider roared.

Jasper broke into a shuffling run. The others ran with him, a wall of flesh rushing away from the rising sun.

It was going to be a good day.

On this day Baron Alrod, the crown and glory of Traxx, jewel of the east, would watch his newly hatched gargants jump over the Narrows and into Slade. His pleasure would be complete when he personally stuffed Prince Treffyn's spine down his throat and took over that goat's stronghold as his own.

His valet, Sado, dressed him for battle, his hands gnarled but skillful, eyes dim but nevertheless seeing to his master's needs. Sado was a royal retainer, having risen from the ranks of drudges to a limited freedom and the privilege of serving an exalted master.

Alrod had taken no breakfast this morning. He was prone to airsickness, though he would sooner slash Sado's throat than allow one inkling of that minor flaw be known. He slipped into a high-necked shirt and long pants, admiring his own muscled body, an original masterpiece with no need for transmogrification.

He held his arms out so Sado could strap his armor to him. An elephant could drive its foot into Alrod's chest and this armor, mogged from the skin of a crocodile, would not buckle. His strong-arms had to make do with lizard-skin armor, but the Baron insisted on rare transmogrifications for himself.

Before fastening his master's helmet, the old man held the water bottle to Alrod's lips. "Are you sure, high and mighty, that you will take not one bite of fruit?"

"No. Send for my mount." Alrod's master sorcerer, Ghedo, had mogged Nighteye from a bat. It was an exquisite transmogrification that had taken generations to bring forth, but it produced the perfect flyer for the baron of Traxx.

"Nighteye is at the ready. Hanging off the royal turret, ready to fly."

Alrod swung his arm around, whacking Sado full in the chest. "Nighteye is not to be taken from her perch until the moment I am ready for her."

His valet went to his knees, his face as low to the floor as his injury would allow. "Beg pardon, high and mighty. I did not know. I was simply . . . anxious . . . about what this day would bring."

"Up, man. I give you pardon. But if she falters, it will be your head. Now get that lolly you've acquired . . . what was her name?"

"Dawnray."

Dawnray. How fitting. "Take the girl up the west turret. Make sure she has full view of today's battle. Do it now—I want her to see me take flight on Nighteye."

Sado hastened away. As Alrod climbed the stairs, blood rushed through his belly, making him burn for battle. The gargants were mighty, both in size and number. He would watch it all from Nighteye's back, winging high above the carnage, enjoying the moment they did what his strong-arms were too frightened and his hoornars too few to do safely—cross the Narrows and stomp into Slade territory.

By noon today, he would have Prince Treffyn's head on a stake and his liver swinging in the breeze. By the time the sun set, Alrod would rule both Traxx and Slade.

In the cool of night, he would seek out the new lolly that Sado had brought to the palace. Word was that she was a rare find—a peasant by birth but royal in her beauty. His wife, Baroness Merrihana, had failed him over and over, but perhaps by the time the sun rose again, his heir would already be brewing in Dawnray's womb.

Indeed, it would be a good day.

THREE

THUNDERHOOF JERKED AGAINST HER BRIDLE, SPOOKED by the shaking of the earth. Brady patted her glossy black neck as he looked up at Kendo. "How many?"

"Too many to count. Hundreds, at least." Kendo peered east from his perch in a lofty sycamore tree. A hard-muscled man with black hair and fierce eyes, he was never excitable, speaking in a placid tone even now. "Strong-arms on hoornars are driving them. I see only two hoornars—no, wait, there's another. Ah, mate, there's at least six of them, stinging the poor souls. Plus a full division of strong-arms behind the gargants."

"How big are they?"

"Fifteen feet tall at least, some bigger than twenty. Strike that—*most* are bigger than twenty feet."

As Kendo scrambled down, Brady busied himself with his armor. Unlike the iron mail of ancient knights or the mogged thick-skin armor favored by strong-arms, Birthrighter armor was light and flexible. More like fabric than a protective shell, it was woven from silk, wire, and shroud—the heavenly given material that was *out-of-time*. The shroud made it almost impervious to assault—*almost* because shroud armor had to have pores or the wearer would simply be out-of-time and of no earthly good.

Timothy worked with Taryan at the edge of the Hollow, hoisting the scope up and out of the cleft in the cliff. "Brady, did you at least *consider* breaking camp and making a run for it?" Timothy managed to glare and to focus on his work at the same time.

"Got a better plan?" Taryan snapped as she cut open the scope.

"It's all right. Timothy has the right to question." Brady kept his voice even, with no hint of accusation. "And the best answer I can offer is this: this plan we've devised—"

"*You* devised," Timothy said.

Was Timothy's resistance a normal reaction to an extreme threat? Or was a rebellion brewing that Brady would need to attend to? "The plan seems the right thing to do," he said.

"Well, I pray it is," Timothy muttered.

"I pray the same thing." Brady nodded, trying to keep his tone, his face—even the bearing of his shoulders—calm and confident.

"Aye," Kendo said, swinging onto his horse.

"And amen," Taryan said, her eyes shining as she looked up at Brady.

Timothy pulled out the last length of scope. "And amen."

Brady reined Thunderhoof toward the east. Still a league away, the horde emerged from their own cloud of dust, heads bobbing on massive shoulders, arms swinging, legs thudding. He waved for Kendo to get onto his horse. "We've got to get going, draw those hoornars out before the mogs get any closer."

"Hold up, mate. We've got a minor complication." Kendo pointed to a russet-skinned girl standing in the brush that hid the entrance to their caves.

"Ajoba! Get back to the caves and attend to your responsibilities," Brady shouted. Another problem he'd have to deal with later. The gargants took vast priority for now. He nodded to Timothy and Taryan. "Blessings on you both."

"And on you," Taryan said.

Brady raced with Kendo toward the rising threat.

Ajoba disregarded Brady's order to return to the caves. Though he was the leader of Horesh, it mattered not. She took directions from a higher power now.

It had been two weeks since Demas had come to her in the darkest hour of the night. Ajoba had just returned from a teaching mission through the outer villages of Slade, speaking to anyone who would listen. She had collapsed on her mat, praying about the books she had left behind, the mysteries that would unfold as the villagers—especially their children—learned to read. The stronghold princes deliberately kept the commoners in ignorance, killing or enslaving the few stronghold citizens who dared go out into the villages and plains to teach simple math and letters. But the stronghold princes could not kill the hunger of the human mind.

When light flickered in the corner, Ajoba barely had strength to turn her head. The silver spilling across the hard-packed dirt had to be the moon. But the moon was in crescent, insufficient to fill her hut with this spangle of soft light. Manueo must be making puppet magic with his fingers and a lantern. He was a loyal deacon, but far too immature for a man with gray hair and rheumy eyes.

"Who's there?" she asked.

"Sister Ajoba."

Not Manueo, indeed not. This voice was as silver as the light. She sat up, intrigued. "Here I am."

"You can do more."

She pulled her knees to her chest.

"You *must* do more," he said.

"Requesting pardon, but who are you, please?"

An unseen presence pressed the air from her lungs. "You do not know?"

He came clear now, his hair longer than Brady's, his eyes flashing like fool's gold in the water of the Shallows. Folded wings extended above his head, translucent and veined with diamond dust. Without touching her, he pulled her to her feet. "Child, can it be that you have never seen one like me?"

Ajoba lowered her eyes, strangely ashamed that she had not.

"My name is Demas. I have been sent to guide you." His voice was the only thing about him that didn't flow; it was more percussion than woodwind.

Dismay flooded her. "Tell me how I have strayed, and I will correct my ways!"

"You have been good and you have been faithful, young Ajoba. But you can do more, and I will show you how." He dipped his head toward hers. "If you will allow me."

She bit her lip. "Of course."

"Do you hesitate?"

"It's just . . ." She breathed in, smelling her own fatigue. Was that smoke? It must be closer to sunrise than she realized if Manueo was stoking the fire for breakfast.

"You hesitate!" His wings hunched upward. If he opened them, surely he would break through the walls of her hut. "Should I seek another?"

She reached out, surprised that she could close her fingers over his upper arm. "You don't need to look for another."

"So it shall be." He bowed his head and, in a whirl of silver, left her hut. She watched as he flew along the river, a streak of light that cast no shadow.

He had visited her four times since, warning her not to tell the others that she had been singled out. *Jealousy, my child.* He had helped her deepen her tone to preserve her voice and to sharpen her words.

Demas had shown her places where Horesh was weak: Brady's weariness; Kendo's preoccupation; Niki's impatience; Timothy's dissatisfaction. *You must not expect such fragile ones to lead you, my child.* With each visit, he taught her how to lead and how to follow.

In the early haze of this dawn, Ajoba had settled the families and deacons deep in the echo caves and told them what they must do. Then, as she looked for a suitable cleft for herself, Demas had appeared once more. He'd said simply: *Go up and do it quickly.*

She raced along the hairpin route that Brady and Kendo had cut on the face of the east Blunt. She hadn't meant for Kendo to spot her as she snuck into the brush, but his eyes were so sharp. No matter—she still had to obey Demas.

As she watched the horde approach, the ground trembled under her feet. She felt no fear; just the stir of anticipation that she was where she would be needed.

Some willingly submitted to transmogrification, wanting to be stronger or more beautiful. But not this, surely not this. These people charging with Jasper had once tickled children and hugged mothers and kissed lovers. Now they were monsters rumbling across the plains toward the Grand River.

They intend to drive us right over the Narrows, Jasper realized. At their closest point, the Blunt cliffs were only twenty feet apart. Both Slade and Traxx had tried to build bridges over that gap, but the ghouls that lived between the cliffs punished all attempts. No man or beast dared try to cross the Narrows.

Jasper and the others were big enough now merely to jump across.

He grabbed the arm of the man next to him. "Kinsman, let us slow down, turn to the side." Or that is what he meant to say, but the words came out thick and halting: "Slow. Turn."

The man turned his head, one eye rolling back, the other slowly fixing on Jasper. He opened his mouth, trying to form words as well, but his tongue was as thick and prickly as a roll of hay. Howling, he raised his fist and battered his own face.

Jasper stepped away, pushing against what surely must be a woman, but her face was craggy, as if someone had set rocks under her skin. "Change. Course," he struggled to say, nodding toward the north. "Maybe. Mountains."

She reached for him, her eyes sparking with comprehension. As he grasped her hand, her fingers snapped in his grip like twigs. She shrieked in pain and tumbled away. She would not survive this mad rush but be crushed under the feet of the horde.

Within hours, the animals would begin to feed. After a few days, she would be a pile of broken bones and little else.

Such was the fate of failed mogs.

Jasper bumped against a man with a head the size of a full-grown bull on a neck that was too slim and would surely break soon. Another man had no neck at all, his beard and chest hair one continuous mat, his arms short and with no hands—no, he did have hands but they hadn't mogged with the rest of the body. Tiny fingers wiggled at the end of arms the size of tree trunks.

How long had it taken for the sorcerers of Traxx to make them like this? Had it happened overnight or over a decade? Was Jasper's wife still crying for his return, or had she gone to dust?

Heat striped his shoulders, and Jasper turned, expecting to see his back dripping with hoornar poison. But it was a flare of light that sizzled on his skin as morning broke the horizon behind them. What would this day bring? If he survived the leap over the Narrows and broke through the armies of Slade, people—children—would die.

Jasper could not live with that, nor could he live like this—a human transmogrified to something that surely was never intended. He vowed to be the first to reach the Narrows, the first to greet the ghouls face-to-face by plunging off the east Blunt and into the darkness below.

Brady had faced death many times but never with Horesh at stake. He laid out his fire arrows, swallowing back fear, remembering Niki's face over the fire of the forge, the iron in her voice as she asked—never would she beg—not to be sent on transit. If he had gone and she had stayed, would she have chosen a different course?

Timothy had opposed this plan. Yet he and Taryan stood at the edge of East Blunt, armed only with the scope. Brady tried to push the image of Taryan's sweet face from his mind. She would be all right—the plan was a good plan. Unorthodox perhaps, but wasn't that true of all their plans?

Kendo had cut free the large mirrors upground that fed light to his omniscope. He and Brady stood on opposing ridges, where they would deflect the rays of the rising sun westward. Timothy and Taryan had the trickier task; finding the right angle with the length of scope to catch and magnify the light. All this while the ground shook and the horde of gargants thundered down on them.

First Brady and Kendo had to take down the six hoornars driving the horde. The most they had ever battled before was four, and that had been with a full crew of outriders. Would Kendo's fire arrows even work? He had been experimenting with explosive powder all winter, but that was under controlled conditions.

No time for doubts now. The moment was upon them. Brady slipped on the silk-and-shroud mask that completed his armor.

The ground shook as the leading edge of the horde drew near to the neck of land between the two ridges. Flames flashed across the way—Kendo taking down the first hoornar with an exploding arrow into its eye. With a scream, its strong-arm rider plunged into the trampling horde.

Brady lit his first arrow, praying that Kendo had wound the packed tip correctly and it wouldn't blow up in his hand. He nocked the arrow and let it fly.

Fire exploded harmlessly an arm's length from the hoornar's face. A near miss—but it might as well have been a hundred paces. The creature dove at Brady, its buzz rattling his eardrums.

Brady drew his sword and slashed. His blade bounced off the stinger with a loud clang, as if it had struck granite. The sorcerers had been at work again, refining the hoornars so their stingers were impenetrable. The hoornar tipped but righted quickly, curling its stinger, ready to deliver a killing blow.

Brady grabbed the hoornar's legs and swung up so the stinger curled under him. He wrapped his legs around the hoornar's underbelly and thrust with his sword, finding that tender spot between the abdomen and thorax where the rider's saddle was fastened. The strong-arm jabbed at him, but the hoornar's frantic wings shielded Brady. He yanked, bringing the saddle free and tumbling the strong-arm off.

As the dying hoornar spiraled downward, Brady leaned sideways, using his weight to spin the mog back toward the ridge. He jumped off and was about to load another fire-arrow when two hoornars came for him. He hacked, severing the head clean off one. Its strong-arm rider jumped onto the ridge, but Brady shoved him to the edge and over, where he tumbled into the horde, now passing between the ridges.

Time was running out—the gargants were less than half a league from the Narrows. If Brady and Kendo couldn't clear the sky of hoornars, nothing would persuade the gargants to turn away. Brady quickly nocked another arrow, lit it, let it fly. It found its mark, exploding into the underbelly of a hoornar and bringing it down.

Kendo signaled from across the ridge—the sky was clear of strong-arms. Brady picked up his own mirror and positioned it so the broader curve caught the light from the rising sun. The light coursing across the length of the mirror—no longer than his arm-span—was enough to almost blind him.

Then a broad shadow swooped down on Brady, blocking the light from the east. Alrod, riding the mogged bat called Nighteye.

Brady carefully put the mirror down—if it broke, the plan would be in severe jeopardy. He lit a fire-arrow and swung it in the bat's face, blinding its light-sensitive eyes. Alrod sliced the arrow in half, then reined the bat in a tight circle, intending to slice Brady in half as well.

He rolled under the sword, then leaped immediately up so he could grab the underside of Nighteye's harness. Alrod laughed and yanked Nighteye's tether. As the bat rose high above the horde, Alrod leaned over her head and jabbed with his sword, trying to dislodge Brady.

He kicked sideways with enough momentum to swing up onto

her wing. Her wing convulsed, turning her body sideways. Brady grabbed a fistful of sleek fur and crawled onto her back. Alrod sat in a combination harness-saddle, mogged from cowhide into livery softer than any leather and almost as strong as iron.

Alrod raised his sword, but Brady was quicker, jamming Alrod's blade back with his short blade. He slammed his shoulder against the baron's, causing him to drop the sword. Brady jabbed with his short blade, pain shooting up his arm as the blade slammed against impenetrable armor.

With Alrod slashing back at him, Brady dug his heels hard into Nighteye's ribs, trying to drive her back toward the ridge. She squealed in protest, and a small part of Brady felt pity. She hadn't volunteered for this battle, any more than those poor souls who had been mogged into gargants. Still, he had to force her back to the ridge. Time was short. He needed to lift his mirror to the light—Alrod would have to wait.

Nighteye refused to fly downward. Her instinct prevailed, and she flew straight up. Almost in the clouds now, Brady could see the field of battle stretched out below. Mammoth heads bobbed as the gargants continued to move west, even though the hoornars that had been driving them had been cut from the sky.

Light sparkled at the top of East Blunt Cliff, where Timothy and Taryan stood with the scope, waiting for him and Kendo to shine a brilliant light back to them. Directly below, arrows exploded in harmless bursts. Even Kendo wasn't strong enough to shoot an arrow this high.

Alrod had a scimitar out now, hacking at Brady. As they grappled, the razor-edged blade cut through part of Nighteye's leathery wing, causing the creature to cyclone sideways. Brady swung a leg over Alrod's shoulder and stomped hard. It was like kicking granite, but the shock of his foot was enough to make the baron drop the sword.

Alrod pulled Brady into a headlock, but thankfully his armor made it impossible to form a tight enough vise to choke Brady. "Surrender, outrider," Alrod roared.

"What? And spoil all this fun?" Brady inched forward and yanked Nighteye's ears, pushing her head down so her struggles took them groundward.

Below, Taryan and Timothy still stood their ground, waiting to raise the scope. The gargants were drawing close, but Brady was a hundred feet over where he needed to be. He reached down, buried his hands deep into Nighteye's velvety fur, found the harness that kept Alrod's saddle on. When he secured a grip, he drew his legs up and rolled onto the creature's head. The momentum carried Alrod up over his back and onto Nighteye's snout.

The disoriented animal shook its head, chittering in distress as she continued to spiral downward, injured wing fluttering wildly. The baron grabbed fur on both sides to hold on. Brady clung to the harness with white knuckles as wind whistled past his ears.

"Save me, and I will spare you," Alrod gasped.

"High and mighty—you are about to become low and trampled." Brady kicked hard, dislodging the baron. He caught a fleeting glimpse of Alrod bouncing off one gargant's back onto another on the way to the ground. Then a wrenching shudder from Nighteye grabbed his attention.

She was trying to fly upward again, but the slit in her wing had lengthened. She veered wildly to the right, heading straight toward the cliff. Brady reached for her ears, yanking backward, trying to keep her on a straight line with the cliff, but she had lost all ability to respond. With a panicked screech, she crashed headfirst into the rock.

Brady just had time to leap from Nighteye's head and roll clear before the wounded mog toppled to earth and into the path of the panicked gargants.

The horde drove at them, the very ground buckling under Timothy's feet. The noise was immense: hammering feet, rushing water from deep in the Narrows, cries of fear and fury. Timothy wanted to scream with the same fear and fury, to ignore Brady's plan, to drop the scope and run for his life.

Suddenly both ridges came alive with light. Brady and Kendo had raised their mirrors, caught the rising sun, and fed it toward the Narrows. Even now doubt gripped Timothy—*could this possibly work?*

"Now!" Taryan called. "Lift it high!"

He raised the scope, shifting the array of mirrors to catch the flash of the sun as it rose behind the backs of the gargants and was magnified by Brady's and Kendo's mirrors.

The long shadow cast by the horde crept toward them.

"Angle higher," Timothy said, hoping they would get this right in the moments they had before those massive bodies roared over them. Why had Brady ever thought this insane idea would work? And yet, as Timothy strained to change the angle of the woven cord, he hoped, prayed that it must. As always, his prayer took the form of music.

"Glorious," he sputtered, lifting the scope over his head and trying to catch a reflection of the mirrored light—itself merely a reflection, a shadow, of the truly glorious.

Timothy smelled the gargant's sweat in fetid waves, but he sang even through this thought: *At least I'll die like a man.* Somehow his music took hold, keeping his feet in place, his hands tight on the woven cord:

Can you hear the distant thunder?
Can you feel the tremble of the earth?

The scope caught the sun, exploding light in the faces of the gargants.

The mogs twisted, their shoulders following the instinctive turn of their heads. Yet their feet still carried them straight at the Narrows, so panicked they had been by the stings of the hoornars.

"Scream!" Taryan shouted. "Now!"

Screeching rose from the echo caverns that laced the Blunt

Cliffs. The voices of the deacons and the rescued ones, magnified by the steep hollows and clefts of the Narrows and accompanied by the din of sticks on pots, rose unearthly and incredibly loud, as if the Grand River itself was howling. Timothy bellowed along with them—so hard his lungs seemed to turn inside out.

The poor gargants groped at their heads, unsure whether to block their eyes or cover their ears against the barrage of light and noise.

"They're turning," Timothy said. "They're turning!"

One gargant after another turned away until the heart of the horde had turned toward the rising sun. They resumed their headlong rush—just as Brady had promised—this time back toward Traxx. They paid no heed to the panicked soldiers who had sheltered in their wake, but simply stormed over them.

Timothy and Taryan held the scope high until the dust cleared and all they saw was a mountain of flesh receding back into the east.

"We did it!" Taryan cried.

Timothy grinned and let the song come back:

Glorious! You are glorious!
We sing your praise in all the earth!

Suddenly there was a heavenly choir singing "Glorious" as well. But no, it was just their comrades in the Narrows, their singing magnified as it echoed between the Blunt Cliffs and rose into the dawn.

Timothy and Taryan hugged and danced, laughing and whooping. Then she pulled away, shading her eyes.

"What's wrong?" he asked.

"That." She pointed east.

A lone gargant staggered out of the retreating horde, his head lowered as he wheeled back around to his original course.

He has no intention of leaping across the Narrows, Timothy realized. The poor soul was on a determined sprint to death.

Ajoba had just slipped out of her hiding place when she saw the gargant charging down on her. She raised her hands, palms open, hoping he could see her. "Friend, I ask you to stop!"

The gargant stumbled, then came to a lumbering stop, swaying before her. His words sounded like ragged explosions. "I. Can. Not."

Something whisked overhead. The gargant yanked a fistful of arrows out of his arm as if they were splinters. Taryan stood to the south, bow up and ready to shoot again. Timothy ran in from the upriver side. Kendo hopped off his horse, ran for the cliff. They meant to trap the mog and fell him away from the Narrows.

Ajoba stepped between the gargant and the cliff's edge. "There is hope, brother, if you would only stop and turn north."

His misshapen face was soaked with tears. "No. Hope."

"Ajoba, get away from him," Brady said as he moved in behind the gargant. Taryan edged closer, her brace of arrows aimed at the gargant's throat.

"No! I beg you, Taryan. Don't." Ajoba stepped between the giant and Taryan, knowing it was a ridiculous gesture. Kendo had sheathed his sword and now aimed a spear at the man's face. Ajoba circled the gargant, trying to block him from each of her comrades.

"Tell them. Don't bother," the gargant muttered. "I. Will. End myself."

Ajoba wrapped her arms around his leg, the size of a tree. "While there is still hope?"

Brady spoke softly but steadily: "We pity him as well, Ajoba. But if you will not think of us, think of the ones in our care."

The gargant reached down with fumbling fingers to pry her off. "Let. Me. Die."

"There is hope," she told him, realizing as she said it that this was why Demas had sent her upground. It was for this moment that she had been called.

"I promise you," she added with growing confidence. "Head north and you will live. I know this, and I swear it."

Brady gave her a quizzical look but lowered his sword, his forearm still tensed and ready to strike. "Friend, if we put down our weapons, will you do what she asks?"

The gargant slowly bent at his waist so his face was almost to Ajoba's. "No place to go back to. Only. Death."

"There is life. I—"

"A troop of Traxx strong-arms have broken out from horde and are heading this way!" Timothy said.

Ajoba held fast. "Friend, hear me. If you head to the Bashan Mountains, you will find hope and you will find life. Will you do that?"

Kendo's voice was barely a whisper as he hefted his spear. "Brady, shall I?"

"Wait," Brady said. "Friend, will you leave?"

The gargant fixed his gaze on the deep gulf that was the Narrows. For a dark moment, Ajoba thought he was going to lean forward and tumble in.

Instead, he bent to her and touched the crown of her head. "Is this true, little one?"

"It is. I swear it on my life."

The gargant nodded his ponderous head, straightened, and turned north. Gradually he broke into a thunderous jog, heading for the foothills of Bashan.

Four

A blizzard had swept in from the south. Niki looped a rope around the rooks' waists and anchored them to each other and herself so they wouldn't stumble away in the snow. It wouldn't do to lose them just hours after coming out of the whale.

"What do we do?" Anastasia muttered, trying to disappear into her parka.

"Stay by the sled." Niki strained to make herself heard over the howling wind. She pulled an ax from her pack and began to hack at the ice.

"I'll help," Kwesi said.

"I said to stay there." Brady would not be pleased if she brought these kids back with fingers missing from frostbite—or worse. She worked feverishly, grateful for the labor that brought heat back into her chilled limbs. In a short time she had hacked out crude blocks of ice. She allowed Kwesi to help her stack them while the other two unwrapped the tarp that covered most of the top of the sled. She had them turn the sled on its side and jam it against the blocks to form a small lean-to. They stacked more blocks around the back of the sled and used an extra length of tarp to form a windbreak for the dogs.

Niki hustled the rooks into the shelter.

"Shouldn't we bring the dogs in with us?" Anastasia said.

"This is their natural habitat. They *want* to stay out." Niki pulled the flap over the opening, thinking how few natural habitats were left in this world. She tossed the rooks food packets, told them to eat, and then went outside to plug the cracks of their lean-to with snow. The dogs huddled in a tight circle behind the windbreak to chew on their provisions, unconcerned with the storm.

An hour later the shelter was warm from their body heat. The air smelled like the soy paste that Niki had insisted the rooks eat. After being inside the whale for who knows how long, they needed nourishment. She had forced herself to eat it as well—it would have more calories than the dried meat she preferred and thus help her stay warm. She had expended what little reserve she had had building this shelter.

Niki was still naked under her jacket and snow pants while she waited for her unders, pants, and shirt to thaw and dry. Anastasia had asked how they had gotten wet. "Stupid accident," was all she would say. It wouldn't do to let the rooks know—especially the silent Cooper—that something had gone wrong with their transit.

"Since we're just sitting here, let's do some transit business," she said. "Letters first."

The letters were the only contact birthrighters had with their loved ones on the Ark, often more welcome than the rooks themselves. As the kids passed them to Niki, she tied them into one bundle, wrapped it in shroud, and stuffed it into her jacket. Letters from her parents and brother Rian would be among them, but right now she needed to be leader and not daughter or sister. The letters pressed against her side, a cold reminder of all she had left behind to come out into this world.

"All right. Now, can someone start the need-to-knows?"

The rooks stared at her. Their faces were paler than she'd realized a human face could be. Even Kwesi's ebony skin seemed washed out, like a dark cloth that goes to gray when left too long in the sun.

"Anytime now," Niki said, trying to sound friendly.

Cooper kept his gaze fixed on his knees. Anastasia poked Kwesi.

"Grab this one, ma'am," Kwesi said. "We're bridgin' on—"

"Not *we*," Anastasia said. "The builders. We're birthrighters now."

"Yea, that we are. Anyway the builders are bridgin' this road of weightlessness. Low *gs* on their way to zee *gs*."

"What? What did you say?" Niki's head pounded already; she didn't need Kwesi's jangle to confound her. And when had she become a *ma'am*?

"The builders are bridgin', I said."

"She's not gleanin'," Anastasia whispered. "Speak it old."

Old? Niki was a ma'am *and* old? The rooks were sixteen. She was only six years older.

Kwesi rolled his eyes. "It's like this. They're um . . . making great progress on weightlessness. Do you glean it?"

Niki grabbed his head, pulling his eyelids up with her thumbs.

"Youch! What?" Kwesi yelped.

"The way your eyes were rolling, I thought you might be having a seizure. Because I know you would never be so rude as to make that expression in the presence of a camp elder."

"No, of course not." Kwesi shrunk back, rubbing his eyes.

Niki sat back down, suppressing a smile. "Now can one of you tell me what the builders need us to know?"

Kwesi opened his mouth to speak, but Anastasia hushed him. "Sorry. What Kwesi meant was that the builders have jammed . . . I mean . . . we have been gifted with a form of weightlessness. The prophetics have been coming for a couple of years now, but until someone tried engineering the antigravity thing, no one realized it would actually work."

Niki rubbed her own eyes now, trying to get her mind around the concept. "You saying that the Ark is going to sail up to the stars? Is that the plan?"

Anastasia shook her head. "The mission is the same—wait to be called back up into this world. The builders think maybe that the weightlessness will allow them to cross the toxlands when the Ark is called to sail."

"It's so *fame*," Kwesi gushed before wilting under Niki's glare. "I mean, cool. I mean . . . um . . . neat . . . jammin' . . ."

"I get it, rook," Niki said dryly.

"We get to play in it," Anastasia said, her hands fluttering her enthusiasm. "You can dive in headfirst and fly, without falling . . ."

"Is there any practical purpose?" Niki said. "Anything we can use out here in the world without compromising the Project?"

"No. Sorry." Anastasia said.

Niki shrugged. The only thing birthrighters had ever been allowed to take off the Ark was the spindle for spinning shroud and their letters. All birthrighters had to live in this world with only the tools found here. If need ever arose, the Ark had lasers for defense. But her children fought with swords, spears, and their own ingenuity.

"That's all I need to know on that. You can report in full back at Horesh. Is that it for the need-to-knows?"

Kwesi poked the skinny redheaded boy. "Didn't you have the *solitary*, Coop?"

Cooper looked up, his brown eyes still glazed. He hadn't spoken one word aloud yet, having simply nodded when Niki had asked him if he had come through transit all right. It was Kwesi—the apparent leader of this group—who had introduced himself, Anastasia, and finally, as if he were an afterthought, Cooper.

"I had to listen to your garbage about diving headfirst into some useless chamber and all this time there was a solitary?" Niki felt like throwing all three out into the snow.

Anastasia punched Cooper. "Nice blow, joe. You got the call, so give it a roll."

"Sorry," he said hoarsely. "I . . . um . . ."

"They had you memorize it, right? So just go ahead; say it." Niki was surprised at the motherly gentleness in her own voice. Something must have happened to this boy in transit. Why else would the bowhead have dived before spitting out his husk? When Niki cut through the shroud, his eyes had been wide and his hands trembling.

Cooper took a deep breath. "The Ark has lost contact with Arabah."

Anastasia gasped. Niki put her hand to her mouth, trying to keep back her own shock. "Are the builders sure?"

Cooper nodded.

Niki was rocked to the core. Camps were attacked, birthrighters killed. But someone always survived to send the collections back and report in. Each camp was on its own; they weren't allowed to know the locations of the other camps. It was too dangerous to each other's security and, ultimately, to the security of the Ark.

Never before had an entire camp lost contact.

The builders must be very concerned if they were sending this news to Horesh. Their camp had survived the longest and had the largest troop of seasoned outriders. If a rescue was to be mounted, it would be Brady and Niki who rightfully would be asked to take it on.

She leaned forward. "How long have they been silent?"

"At least three months. They missed a collection call—"

"Which sometimes happens," Anastasia said.

Niki gave her a withering look. The girl shrank back, pulling her hood tighter around her face.

"Just one?" Niki asked.

Cooper nodded.

Niki had guarded crews who had missed a collection drop because of rampaging mogs or battling strongholds. "Anastasia is right; that does happen. So there must be something else."

"Arabah was scheduled for a transit. The builders sent out eels and got the sharks in return—Arabah's signal—so they figured the camp was ready to receive the rooks. They signaled for a whale, shrouded the rooks in husks, and sent them out."

"My cousin went out in that group," Kwesi said, his eyes dull.

Cooper raised his eyes, seeming to draw strength from Kwesi's concern. "Weeks later, a bowhead knocked against the collection port. Someone thought it was marked as the bowhead who had done the transit, but everyone said no, it couldn't be. Because the whales do it just once."

Cooper coughed. Niki passed him the water bottle. The Ark was kept at perfect humidity. But out here, even in a snow squall, the frigid air could dry a body out quickly.

"What happened?" Kwesi said.

"The divers signaled with the light, to release what they thought were collections. They expected it to be an Arabah shipment, weeks late. The bowhead coughed up the husks at the collection port with the rooks still in them."

Cooper finally looked at Niki. "They debated halting the next transit—ours. But they needed to get the word out to Horesh. They kept it as a solitary so Anastasia and Kwesi wouldn't panic."

"That's insulting. I wouldn't panic." The gooseflesh on Kwesi's neck said otherwise. "What happened to the rooks?"

Cooper rubbed his temples. "The builders had to keep them shrouded in the husks, like they were any other collected species."

"They put them in storage?" Anastasia's voice squeaked with indignation.

"How could they do that?" Kwesi narrowed his eyes at Niki, as if this were all somehow her fault.

"They would have to," Niki said. "They'd been out into the world, even if they hadn't been picked up or opened. There would be no way to ensure they hadn't been contaminated. Cooper, what are the specific instructions for Horesh?"

Cooper wrapped his arms tightly around his chest. "They gave me the coordinates so Horesh could check out the camp. The builders want to know what happened and why. They're still hoping . . ."

Against hope, Niki thought. "Is that it, Cooper?" She swallowed back a bitter taste, struggled to keep her voice calm.

"One more thing," he said, his voice low.

"What?"

"They've received a strange prophetic. It's simple, but they're not sure what it means. Perhaps you will."

She nodded. "Go on."

He caught her gaze for the first time since coming out of his shell. He was so young, but the haunted look in his eyes seemed ancient. "This is what they were told: *The seams are loosening . . .*"

"Seams? What seams? You mean the Ark?"

Cooper looked down at his hands. "No."

"Then what?"

He clenched his hands, worrying his knuckles. "They worry that it has to do with the earth's magnetic core. The instruments indicate an impending shift."

"I don't understand," Niki said.

"They don't either. If the poles reverse . . ."

"What?"

Cooper's mouth was tight, his hands like rocks against his chest. "They don't know. The world could just blow apart."

Kwesi and Anastasia glanced at each other but wouldn't look at Niki. Better that way—she had no assurance for them.

Niki closed her fingers on her sword, uneasy though it lay close by her side.

Cooper still hadn't seen open blue sky.

When Niki cut him out of the husk, she had yanked him to his feet and shoved him into some sort of shelter. He wanted to say, "Hey there, I am not a sack of seaweed," but he couldn't find his tongue.

Anastasia had sat with her back to Kwesi as he dressed. A set of clothing lay out for Cooper. After he had slipped into a set of unders, he tried to make sense of the trousers. He felt small, thin, and very white—completely unlike Niki, who was tall, muscled, and ruddy. Her eyes were bluer than anything he had ever seen.

Why was she here anyway? They had expected to be met by

Brady, but no one had the nerve to ask why his second in command had come instead.

While they dressed, she dragged their husks into the shelter.

"You should get into dry clothes, ma'am," Anastasia said.

"You should not be telling me what to do, rook." Niki slashed through the husks and stretched the shroud until each piece lay flat. She tied the pieces with twine and stuck them into her pack.

When Cooper had finished dressing, she sent the three of them outside. The ice and the sky seemed the same color, a milky white without texture. The only color was the dark spot where the bowhead had come up, now a slick of new ice. The dogs heard the activity and emerged from their windbreak, shaking flurries of new snow from their plush coats.

"Samoyeds," Anastasia whispered. "I've seen pictures of them."

"Not purebred, though. No purebreds in this world." Kwesi tried to pat one of the dogs. It snapped at him.

Niki stuck her head out of the shelter. "Leave them be. They're not lapdogs."

"I was just being nice—"

"How about I be nice and let them eat the fingers off your hand? Now, keep away from them." Niki ducked back into the shelter, with Kwesi glaring after her.

The wind howled. Whites specks fluttered from the mist.

"Snow," Anastasia said.

Confetti, Cooper thought. *Celebrating my arrival.* But when he tried to say the joke aloud, his tongue seemed frozen to the back of his teeth. Would he ever be warm again?

"All right, rooks. Let's go." Niki packed them onto the sled. They drove for hours into the storm.

"How do you know where you're going?" Kwesi had the jingle to ask at one point.

"I don't. The dogs do," Niki said, standing tall on the back of the sled.

They finally stopped, because of the storm. After she had fed them and taken report, Niki told them to get some rest. Even though they were packed tight in this makeshift shelter, Cooper curled into himself, feeling as alone here as he had in his husk. He would never go back to the Ark. He would never see his parents or his grandmother again. He was going to die in this hard world. And if its seams were slipping, as the prophetic had said, then he likely would die before he learned what it meant to truly live.

He thought of the shroud that Niki had salvaged from their husks. Maybe he could sneak out a sheet while she slept, wrap himself back into it. He could sleep out-of-time until the end of time, like those poor rooks who never made it to Arabah.

But this woman named Niki would slice his husk open and yank him out. He knew her voice already—her tone was husky, her words like sling stones, finding their mark. She'd say, "Be a man, rook," which was what he'd claimed he was when he'd sworn his oath to the Birthright Project and let himself be shrouded into a husk to be dropped onto the bottom of the ocean for a whale to retrieve.

Maybe if he could finally see the blue sky, he could be brave. Maybe then the tears wouldn't freeze on his face while fear flickered hot in his gut.

The rooks were finally asleep.

What had Niki ever done to deserve this? She was more worn out after a day with them than she would be in a protracted battle. To be fair, it was less them and more Arabah. To think that a camp could go without contact—she couldn't think it, because it was unthinkable.

She had pulled on her snow pants and boots, needing to get outside. The storm had passed. The night sky was studded with stars, and the air was crisp and clear. *The seams are loosening.* Niki swallowed back the image of this world with its monstrous wickedness spilling out into that perfect sky. Was that what the prophetic meant? Or was it more personal? This transit Brady had forced on her had stretched her to a limit she hadn't known existed. Easier to swing a sword against a vicious enemy than to live with herself in frigid silence for all this time.

The dogs stirred in their circle, finding her by her scent. She rewarded their attention with scraps of dried blubber. Good fuel for cold nights. She tried to think of Chiungos and the rushing river that would take her south to Horesh, but all she could think of was Arabah.

A missed collection and a missed transit.

Any birthrighter could send a collection from anywhere in this world. All that was needed was a scrap of shroud and a call into the wild. If Niki were halfway around the world, she'd simply need to wrap her collection—be it a tortoise egg or an alligator ovum—in shroud with the out-of-time side inward and then wait. Letters were sent to the Ark the same way. Sooner rather than later, some bird or fish or even bear would appear to take the bundle. It might take time, but eventually the bundle would get from the desert or mountain to a river. From the river, the bundle would somehow get to the ocean, by fish or otter or some willing creature. Once in the ocean, such a bundle could be carried even from the southernmost polar caps to the opposite end of the world to where the Ark lay under the ice, hidden for generations.

Niki rubbed her arms, gripped by fatigue that was nowhere near strong enough to blanket a rising fear. What if she finally got the rooks back to the Narrows and found that Horesh, too, was gone—obliterated by whatever had taken Arabah?

A deeper worry trickled out now, born of fatigue and isolation and stress, but this thought pierced her: What if Brady sent her north so he could pack up Horesh and leave her behind?

Impossible, Niki told herself. But what had happened today on the ice and under the ice had been impossible, and yet it came to be. She turned to duck back into the lean-to, resolved to put all this foolishness away.

Something moved on the other side of the lean-to. Without thinking, her dagger was already in her hand. She crouched low, smelling an open wound. And something deeper—the scent of loss. The wind gusted, and she lost the scent. Snow blew up in a sudden curtain, then drifted as the wind died. Whatever Niki had seen had disappeared.

Was that a terrified animal she had sniffed out? Or perhaps it was just the wind, blowing her own fear back in her own face.

Once he had been sharp of fang and strong of bite, howling his might against the full moon with pride and assurance.

Until the night they turned on him.

He had held on as long as he could, taking on each challenge with courage and cunning. But they'd kept at him until he was too bloody and broken to go on.

He knew this: he could die or he could leave.

He crept away, wanting to die, because this humiliation was too much to bear. Some unseen hand pushed him north. When all he could smell was his own life leaking out, that hand tugged him into a hollow in the ice. He lay there, waiting to die. Instead, he found himself waiting for something else.

Now that something flashed by him. Bundled in skin and fur not her own, nevertheless he knew this creature was a female. Her scent filled him with courage, because he knew, through his blood and bone, that she overflowed with courage.

He watched as she leaned into the wind. Her scent dominated the night, a mixture of the salt water he never dared to cross and her own yearning, so battened down that it created a strength of its own.

He was a cousin to her dogs by blood, but by the spirit it was she who was his sister.

She went back into the shelter and he started to follow. The dogs stirred, knowing he was there, but also knowing that they were safe because they were well fed and strong.

Even inside her den, her scent was so strong it pushed into the storm. Others were in there, but they were a wisp compared to her. He dug and circled until his back was against the wall where she lay.

Only when he sensed her sleep did he grow still and sleep as well.

FIVE

Be he ghoul or flesh, the outrider would pay.

That fiend with the strange eyes had dumped Alrod off into the horde as if he was a piece of manure scraped from the bottom of his boot. Thankfully his croc armor kept him from being crushed as the gargants stomped by him. But his skin was battered, his jaw misaligned, and his nerves shot through with pain.

Even worse, his surviving troops had been forced to slaughter many of the surviving gargants to keep them from trampling into the Traxx stronghold. He had lost most of the mogs and too many of his troops in what was supposed to be a glorious victory.

Alrod sank deeper into the cushions, suppressing a groan. It would not do to have his palace staff know how battered he was, and it certainly would not serve him well to have the baroness see him in this pitiful state. On his orders, Sado had locked her in her suite for the night. She knew better than to protest, though no doubt she would make him pay for the indignity. No matter. He would worry about that later.

The bells above the door jingled. Ghedo entered with a steaming mug.

"No," Alrod said.

"It will ease the pain."

"I don't want to ease my pain. I want to cherish every bitter moment."

"So you can pay it back in kind?"

Alrod smiled as much as his sore jaw allowed. "Tell me—what can we do against these outriders?"

Ghedo waved his hand in dismissal. "Gnats. Pay them no mind."

"Gnats?" Spikes of pain dug into Alrod's chest, driven as much by outrage as injury. "They foiled a full strike force, cost me what—hundreds of mogs? Not to mention the front ranks of my best fighters."

Ghedo smiled. "They did us a wondrous favor, Alrod. You should be offering them gold and lollies, not curses."

Alrod groaned, his anger tearing through every nerve.

"You sure you won't drink?" Ghedo held the mug out again.

"You can't enchant me." Alrod trusted Ghedo with his kingdom but not his self. Never his self. The other stronghold princes submitted to transmogrification out of vanity or fear, but not he. The jewel of the east ruled with a clear head and a body that was his alone.

Ghedo slumped onto a cushion. "I have no desire to do anything other than serve you. I only offer you a day of bliss while your bruises settle."

"Does this bliss include your ludicrous suggestion that the outriders actually did me a favor today?"

"Allow me to help you gain some perspective. First of all, that croc armor I mogged for you—at the risk of my limb and life—served the need superbly. You have strong-arms on the plains so trampled as to be unrecognizable. You sit here with a few bumps—"

"Bumps? I can hardly breathe, man."

"The battle was lost once your hoornars were taken down. You should have had the sense to return to the stronghold then. Leave the outriders to their little games of hide-and-seek. I tell you, friend, they are not worthy of our notice."

Alrod closed his eyes, letting his pain and rage take him to a place where a lesser man—indeed, most men—would fear to go. He slipped into the familiar well of darkness that never ended, and yet, to drink from this well was to seize unimaginable power. He poured his agony in, grasping the darkness with both hands so he would not slay his own sorcerer. Who was better equipped to take him to great glory than the sorcerer who hid behind a bland face as he drank from his own well of darkness?

Alrod breathed deeply, pain like shards in his spine. This, too, would be to his glory, he vowed, as he opened his eyes. Ghedo had taken off his cloak with its veiled hood and now lounged on a satin settee. The master sorcerer never used a valet and only enjoyed lollies who were either blind or had their eyes covered. Even his underling sorcerers had never seen the man under the cloak. Only Alrod ever saw him like this, in the gold tunic of Traxx royalty but otherwise unadorned. Once he put on that purple cloak, the sorcerer became not a man, but an object of wonder and terror for Traxx citizens and beyond.

The sorcerer's sandy brown hair hung in a thin braid that snaked over his shoulder. His eyes were pale blue, his face clear because he could not grow the beard that Alrod decreed for his court. He was only a few years younger than Alrod but still looked little more than a boy. He could become mighty of muscle or fair of face but, like his master, Ghedo scorned self-transmogrification.

The weapon must never wield its master.

Ghedo's father had served the first baron of Traxx, and his son would serve the next baron of Traxx, assuming Alrod recovered his vigor before this new lolly was gray as ashes and moldy as a rotted apple. Such a lovely name—Dawnray. Such an outrage to keep her waiting.

"You cherish your head, friend?" Alrod said.

"Indeed I do, master."

"Then tell me quickly why today was a good day."

"Survival of the fittest will work to our purpose. Only the strongest and smartest of the gargants survived today's mishap. They scattered north, toward the mountains. I ordered your men to go after them and round them up before they perish. Alrod, you must see how glorious this is!"

"I warn you, Ghedo. Your head is tottering . . ."

"You know my position on conquest—a big army is useless. Today proved that force and size alone buys us nothing. I will tweak these surviving gargants to give you a powerful, intelligent, and loyal fighting force. This I promise on my own head."

A warmth trickled between Alrod's ribs. He could indeed see the advantage in these circumstances, though he would more like to skewer the outriders than have to thank them for forcing a shift in strategy.

"Should I order the gargants brought back to your compound, Ghedo?"

"No. By now Treffyn knows about the gargants. But he'll also hear about how they all died in the mishap. The little fool might even do a flyover to see their rotting bodies. We don't want him or his spies knowing that the best survived."

"I hate how that little sugar-sucking ant flies over Traxx at will. You need to mog something to take on his buzz-rats," Alrod growled. "Then we wouldn't need to play this game of trying to sneak across the Narrows. If Treffyn didn't have those buzz-rats, we could cross the Shallows at our leisure and kill him and his strong-arms the same way."

Ghedo stood, sliding his cloak over his shoulders. "Better to conquer them than to kill them. Then we can add Slade's flying rodents to our fleet of hoornars."

"We lost more than half our hive today. We can ill afford such losses. And Nighteye as well—my beloved Nighteye. I swear, Ghedo, if I ever lay eyes again on that outrider with the strange eyes, I'll throttle him with his own skin."

"Nighteye was the crown of my craft. But I'll dream up something even better for you. I promise you, my friend and my master, than one day you will rule all the strongholds, nay—the whole world." Ghedo bowed, one knee to the floor, a sign of abject submission for a sorcerer.

"Up, friend. I believe you. What next?"

Ghedo stood, tying his cloak. "I need your provisioner to

send foodstuffs north. You've got a very large army to feed. I'll be going as well. As soon as you are able, you must join me."

Alrod rubbed his jaw, trying to will the pain away. "Death seems more inviting than a trip into the mountains."

Ghedo grinned, looking truly like a lad. "It will be worth it. But first, you must appear at court tomorrow. Your subjects and Treffyn's spies must see for themselves that you are still alive."

Alrod rang for Sado, waiting for Ghedo to pull up his hood before admitting his servant into the chamber. After issuing the appropriate instructions, he sank back on his pillows, sweating from the pain.

Ghedo once again offered the mug. "You sure you don't want this?"

"No. Leave me."

"As you wish." Ghedo nodded and left Alrod to his misery.

Ghedo had proposed a sensible strategy. The outriders truly were gnats, striking at an occasional mog camp but too few in number to hinder Traxx's mighty war machine.

Until yesterday.

Alrod would not rest until he found the outrider who had bested him in the sight of his troops. The brute would face a fate unimaginable to all but the most creative of avengers.

And he was certainly that.

A howl ripped through the crisp morning air. Timothy unsheathed his sword while Brady reined Thunderhoof to a stop.

The cry was as nerve-shaking as the sight of dead gargants left to rot on the plains of Traxx. In the midst of the carnage lay scatterings of charred flesh. The surviving strong-arms had at least shown their dead comrades a small measure of respect by burning their corpses.

"Over here." Brady dismounted near one of the gargant bodies, his sword still in its sheath. He waved his arms and hollered, driving off a small flock of crows.

Timothy climbed off Ranger and slowly approached, slipping his short blade into his free hand. If Brady wasn't going to take precautions, Timothy would have to double his own.

The mound of flesh stirred. "He's still alive," Brady said.

"Careful, mate. It might be a trap."

With no heed to Timothy's warning, Brady moved around the gargant until he was face-to-face with him. Timothy rushed to his side, pressing the tip of his sword to the gargant's throat.

"No need for that," Brady said.

"If you won't be defended, I will at least stand on the right to defend myself," Timothy said, keeping his sword in position.

"Aye, the modus on unknown encounters provides you that right."

The modi were the protocols that governed camp life; each camp developed their own and submitted them to the builders for approval. Within a year of coming to Horesh, Timothy had decided that Brady erred on the side of laxity in regard to Horesh's rules and practices. More stringent modi would serve the camp well.

The gargant lay on his side in a puddle of blood. The pike piercing his chest was marked with the Traxx insignia—a hornet curved to sting. His face was swollen to bursting. The pores in his forehead leaked fluid in sour, rain-sized drops. Imperfectly mogged, the gargant's arms were studded with scores of tiny fingers. One eye was larger than the breadth of Brady's chest, while the other was a gaping hole. The tracker in Timothy recognized the teeth marks of a coyote on his cheek.

"Monstrous," he whispered.

Brady held his water skin to the gargant's mouth, prying his bloodied lips apart so he could drink. The gargant drained the sac quickly. Then he spoken in stuttering breaths. "Kill me. I beg . . . you. Kill . . ."

Brady shook his head. "I am sorry, friend, but I can't."

"You have . . ." The mog exhaled, a rumble of fluid deep in his chest. "Sword. Kill me."

Brady brushed the back of his hand across the gargant's

forehead, like a tiny child soothing a parent. "I am sorry, brother. But I cannot raise my sword against you."

The gargant's eye rolled back. Timothy thought he had died. But no, his larger eye opened again, fixing on him. "You with . . . sword . . . raised. You do it."

Brady looked up at him, his face unreadable. "You owe him the courtesy of an answer."

Timothy lowered his sword.

"Don't," the gargant gasped. "Use it. Kill me."

Killing this man who had been made grotesque—against his will, for a horrible purpose—surely that would be a mercy. The gargant had no hope for survival, no hope for anything beyond having his living flesh gouged by carnivores.

But Brady had refused. Was it because he would not kill except in battle? Yet they had no way to move a mog this size and, even if they did, his wound was obviously fatal. Wouldn't grace at least decree that they put a sword in the gargant's hand and let him take his desired course? Why didn't Brady offer some guidance here? The man was infuriating, always testing Timothy, far more than the other birthrighters under his authority.

"Kill. Me. Please . . ."

Brady's face was hard now, his eyes dark. "The man waits for your answer, mate."

Trying to take a cue from Brady, Timothy retrieved his own water skin.

The gargant refused to drink. "Use. Your sword . . ."

Timothy put his hand to the gargant's cheek. "I have the sword. But I do not have the right. I am sorry."

A seizure shook the gargant. Timothy prayed this was the last gasp that would put the man out of his distress. But the eye opened again, searching out Brady this time. "No hope . . ."

Brady glanced at Timothy. "Get back on your horse and stand guard."

Timothy sprinted to Ranger, relieved to be dismissed from this dilemma but ashamed by that relief. He circled the area, eyes alert for strong-arms on the horizon or coming from the sky. A day ago, the first signs of spring had burst forth on these plains, but now the greening grass and budding trees had been trampled into dust. After the scavengers had their fill, the gargants would be skeletons, more debris on the killing fields.

Brady knelt by the gargant until the sun was high in the sky. He finally waved to Timothy.

"Is he gone?" Timothy said.

Brady nodded. "To glory."

He urged Thunderhoof into such a rousing gallop, Timothy could barely keep up.

Peace came with nightfall. Brady leaned against Taryan's knees as she braided his hair, taking in the only home he had known outside of the Ark.

Moonlight dappled the shroud strung over Horesh, creating a gossamer rainbow against the night sky. The out-of-time side of the net faced upward, so that anyone daring to stand at the edge of either of the Blunts would see an unworldly shimmer but no sign of the camp below. The ghostly howling in the background—so familiar now that Brady scarcely heard it—came from a variety of wind-flutes Kendo had hung deeper in the Narrows, in the same echo caverns where the deacons and rescues had hidden yesterday. The magnified noise of the flutes, along with carefully cultivated stories of ghouls, was enough to keep even the most daring of strong-arms away.

A pot of stew hung over the cooking fire, and puff-bread baked on stones. Two children ran about, chasing a ball while their parents and grandparents watched, careful to keep them away from the river. Kendo sat on the far side of the Grand, repairing the scope and enjoying the solitude the rushing water gave. He would be taking the two families to sanctuary the next day, and after that Brady and Timothy would leave for Traxx.

Ajoba sat in her hut, spinning shroud and avoiding yet another lecture from one of her elders. Timothy's lyre rang from the men's hut as he worked on a new song. With so many birthrighters on mission, he had the barracks to himself. Once Niki got back from transit, Timothy would take the rooks out for training. Brady smiled at the thought—the young tracker had even less patience for mistakes than Niki did.

"What are you laughing at?" Taryan said.

"Life."

"Better laugh than wail, I suppose."

"I'm taking Timothy to the stronghold with me."

Her hands tightened in his hair. "Neither he nor you should be going. It's too dangerous, especially with that snake-faced Alrod dead."

Brady twisted so he could look up at her. "You think he's dead?"

"The merchant caravans coming from the east say no one has seen him since the battle."

"Doesn't mean he's dead."

"Doesn't mean he's not." Taryan sighed. "All right, I suppose it's wishful thinking on my part."

"It's my job to find out what is going on. And I need Timothy's help. And, lass—if you tug any harder, I'll be bald and barred from court."

No response.

"Taryan, I also have to find out if the gargants are still a threat. There were survivors—and not just the one Ajoba turned. You heard Kendo's report. He tracked the survivors north to the mountains, and the troop of Traxx strong-arms were right behind. We have to know what's happened to them."

She rested her hands on the crown of his head. "I know, Brady. I know."

He pulled her hands to his face, stopping himself a moment

short from kissing them. He had no right to—not yet anyway. "So do I get the rest of my braids?"

"Of course you do." She ran her fingers into the hair on the nape of his neck and got caught in a snarl of curls.

"Youch!"

Taryan laughed. "What? The lad who rode a hoornar into the ground can't stand to have his hair arranged?"

"I love your efforts, but truthfully, I hate having my hair primped like some lapdog."

"If you show up at the hopefully deceased Alrod's court—"

"Trust me, lass—he is alive. I feel it in my bones. That snake is too nasty to die."

"At the very least, he's going to be in a foul mood. Even when happy, Alrod orders men whipped on the spot for appearing with less than six braids. The eighteen I'm giving you may get you a seat at the royal banquet table."

"Wonderful. Braids and indigestion. It's about time that blooming fool Alrod set a style of hair that a working man can be proud of."

"That's *Baron* Alrod to you. And when you bow before that blooming fool, make sure your nose is down to the ground—"

"—and my backside is up to the sky." Brady waved his hand in mock subservience. "I know how to fawn quite well, thank you."

Taryan tweaked his ear. "I'm not so sure of that. Perhaps you should practice. I could stand a bit of fawning right about now."

"I bow to you, everyone else in camp will want fawning. I'll never get my backside back down to earth."

Taryan rested her hands on his shoulders and they sat in silence, letting Horesh life flow around them. Manueo sang off-tune in the armory, the ragged harmony of his saw punctuated by the occasional hammer blow. Magosha shooed the kids away from the honey she brushed on her puff-bread, then called them back for a chunk of sweet cane. Rescued from a mog camp, the couple had asked to stay at Horesh rather than be moved to a sanctuary. Brady had been shocked but pleased when the Ark actually granted permission. Magosha's cooking and Manueo's carpentry skills had since become indispensable to the camp.

Horesh was broken in two by the Grand, rushing by in a roar so constant that they seldom took note of it. Sometimes it was easy to forget about upground, where stronghold princes battled each other, where the original creation was being transmogrified out of existence, where the winds of despair ran hard and steady. Yes, there were regions that had escaped the wholesale devastation of the Endless Wars or regenerated in the aftermath. But the corruption of the strongholders seemed to spread wider with every season.

Taryan slid her arms around his chest and hugged him from behind. Her hair fell across his shoulder like a sash of wheat-hued silk. "Put it behind now, lad. Just take in the night and let the rest of it go."

Brady took a tress of her hair and plaited it with his, wishing Alrod's style masters would decree a shaven face so he could be done with his beard and feel Taryan's cheek next to his. In another time or another place, he would let his fingers dance across the freckles on her nose. He would tease until the dimple in her left cheek deepened. And if she were willing, he would put his lips to hers . . . but no, he couldn't think about that. Not yet.

Brady held out the braid he had made, keeping his tone light. "Interesting new fashion, don't you think?"

"Indeed. Alrod's style masters could learn a thing or two from you."

"That's 'blooming-idiot Alrod' to you, lady."

Her dagger flashed. Brady reached for his, ready to leap against the unseen enemy, but Taryan whispered, "Keep still." She snipped the tress from her head so it could remain in his braid.

"Taryan . . ."

"Just don't lose it this time, or I will cut all those braids off your jolly head."

"I won't," Brady said. "I promise. And I always keep my promises."

Her fingers stiffened.

"What?" he said.

"I can't ask you to promise you'll come back safely from Alrod's court, can I?"

"You cannot."

"Then I won't." Taryan went back to braiding his hair,

Brady leaned back against her knees and watched a night he wished would never end.

The *glint* wafted out of the night, tiny sparks pirouetting from Ajoba's palm and onto the spindle of her spinning wheel. She would turn the wheel with the glint, a true gift from heaven, until the spindle filled. Then she would move to the loom to weave shroud from the thread she had spun. Tracking crews were due from the field. Niki would be arriving soon from transit, bringing the new collection lists. Ajoba must be ready with shroud for the missions.

It seemed a lifetime ago that she had made her own transit, though it had only been a bit over a year. She had only been in Horesh for five months when she was anointed as the new teacher to replace Tylow. He had been a serene shadow of a man with a faint presence but a strong spirit. A mogged vine had burrowed into his feet, snaking into his internal organs and taking a week to kill him.

In addition to teaching, Tylow had also been the one who made shroud. So after Tylow died, Brady had made everyone take a turn at the spinning wheel, from snappish Niki to Magosha and Manueo, who had not come from the Ark but had been adopted into Horesh as deacons, or helpers. Camp was full on that day, with the eighteen outriders and the thirteen trackers all back from mission.

Ajoba had felt so tiny, standing between Bartoly, with his shaggy beard and broad shoulders, and Jayme, with her long legs and piercing eyes. Kendo smelled like the fire-powder he experimented with constantly, while Niki smelled like fresh air, her curly hair still wet from swimming in the river. Though they had been in a training class two years ahead of her, Timothy and Dano barely spoke to her. Brady said it was because two years out in the world were like ten on the Ark.

When Brady came back from a mission with the news that Tylow had died, the birthrighters had run to one another to offer comfort.

Ajoba had no one to hug.

She had come on transit with one other, but Dirk had quickly dropped out of camp and been sent to a southern sanctuary. She longed for the next transit group to arrive at Horesh—rooks she had been in classes with—so that she would not feel so young and so alone.

As she stood in the group on that day, watching everyone take a futile try at the wheel, Taryan had taken her hand. "It's like that old story my grandmother told me," she said. "A prince looks for his lost love. All he has is a single shoe, and he tries it on every foot in the kingdom until he finds the one it fits."

Niki glared across the hut. "This isn't a stupid fairy tale."

Taryan simply smiled.

Ajoba's turn came. Brady placed her hand between the wheel and the spindle, turning her palm up.

"This is not going to work—" she started to say. The spindle hadn't turned for any of the others. How could it possibly work for the youngest tracker in camp?

A whirl of light glimmered across her palm. Pain seized the bones of her hand, as if they were being crushed and remade inside her skin. The wheel turned and the spindle spun, filling with glitter and shadow—the here-and-now and out-of-time fibers that could be woven into shroud.

An hour later Ajoba looked up from the wheel. Only the camp leaders, Brady and Niki, remained. Niki studied her, eyes narrowed. "You're very young."

Ajoba nodded, letting the wheel slow. She was still sixteen.

"But this is not our choice to make, and Niki knows that." Brady said. "It is, however, your choice to accept or decline, Ajoba."

Words came from her mouth, though she scarcely knew how they had come to be there: "I am the Lord's servant."

Brady cupped his hands over her head. His words of anointing were distant as her heart filled with a fierce joy. Ever since then she had spun glint, woven shroud, sung praise, and taught hope.

"Some teacher you are." Demas's harsh words knocked Ajoba out of her memories.

She leaped to her feet. "I didn't hear you come. Otherwise I would have greeted you."

"You spin at a time like this?"

"The missions are expected back soon, plus the collection lists from the Ark. I need to be ready for them."

Demas circled around her, his finger to his temple as if deep in thought. His face seemed carved in fine marble with its high forehead and elegant nose. His long hair was very dark, catching every glimmer of light in the room.

"So it is your *mission* to be a simple spinner and weaver?" he asked.

"I spin glint; I weave shroud. Manna for this dark time." Surely he knew this. He must be testing her.

Demas slowly smiled. "Very good. You understand this part of your gift well. But you have left your real mission wanting."

"Requesting pardon, but I don't understand."

He put his finger to her chin. Her jaw went numb, but she dared to gaze into his eyes, startled to see her own image on his face and hear her voice that came from his mouth. "Friend, hear me. If you head to the Bashan Mountains, you will find hope and you will find life. Will you do that?"

"He went," Ajoba said, her voice weak.

"He went *alone.*" Demas folded his wings and vanished into the night.

Six

Baron Alrod was a hard man, all bone and sinew with no measure of softness. His face was narrow, his cheekbones angular, his eyes set so deep that Dawnray could not determine their color. His hair shone silver, plaited into tight braids that suggested chains around his head. His nails were clipped and decorated with precious stones, but his knuckles were gnarled. With those hands he had killed countless men, most of them innocent of anything other than being in his way.

From early childhood, Dawnray had been taught to hide each time the Traxx strong-arms rampaged through their village. That rat Sado had taken her by guile a week ago. He came to her door in tattered rags, begging for bread. She showed him mercy, and he repaid her with a dose of sleeping draught. Since then, she had been held in the baroness's treatment rooms, being bathed, shampooed, perfumed, clipped, trimmed, and painted.

She had come away feeling filthy.

The baroness had brought her to Alrod's private rooms this morning for his inspection. "You'd better hope to please the high and mighty one, drudge," Merrihana had said. "Rejects go to the officer's barracks for their pleasure. Or sometimes my husband favors the kitchen staff with your kind. And then there's the sacrificial altar . . ."

The sacrificial altar, where virgin blood was collected by the sorcerers to add to their potions. *Oh, Papa,* Dawnray wanted to cry. But Papa had died trying to save her from being taken.

Merrihana jabbed her in the ribs. "Stand straight, drudge."

Alrod brushed her face with his fingertips. "Her skin is soft, her lips full. Are you sure she has no mog about her?"

Merrihana stood straight, her chin up. "None, husband."

Alrod locked eyes with Dawnray. Her knees trembled, but she kept her gaze on his face. "Such eyes," he said. "Would you say they were blue? I've never seen such a shade."

"I would deem them as cobalt, dear heart." The baroness's own eyes were a golden topaz. It was said in the villages that they had been mogged from a cat's so she could track her husband's comings and goings in the dark of night.

The baron opened Dawnray's robe. Her face flamed. No man had seen her body since she had come out of diapers. "You attest that she is not mogged in any way?"

"If you ask me that one more time, I swear I will slash her throat and be done with this."

Alrod took Dawnray's hand. "Sweet one, I am a bit under the weather right now. A hard-won victory that left me bruised and hurting. But shortly, I will bless you."

Dawnray lowered her gaze, sickened to have him so close.

Alrod brushed her cheek with his lips. "Modest as well as beautiful. That quality will suit the mother of my son."

Dawnray held her breath to hide her shock. She couldn't think of anything more despicable than carrying the spawn of this weasel.

Merrihana pinched her side. "She is young and strong. She should be a suitable breeder, my husband."

Husband. The word dropped like a rock onto Dawnray, as if she needed a reminder that she was a drudge—soon to be a lolly—while the topaz-eyed woman had a rightful claim in Traxx succession.

Alrod snapped his fingers.

Sado shuffled into the chamber, his pitted face bowed in reverence. He wore a gold silk sash over cotton shirt and trousers, marking him as a favored servant.

"Find her a suite of rooms. Nice ones with fresh air. Assign a competent girl to attend her."

"Yes, high and mighty."

"And find her something suitable to wear. Dawnray will join me and the baroness at court tomorrow."

"As you wish." The servant bowed and nodded for Dawnray to follow.

Timothy had seen the Wall of Traxx many times, gleaming like a stack of ribbons in the afternoon sun. Today, he would see it up close for the first time.

Anticipation mingled with anxiety as he and Brady walked the last three leagues to the stronghold, leather bags slung over their shoulders. They had left their horses with a trusted farmer in the closest village.

The wall surrounding the stronghold was fifteen feet high and twice as deep, Brady had said, and made of something unusual, but he refused to tell Timothy what it was. "I want to see your face when we get up close, Tim. You're in for an interesting surprise."

They were ten feet away now, and Timothy could scarcely believe what he saw.

Flowers.

The mighty stronghold of Traxx was defended by blooms of every hue: sun-yellow daffodils, crimson roses, lavender orchids, chrysanthemums of every color from stark white to night-sky blue.

Brady laughed. "Better close your mouth, mate. The flies around here are bigger than my head."

"This is what keeps out the enemy? Alrod hunkers down behind a wreath of flowers?" Timothy traced a line of pink phlox through a patchwork of purple and white tulips, enjoying the flutter of velvet petals under his finger. The scents were intoxicating, from the subtle sweetness of honeysuckle to the sumptuousness of lily.

Brady clamped his hand on his wrist. "Don't."

"Why not?"

"Watch." He hacked away until the ground was littered with bright blooms. Thick stems and woody growth tangled behind the flowers.

"So there's thorns. So what? Vegetation is easy enough to burn away or to cut through. You just proved that. I don't see how this can be any defense for Traxx."

"You knock down a stone wall, it stays knocked down unless someone rebuilds it. You cut through this tangle and it grows back on its own. Very quickly." Indeed, the wall had grown back in little more time than it took Brady to draw back his sword. Flowers budded, then bloomed, before their eyes.

"Are you telling me this fortress is impenetrable?"

"No. You just need to know how to . . ."

Brady's words faded away. Somehow Timothy's sword had gotten into his hand. He slashed and hacked, moving forward, confident that he who scaled cliffs and tracked lions could slice through this riot of petals. Somewhere, from far away, Brady was calling *no*. But Timothy breathed in *yes,* because that's what the wall called to him.

Yes, Timothy. Share in our beauty.

Surely this kind of transmogrification couldn't be wrong, not when the sorcerers could cast a spell of satin and fragrance. It must be the birthrighters who had judged it wrong and had collected and fought and kept the faith for nothing.

Let this be your faith . . .

Satin arms slipped around his chest. Soft fingers encircled him from his biceps to his ankles. Timothy fell back into the embrace, thinking perhaps that at long last, this was love—

Let this be your music . . .

—even as the arms squeezed out his air and crushed his ribs so surely he would be a bag of bones if someone didn't help. But he had no voice to ask for help, no will to resist.

Become our secret. Become our beauty.

A blade flashed by his face in a steady *thwack-thwack,* hacking the sweet-smelling velvet arms. Timothy was yanked backward. He found himself sitting on the hard ground outside the wall, watching as flowers closed in once more over the tunnel he had cut. "What happened to me?"

"The flowers are mogged to produce a humanlike pheromone. Draws you in like a butterfly or bee."

Timothy was indignant. "Why didn't you stop me?"

"I told you no."

"I didn't hear you. No, that's not right. I did hear you . . . but I didn't believe you." Timothy rubbed his ribs, taking in air to fill out all the spaces between. No sooner did he breathe than—

Yes. Come and taste of this forever sweetness.

"No," Brady said.

Timothy moved again toward the wall, summoning only enough will to reach his arm back. Brady yanked him back.

He rubbed his face, trying to get his bearings. "How can you resist it and not I?"

"By holding on to the truth. And by breathing through my mouth instead of my nose."

"That simple?"

Brady laughed. "The Traxx sorcerers are far too clever to rely on one device to keep intruders out. Watch." After a minute of hacking into the wall, Brady motioned Timothy to look deep into the niche he had cut. This time he was careful to bring air in through his mouth and not allow the sweet odor to drift into his nostrils. *This beauty is treacherous,* he reminded himself. *A ruse, a lie, a trap.*

Beyond the flowers was a tangle of branches studded with thorns sharper than an outrider's sword. Between the intervals of thorns grew nettles and briars. "How can we possibly pass through that?" Timothy said.

"Start singing."

"What?"

"Use your gift, lad. That fine voice."

"Why do you insist on confounding me? Can't you just explain for once?"

"The reality tops any explanation I can give," Brady said.

"Fine," Timothy said, grinding his teeth.

"Timothy—"

"I'm getting to it. Give me a moment." He closed his eyes, letting music rise from within, waiting for song that would capture this wall that determined to capture him. The tune came first, with words rushing to catch up.

Dark may rule the day. Deep may be your pain in this place.
Hide, you slip away . . .

There was a rustling from within the wall. A misshapen lump shuffled out.

"What is that thing?" Timothy whispered.

"Keep singing."

Even though Timothy took care to breathe through his mouth, the creature's stench made his sinuses curdle.

Flowers may fall and fade, memories of life, better days
Fire, there burns a flame . . .

"He's a *slung*," Brady whispered.

The creature had stumps for legs and arms, but Timothy couldn't be sure if it had a face, not with its head bent almost to its knees. "Is it—was it—human?"

"He is."

"Mercy."

"Something Baron Alrod is notoriously short on. These poor souls are mogged in infancy with tortoise potions so their skin is rock-hard. Their job is to keep intruders out. Oh, and to keep the wall fertilized."

"With what?"

Brady laughed. "You surely don't want to know that, mate."

"So what is the music about?"

"These little fellows love music. In past times, as long as I sang to him or his brothers, they would lead me through happily. But slungs can only hear a limited pitch—a man's tenor or woman's alto. My voice has gotten too deep for a slung to hear. So keep at it."

As Timothy sang on, the slung hobbled up to him. His eyes were dim and filmy, his skin like pitted stone. His stench was overpowering. Timothy covered his nose and mouth with his hand.

Brady pulled it away. "Don't. They resent any implication that their odor is less than pleasing. Our friend thinks he is one with his flowers."

That the pitiful creature smelled like maggoty meat was not his fault, Timothy supposed.

"Follow me," Brady said. "And I'll follow him. Stay very close. The slung is our battering ram through. If we get separated in here, I won't be able to pull you out. And remember—hold to the truth."

The slung charged forward, never flinching as thorns the size of spears broke off against his rock-hard skin. Timothy slipped his hands through the back of Brady's belt and followed. Behind him, the broken thorns already sprouted new growth.

Their feet made a sucking sound with each step. "I hesitate to ask, but what am I stepping in," Timothy said.

"That's why I told you to wear your thickest boots and tuck in your trouser legs. We are up to our ankles in what makes this wall thrive. The slungs bring it in by the bucketful, spread it constantly."

"Manure?"

"That and more."

"What more?"

"When we get through this wall and into the stronghold, you will see beauty that you have never even imagined. But it comes at a price, and that price is paid not only by the enemies of Traxx, but by the poor souls of its villages. I honestly prefer not to go into any more detail than that. Understand that if we were able to enter through the gate like a proper Traxx strongholder may, we would have."

A shudder seized Timothy. All birthrighters were inoculated against transmogrification before they left the Ark, but they were still vulnerable to original illnesses, anything from pesky colds to murderous plagues. Any manner of foul organism could thrive in this place.

"Fix your eyes on my back and keep moving," Brady said. "And do not—on your life and mine—stop singing."

Timothy sang on, but he couldn't resist the urge to glance about. Stems, stalks, and branches knotted into a solid stockade. Slowly he discerned shapes in the tangle. He started—a man in full Slade armor stood to his left. No, not a man, but a skeleton, its armor pierced through the chest by a massive thorn while vines twined out of the eye sockets. A marrow bug poked along the jaw.

The torturous brush was clogged with bodies—some men in armor, some mogged creatures pathetic in their skeletal states, one man with muscle still on his bones but his skin rotting away. Timothy didn't realize he had stopped singing until he heard Brady's voice, straining into falsetto. "Deep may be your pain in this place."

"Still believe that love remains," Timothy chimed in.

He tightened his grip on Brady's belt. There were times when it was blessed to follow. Surely this was one of them.

Seven

After nearly a week of travel, Niki and the rooks had come far enough south to smell spring. Cold air swirled around their ankles, but the sun on their backs was warmer with each league south. Bits of tundra poked through the snow, now soft with melting.

God speaks clearly over the ice, Brady had said. Niki had left most of the ice behind, and He hadn't spoken yet. Maybe He had nothing to say—unlike Kwesi and Anastasia, who wouldn't shut up.

"Can I drive the sled?" Kwesi nagged. "I want to be grabbin' and shakin' this trip with both hands."

"I keep twisting my ankle," Anastasia moaned. "The ground is so rank."

Grabbin' and shakin'—experiencing to the full. *Rank*—anything that made Anastasia unhappy. Niki didn't know which was worse: the rooks' jangle, or the fact that she had begun to understand it.

Cooper was silent but still a nuisance. When he tripped for the third time that afternoon, Niki snapped at him. "Get your head out of the clouds. You're acting like you've never seen blue sky before."

The words were out of her mouth before she realized that of course Cooper hadn't seen blue sky before, except in the moving pictures they showed on the Ark. What was the term for those images? The longer she lived in this world, the more it seemed that the Ark had been just a dream. Once-familiar things had become wisps of memory, dissolving like vapor under a rising sun.

Holovids. That was the term. The moving pictures of the world as it used to be, preserved on those tiny little slips of . . . something. Oh yes. Silicon chips as small as her fingernail could store images and information that would take a thousand books to preserve. The first time Niki saw a holovideo of open sky and gleaming water, she hadn't been much older than three. Afterward she had run down one hallway and up the other, demanding to be let out so she could see sky. Even as the builders doubled and tripled the size of the Ark, it never got big enough for Niki, not when she knew there was a whole world outside.

Long-forgotten words flooded back—*holograms*, *electricity*, *superconductivity*, *fusion*, *microprocessors*, *lasers*. Images came next, with full sound effects: whirring motors, churning engines, thinking machines with tiny blinking lights.

She shoved them all back into the mental fog. It was safer to forget. If any of the warring nobles learned of the Ark's existence, they would skin every birthrighter alive to find it and grab the science and technology that mankind had blasted out of this world eons ago. Is that what had happened to Arabah? Were the camp's birthrighters now on the racks of Slade or in the cauldrons of Brennah?

A small animal flashed in front of her. Too big to be a mouse. It scurried back her way, startled by the presence of humans. A lemming—the first land animal she'd seen coming off the Ark on her transit.

Things had been so different back then. There had been no dogs to carry them south—she, Brady, Kendo, and Tylow had walked for weeks until finding the first settlement. The people of Kinmur had welcomed them and continued to provide assistance on Brady's trips north.

She and her comrades had made collections along the way, wrapping tundra grasses, mice, even moss in shroud and leaving it for larger animals—sometimes bears, sometimes wolves—to pick up and take to the ocean. The angel had instructed them to do this, but Niki had not believed it would work until she saw it for herself.

These rooks needed to make their first collections, too, as soon as possible. Brady had reminded her of that: "They need to be more than spectators, even on their first journey."

How many cold-climate rodents had been sent back to the Ark by now? Perhaps not as many as Niki and her campmates supposed. She didn't know for certain that all the transits were made in the far north. If collections could be made all the way down at the equator, couldn't rooks be delivered the same way to the southern camps?

Birthrighter camps had been scattered around the continent so trackers wouldn't have to travel extreme distances to make collections. Solitary birthrighters, known simply as scouts, were needed to find fauna and flora that neared immediate extinction or had migrated because of the Endless Wars. Otherwise, the builders sent lists based on the geographical, botanical, and zoological records of each camp location. Trackers worked in increasingly larger circles from their campsites. Horesh had long ago collected species from the south side of the Bashans and throughout the bordering strongholds of Traxx and Slade. Their tracking crews now ranged long distances to collect the items on their assigned lists. The day was coming when Horesh would have to move to be productive—perhaps even to another continent.

Niki signaled the rooks to stop. Cooper was the only one riding in the sled—the snow had grown too soft for the dogs to pull all of them at once. "Do you see those tracks?"

"What? Where?" Anastasia asked.

Kwesi was already bent over, searching the snow. "This?"

"Yes," Niki said.

Cooper bent down next to his companions.

"A rat, right?" Anastasia said. Kwesi nodded his agreement.

"No, it's a lemming," Cooper said, reddening as Niki smiled her approval.

She unwrapped a piece of shroud. "Track it and collect it."

"Yea!" Kwesi said.

The rooks moved in a cluster, their faces almost to the snow as they followed the tracks. Niki laughed aloud at the sight of their noses near the ground.

Anastasia stood up, glaring. "What?"

"You're going to drive it to ground if you all get on its tail," Niki said. "Remember your training. Figure out where it's heading and find a way to trap it." Birthrighters were trained on the Ark with the domesticates that had been onboard when they first went under the ice. The training corridors often swarmed with mice and goats as the first-year students tried to find and trap them.

Kwesi motioned Cooper to the left and Anastasia to the right. He tiptoed along the track while Cooper and Anastasia moved silently into position. Kwesi let out a loud "Ooh-hah!" and the lemming rushed between Anastasia and Cooper. They raced straight at it, so intent on covering the lemming with their scrap of shroud that they collided.

Niki collapsed in a fit of laughter.

"That's not funny!" Anastasia hollered. "You have no right to mock us when—"

"Stasia, hush." Kwesi put his hand to her mouth, his eyes searching out Niki. "Niki, look to the northeast. "What's that?"

A faint radiance danced beyond a hillock, casting an eerie glow in the bright light of day. Niki had seen this countless times and always with dread—and, if she were honest—some measure of anticipation and excitement. She unsheathed her sword. "Come here. All of you. Now! Tell me what you see."

"Are those lanterns or torches? Do people live there?"

"Not this far north," Niki said. "Come here. Quickly—come to me. Come on, move it, rooks."

"What is that? It's . . . too strange," Anastasia said. "Like that color just isn't right. Green, then blue. Shifting."

"Mogs," Cooper said. "It's the glow of transmogrification."

The rooks stared, transfixed by the glow—their first manifestation of the divine gifts that all birthrighters had been blessed with to one degree or another. Identifying mogs by a glow only they could see. Speaking or singing messages to birds and knowing they would be carried and repeated to the proper person. Trusting land or sea animals to pick up shrouded collections and transport them to the ocean.

"Aren't we too far north to see mogs?" Kwesi said. "What would they be doing here?"

Niki motioned them over to the sled. "The failed ones don't always die. Sometimes they drift away. It's usually the outdwellers who are bothered by them. Kwesi's right—I've never heard of them this far out before."

She dug out her spyglass and sighted on the hillock. "Curved horns, wooly backs. Musk oxen. Looks like three of them. Get your short blades out of your packs."

"Are we going to fight?" Kwesi said, his eyes bright.

"Not if we can help it. We'll just make a wide sweep around them and hope they just keep on with their business." Niki stepped onto the sled and urged the dogs in the opposite direction, keeping her watch over her shoulder.

"They're following," Kwesi whispered.

The oxen lumbered toward them. Niki unharnessed the dogs and shooed them away. Oxen were grazers, but these creatures moved with an intent that made her uneasy.

"What do we do?" Anastasia asked.

"Every single thing I say," Niki said. "Start by listening very carefully."

She urged the rooks toward a ridge that lay a hundred paces to their left. Hopefully the oxen were just curious and this was all just an exercise in preparedness. But the knot in her gut told Niki otherwise. She located the stretch with the sharpest dropoff, with boulders behind which the rooks could shelter. "Crouch down here. Lie down on your back if need be to be as low as you can. If the musk oxen break for us, I'll drive them toward this ridge. As they pass over, thrust your blade into their underbellies. If you miss, group together with your blades outward while I take them on. Whatever you do, don't you try to take them head-on. You hear me?"

Anastasia nodded. Cooper seemed frozen, his short blade clutched to his chest while Kwesi slashed at the air. "I did well in swordsmanship," Kwesi said.

"This isn't the gymnasium, idiot," Niki said. "You can't fence with these beasts like training dummies. You understand, rook?"

Kwesi nodded.

"Stay down and go for their guts. Their skulls are too hard, and the horns will tangle your blades."

The oxen drew near, casting occasional glances at the dogs, who clustered at a distance. They seemed in little hurry, and yet they did not vary their course—straight toward the humans.

Niki helped each rook get into position at the lip of the shallow ridge, placing their weapons so they could thrust against a rushing beast without getting the blades knocked out of their hands. "Whatever you do, don't run away. Even unmogged musk oxen can move fast if startled. If they charge, you keep low and keep your blades high. Got it?"

"Got it," Kwesi said.

"Remember, it is all right to be scared. But do not run away. Don't make yourselves a target."

"We won't," Anastasia said.

"We swear," Kwesi said while Cooper just nodded.

Niki walked about twenty paces in from the ridge, moving at a slight diagonal to the mogged oxen. There were three of them, white coated and black snouted, with horns so massive they should topple the beasts onto their faces. But they moved with such grace that Niki would not consider these creatures as failed mogs. More like dreadful successes.

The mogs crested a mound and stood posed against the sky, their coats a shade darker than the snowy ground, their heads high, sniffing the air. Their broad chests and the powerful curve of their horns formed a startling silhouette against the blue sky. Niki understood, perhaps for the first time, the passion of man to sculpt flesh and fiber to his own will, to cast creation to his own purpose—to become *maker.*

Was her sword, cast for her by Brady in the forge of Horesh, any different from these creatures? Had Brady sent her north because he saw her as a failure, like these musk oxen? How could that be, when she always did her duty and would stop at nothing to do it?

"Attend to business, outrider," Niki murmured. Daydreaming in the face of danger. Stupid way to get herself killed.

Roused by her voice, the oxen trotted off the mound. After a last glance at the dogs, they set a course directly for her. Deliberation, the sure sign of a menace. But perhaps her deliberation would discourage theirs. Niki hefted her spear and shouted, "Go away! Go! Move along, now!"

The biggest one lowered his head and charged.

Niki threw her spear. The animal jerked and tumbled sideways. *Got him—right through the eye.* She waved her sword at the other two. "Hey! Run off now, or you'll be next!"

They charged her, their snouts foamed with spittle. Niki ran toward the ridge. "Get ready, rooks. I got two coming." She jumped aside at the last moment with a hard thrust into the nearest ox as it passed her. Bright blood spurted from its side, but she kept her cheer to herself, hoping the rooks had gotten the other creature.

She scrambled along the ridge. The rooks were not where she had left them. The fools had scrambled up onto the boulders. The surviving beast stood on its hind legs, pawing at the rock.

Niki waved her arms. "Hey! Fleabag! Bring it back this way!"

The ox turned and charged head-on, its horns lowered—an impenetrable target. Niki sidestepped and grabbed the beast by the base of one horn. It jerked its head as it dragged her along.

Niki pressed one foot to its side and used her sword like a lever to kick up onto its back. She grabbed the ox's ears, forcing its head up so she could slash its throat. Too much skin at the underside. She jabbed her blade into the side of the neck. Blood burst out in a red stream.

The rooks were still on the boulders, their faces red. "Hey rooks, you stupid—come down from there now—"

Something slammed Niki from behind. The first beast had gotten back up, the spear still in its eye. It lunged forward, ready to stomp her. She had dropped her sword—no time to retrieve it. She rolled in the snow, somersaulting in a tight ball so it couldn't catch her vital organs. Somewhere in her spin, she spotted Kwesi running at her.

"Stay back. Let me take care of this," she yelled.

Kwesi either didn't hear or chose not to obey. He rushed the beast, Niki's sword in hand. The beast lunged sideways, slashing Kwesi through his coat. He cried out and fell, blood seeping from his side.

The beast turned, coming back for the kill.

Niki leaped, high-kicking at the beast's head. The toe of her boot caught in its horn, upending her. A shadow moved at the periphery of her vision. Another ox? No time to figure that out—this ox was charging back at her.

She feinted to her left but jumped to the right. She grabbed the spear and twisted it in its eye, causing the ox to spin in pain and fury. The spear broke off, leaving Niki face-to-face with the enraged beast. At the last moment she stepped sideways, dodging its charge, and jumped onto its back. She shifted around, digging at its neck, trying to find its windpipe so she could crush it. *These beasts must have been mogged for sport fighting, with all this loose skin and these massive horns.*

And intelligence. Rather than try to buck her off, the creature dropped and rolled. Niki folded her arms across her ribs, trying to keep from being flattened. The ox lifted a few inches, then pressed down. The creature weighed a couple hundred pounds, not as massive as an original but heavy enough that Niki couldn't shove it off her.

With the next rise, she tried to shimmy toward the ox's head, intending to grab the end of the spear still in its eye. But it shifted, trying to cover her face. It would either crush her or smother her to death.

Twenty paces away, Anastasia bent over Kwesi, trying to stem the bleeding from his side. Cooper crept toward Niki, her sword now clutched in his hand. "Drive the blade into its neck," Niki said. "Come in from the side."

Cooper slashed wildly, jamming the sword through the curve of the beast's horn and getting it stuck there. The animal snarled, showing teeth that should be on a shark and not a herd animal. But it did not rise. It had Niki trapped under its side and no intention of leaving this prize to chase another.

Cooper backed away while the beast went back to crushing Niki. Lifting itself a few inches, not enough for her to escape, then pressing down again, harder. Fingers of death crept into her mind, squeezing out thoughts of the rooks and Horesh and her parents, until there was only room for one thought, one face, one last look with her mind's eye—*her heart's eye*—

Something flew across the snow. She saw it when the ox raised itself again—a flash of matted fur, a frenzy of snarling. She felt the shift of weight as the shadow creature tore into its neck.

Now.

With a burst of desperate energy, she gathered herself and rolled out.

The ox had gone still, its hot blood melting the snow next to Niki's face.

The other creature, a scraggly wolf, looked down at Niki, fangs dripping, eyes hot with bloodlust.

"No," she said. "Please."

The wolf blinked and dashed away.

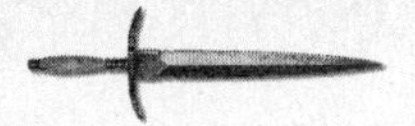

Surely he leaped the back of the beast because he was hungry. No other reason, for she was his enemy and he hers.

He slunk far out of reach of that hard, cold stick that served as her fang. The others huddled behind her, but she stood tall, waving him back. He would not honor her request, at least not until they left.

Then he would feed. Because that was what drove him to do this insane thing, was it not? It had to be, because he would not die for one who was not of his kind.

Or was she?

Eight

TIMOTHY WALKED AS IF IN A DREAM, DRAWN BY GLITTER and lights. "What is this place?"

"This avenue is where the nobles and landowners shop," Brady said. "Lovely in an ugly sort of way, isn't it?"

After they passed through the wall of thorns, Timothy and Brady had scaled the inner wall that kept the strongholders safe from their own defenses and had changed into clothing that suggested rank and privilege. Brady dressed in the sunflower tunic and the gold sash of lower Traxx nobility. Timothy pulled on black wool pants and an orange silk caftan. His straight blond hair and bright-green eyes made him a perfect fit for a Finwayan noble. "The baroness has an affinity for Finway," Brady assured him. "So you'll be welcome at court."

Though the sun had set, the sky over Traxx glittered. Tiny lights sparkled directly out of Timothy's reach, as if the stars had fallen from the sky and hovered over their heads. Even the cobblestones under their feet glowed. "Bioluminescence," Brady explained. "Fireflies transmogrified to hover and give continuous light. The poor things must expend themselves within minutes.

"Not that Alrod or his sorcerers care about that," he added. "Take a long look, mate. This is what the strongholders fight for. What they're destroying the birthright for."

Carts were stacked high with jewelry cast from gold and precious stones. Bolts of cloth were piled on tables—silks, wools, linens, and mogged fibers with that telltale green glow. Other carts were filled with toys, dishes, pots, even weapons.

Everything was finer than anything Timothy had ever seen. Yet Brady had told him the most precious and expensive items were inside, beyond the reach of all but the most elite nobles. Brocade awnings draped the entrance of each shop; flowers carpeted their thresholds. With the sensitive nose of a tracker, Timothy could still smell the wall of thorns four streets away. Would he ever again sniff the wild roses that grew upground of Horesh without thinking of death and decay?

Vendors hawked their wares, not with the coarse calls of the outland gypsies, but with beautiful music, sometimes sung by canaries and sometimes by drudges. Carriages of Traxx nobles lined the street, though it was their drudges who shopped the carts on their behalf while they sat behind diamond-dusted windows, gossiping or flirting.

These people lived as if the world outside their wall of thorns didn't exist. Their luxuries and security were bought at a terrible price—by draining the surrounding territory of its metal ore, its grain, and even its people. Stronghold nobles ruled by the power their mogs provided them. Commoners were nearly helpless to resist.

Timothy often wondered if there had been some point during or after the Endless Wars when mankind could have stopped this pillage, this rape of the environment and one another for selfish gain. He knew the answer to that, just as he knew that, but for the grace of God, his impulse would be to gather the same riches and luxuries the people around him had.

He remembered what he'd learned as a child, back in the Ark. After the Endless Wars, survivors had claimed the remnants of healthy land that was left. Humankind had been thrown back to an earlier, more primitive age, with no recollection of electricity or computers or bombs. Only the ability to manipulate viruses to mutate cells had survived, though the science that explained how these techniques worked had long since been lost. To the sorcerers, the cell lines were potions. And all were commodities, to be used in the consolidation of power. Ghedo had traded his potion for growing human bone for Stynne's potion that allowed vegetation to grow at a ridiculous rate. Given that capability, Alrod had replaced his stone walls with the wall of thorns.

Meanwhile, the commoners living outside of the protection of the strongholds scraped by. Even when a village thrived—with decent huts, bountiful crops, healthy families—strong-arms could swoop down and steal their grain or their wares or their children.

"It hurts my eyes," Timothy said.

"It hurts my heart." Brady scratched his beard. "It befuddles me that strongholders use their incredible talent and energy to corrupt the work of the One who created them."

"They don't see it that way."

"They don't *see* at all," Brady said. "Not when they are blinded by all this."

A woman cried out. A broad shadow darkened the avenue, as if a gargant had suddenly reached over their heads.

Timothy ducked instinctively, his hand on his sword.

"No. Look at the wall," Brady said.

Massive cords, undulating like the arms of an octopus, rose from the top of the wall of thorns. The cords stretched as far as Timothy could see, perhaps over the entire city. At the end of each cord was a bulblike head the size of a carriage, shaped like a massive onion.

"What's happening. What are those things?"

"Cobratraps. Traxx's defense against an aerial attack. They're a transmogrified mix of the Venus flytrap and the cobra lily, grafted with butterwort to provide stickiness."

Timothy had collected seeds from the flesh-eating pitcher plant. Though it was very beautiful, when he opened its flower, he had found a half-dissolved mouse in its trap.

"Now you understand why the geese fly west of the Bashans on their migrations—to avoid flying over the Traxx stronghold. Hoornars make the strongholders nervous, and they're hard to transmogrify. Rather than use them to guard against their enemies' flying mogs, Ghedo and his assistants developed the cobratraps."

The air filled with a whooshing sound, followed by a sharp keening. The heads had opened, emitting a sharp odor that made Timothy's nose water. Tiny specks darted among the heads and stalks, only to be swallowed by the dozens.

Brady passed Timothy the spyglass. "You've got the sharp eyes, tracker. What's happening up there?"

The mouth of the head was ringed with waving cilia. As it turned face-on, Timothy could see creamy satin folds, edged with mauve to form a strikingly beautiful blossom large enough to swallow a strong-arm riding a buzz-rat or a shardwing. The prey would stick in the throat of the flower while the stamen wrapped around it and showered it with acid.

Brady poked Timothy. "Don't keep me in suspense. What nature of invader have we?"

Timothy increased the magnification, trying to hold his hand steady. Focusing beyond the fireflies and into the night was a near impossible task. "Good grief! It looks like sparrows."

Brady squinted up at the sky. "What kind of assault could this be? I don't see any glow."

Timothy watched the little brown bird struggle. The cilia had wrapped around its feet, pulling it into the heart of the blossom. "They aren't mogs. They're original. Like our birds."

Brady closed his eyes, the one man in the crowd not staring into the sky. "They *are* our birds. Taryan must be sending us a message, something that couldn't wait."

"They're not getting through," Timothy said, his stomach sour. "They're all getting swallowed up."

"We'll get them through. Trust me." Brady pushed through the crowd, heading down one alleyway after another. Everyone was in the street, watching the spectacle in the sky and oblivious to two men pushing along.

They came to a dark spot along the wall that protected the stronghold from the outer wall's thorns. "Take off your silks and pull on your shroud," Brady said. Though they hadn't dared to bring their full armor, they did have their masks and gloves, which they quickly pulled from their bags. The shroud in these items would deflect most of the light, rendering them anonymous.

Brady shimmied up to the protecting wall. "Follow me." Timothy did, scaling the bricks to the top.

"Hang your pack here." Brady pointed to the protruding bricks on the inner wall's outer surface—the same ones they had used to scale the wall. Then he grinned, swung his arms back, and leaped on top of the wall of thorns.

"Are you insane?" Timothy said.

"Modus gives you the right to decide that for yourself. But do it quickly."

Dark thoughts seized Timothy, perhaps spawned by the thorns—or perhaps by his own desires. To leap onto the wall of thorns had to be insane, especially without a slung to intercede for them. Why not just walk back through the alleys, fade away into the crowd? He could make a good living with his voice and his music. What would it be like to wear magnificent silks all the time? To marry a lovely woman? To not face loneliness and doubt and death with his daily bread? To be kept safe by thorns and cobratraps?

Brady motioned from atop the wall. "If you will follow me, tracker, it must be now."

Yes, he was a tracker, a birthrighter—Timothy of Horesh. And so he leaped.

The top of the wall was smooth with flowers, no sign of the thorns. Every few paces, the stalks of the unfurled cobratraps rose straight up like tree trunks.

Timothy toed the flowers with his boot. "No thorns up here?"

"They would tangle the cobratraps. This is the only safe place on the wall—at least when the cobratraps are at work. I wouldn't want to be the one to disturb their precious rest."

Like all of Brady's plans, the one he set forth made a foolish kind of sense. Timothy began climbing the nearest stalk, as instructed. The stalk of the cobratrap was ringed like the trunk of a palm tree and about as wide.

Brady ran about two hundred paces down the wall, then clambered up his own stalk. As soon as they spotted him, the sparrows dove right for him. He whistled them back—but not before a cobratrap swallowed another dozen. Brady sang something out that made sense only to his birds, sending them out of reach.

The cobratraps straightened and Timothy clung tight, stunned at the height these mogged plants could reach. Below him, the firefly ceiling looked like a twinkling carpet. In the distance he could see Alrod's palace, with its towers and glowing torches. Only the privileged nobles and merchants—and the drudges who served them—lived within the wall of thorns. Free men and women lived outside the walls, their lack of citizenship making them subject to Alrod's whims but also taking them beyond the immense temptations of the stronghold.

Despite Brady's bizarre plan, Timothy was grateful to be raised above it all. The air was thick with the cloying sweetness of the cobratrap, but above him the stars twinkled, far beyond the reach of man's power to transmogrify and profane them.

Brady waved at him. "Now!"

They brandished their swords and howled. Timothy's cobratrap shuddered, bending toward Brady's stalk. Brady's stalk did the same, sensing Timothy as prey. The heads snapped at each other while Brady and Timothy held tight, waving their swords as needed to encourage this bizarre dance.

Timothy fought nausea as the stalk dipped and swayed. It was one thing to scale a cliff, depending on his own skill and that of his comrades. At least a rock face was stationary. It was another thing entirely to cling to a mogged plant that was intent on swallowing any flesh foolish enough to venture near its head. Below, he heard cries and cheers as the crowds in the streets watched the struggle, spectators engrossed in life and death as if it were all a matter for their amusement. A gong clanged from the far side of the stronghold—signaling strongarms to alert.

Timothy's head snapped back as his cobratrap bashed against

Brady's. "Hold tight, man," Brady yelled, a touch of amusement in his voice.

The cobratraps came together, bounced back, came together again, trying to defend from each other. The cilia on their heads fluttered, eventually becoming tangled. Shadows gathered overhead as other cobratraps stretched to address the threat. One head had snaked over and wrapped itself around the two fused cobratraps as if to strangle them.

Brady whistled for the few surviving sparrows to sail through, then signaled retreat. Timothy slid down the stalk, leaped off the flower wall, and immediately went stomach-down on the inner wall. A troop of strong-arms approached.

Brady and Timothy grabbed their packs and crept on their bellies along the wall. The sparrows kept pace, flitting from roof to shadow to alley as if they made their home in the city. Below, shops yielded to houses, then thatched huts. "The drudge sector," Brady whispered as they dropped from the wall into a shadowed area between a row of houses. "We'll be safe here. Remove your mask and gloves, but don't put your silks back on. We don't want to be mistaken for nobles and mugged."

No one took notice as they moved through the mucky streets. Stronghold drudges had only enough energy to obey their masters, not to worry about other commoners wandering about. Brady ducked around a corner into an empty alleyway and whistled. A trembling sparrow fluttered down and landed on his shoulder while the others roosted along the wall. The cilia had scored through the feathers and into its skin. Timothy checked for breaks in its wings, while Brady sang to soothe it, a strange mixture of praise and whistles.

Eventually the sparrow's little chest stopped heaving. Brady's face darkened as the sparrow sang its message. Some birds had the capacity to repeat communications word for word, incorporating even nuances of speech. Sparrows, with their tendency to twitter, were harder to understand. And this poor creature had been through a battle.

"What's it saying?" Timothy finally said. "Is it from Taryan?"

Brady nodded. "Ajoba left camp by herself. She left a note that she was heading north to try to find the gargant she turned aside."

"On her own? That's insane."

Brady's jaw twitched. "Worse than that. She took the spindle with her."

Timothy felt as though he had been punched, his shock was so great. "She couldn't have."

"No, Tim. She *shouldn't* have. But she could, and she did."

The spindle was never to leave camp. Without the spindle, there could be no shroud. And the spindle in the hands of someone other than a birthrighter was not only perilous to the camps, but blasphemous in the extreme.

"She waited for Kendo and Manueo to leave, taking our guests to the western sanctuary. Taryan would have rushed after her, but she's the only birthrighter left in camp now," Brady said. "By modus, she's got to keep watch there."

"I'll ride out with you."

"No, not yet. We need to stick to our original plan."

"You're going to let her disappear into the mountains? Timothy's tone was sharp, causing a passerby to look at them. "We could be on our horses in two hours and on the move."

"Steady, mate. We're a day's hard ride in the other direction, which means she's two days ahead of us. Once she gets into those mountains, it will be even harder to track her."

"And if she gets any more days between her and us, it will be impossible to track her."

"Exactly. Which is why we stick to our original plan. We will go to court, get an audience with the royal provisioner. If we can get him to tell us where in the Bashans his strong-arms chased the gargants, we'll have a much better chance of finding Ajoba as well."

"How are you going to get them to reveal such information to you?"

Brady smiled. "Not to worry, mate. I have a plan."

Had the wind ever been so cold or the shadows so stark?

Ajoba pulled her cloak tighter, tapping each foot gently before she put her full weight forward. It wouldn't do to stride off a cliff or into a crevasse. Demas had led her along this goat path, where he said the gargant had fled. She had marched with confidence, even as the sun disappeared behind the high peaks, believing she would find the poor soul.

Then Demas had disappeared, leaving Ajoba alone in this world for the first time in her life.

She had been into the Bashans before but always with an outrider, usually Kendo or Bartoly. When her mission was urgent and all the outriders were out of camp, sometimes a senior tracker like Jayme or Dano would strap on a sword to escort her.

When Ajoba became the camp's teacher, she had put aside all her weapons. Even so, she had been grateful for Kendo's sword, which had saved her from that band of raiders, and Taryan's arrows, which had gotten her safely through the valley of bloodsucking owls. Now, walking alone, she felt vulnerable and exposed.

There could be mogs watching now, waiting for the right moment to hurtle from the gloom and rip her throat out. And wasn't it somewhere up here that a murderous vine snaked into Tylow's boot as he dozed?

Upground at the Narrows had been blessed with balmy breezes. Here, as night crept between these peaks, violet fingers of cold strangled the remains of the day. She needed to find a place to shelter, or she could freeze to death. If this were a sanctioned mission, her outrider would set up a tent for her while she attended to a fire. But this trip was not sanctioned. It was an outright act of disobedience toward Taryan, her elder.

Ajoba scampered over a rockfall, grateful that she had traded her skirt for traveling trousers. Indeed, the deep shadow she had spotted was a depression in the cliff face. How far back did it go? If this were a cave, creatures might roost in it, poor mogs who had escaped stronghold tyranny. Even originals could be dangerous. Mountain lions, black bears, and rattlesnakes still managed to survive in the Bashans.

She struck a flint to a candle and moved into the shadow. The flickering flame revealed a shallow curve of rock, a dirt floor, and nothing more threatening than tattered spiderwebs in a high corner. An excellent spot for spending the night.

Ajoba brushed aside pebbles and sat down. She pulled a handful of flatbread from her pack, said grace, and nibbled the dry bread. Her water pouch was slung across her hip in the same fashion that Niki wore her sword. She drank the water in greedy gulps.

Where was the gargant on this night? Had he found a spring to drink from, or was he suffering from thirst? Certainly he would be hungry. She had filled her pack with Magosha's flatbread and a bag of sweet yams. Though it was a heavy load for mountain climbing, it should be enough to at least allay the gargant's hunger.

"Hold on, brother. Hold on." Ajoba spread out her blanket and pulled it up around her, her head resting on her pack. "I'm coming."

NINE

COOPER RACED TO THE FAR SIDE OF THE HILLOCK, throwing up as he went. Something brushed his back. He whirled, fearing another mogged musk ox.

"Put that away," Anastasia said.

He hadn't even realized he had taken out his short blade. Instinct was a good thing—though vomiting at the sight of blood was not.

"Niki wants us to hold Kwesi while she attends to his wound," she said.

He had sickened at the sight of Kwesi's bloody shirt. How would he help if he couldn't keep his own stomach in check? Cooper wiped his mouth and followed Anastasia back to the sled. Even from a couple hundred paces away, he heard Kwesi's moans.

Anastasia took his hand. "Not like the Ark, is it?"

"No." If this had happened on the Ark, Kwesi would be asleep while a surgeon repaired his wound. He'd wake to pain relievers running through his veins and his parents at his side. But this couldn't have happened on the Ark, anyway, because the community under the ice was safe from mogs, sorcerers, stronghold princes, and a world trapped in gloom.

They had been warned about taking care of each other, trained for it, even sewed up wounds on the sides of cattle and pigs. If someone needed surgery, the trainees had been required to observe. Even then, glass had separated them from the open tissue and fresh blood.

Cooper hadn't expected to be confronted with this kind of reality, not a week out of his husk.

Kwesi lay on the sled, clutching a piece of shroud against his side.

"It's not too bad," Niki told them. "His coat took most of the slash. The ox didn't even catch muscle, just a few layers of skin. I need you two to hold his shoulders while I sew."

Cooper's stomach flipped again. He breathed deeply to quell his nausea, and Niki focused his way.

"Look, I know this is nasty," she said. "But it's a hard world, a hard life. You've got to learn to handle stuff like this. See this?" Niki pushed back her curls, showing them the skin behind her ear. "I had to sew this myself. Can't tell you how many times I've stitched up my comrades. I'll stitch you someday probably. Kwesi should be honored to be the first of you three to get the needle."

"I am honored," Kwesi said, forcing a smile.

Niki unrolled a small piece of shroud. Inside were dried green leaves. "Chew on this, Kwesi. It'll help with the pain."

He gagged at the taste but obeyed.

"I'm sorry, Niki," Cooper said. "I was the first one to run."

"Me too. I . . ." Anastasia choked up.

"*We,*" Kwesi muttered. "*We* got scared."

Niki shook her head. "Like I said—hard world. Just believe me next time I tell you to stay put. Now be quiet and hold his shoulders."

Kwesi stared at the sky, still chewing, as Niki sewed. His eyes took on a dreamy gaze, but sweat broke out on his forehead. Afterward he dozed while Cooper and Anastasia gathered materials for a fire, coaxed the damp wood into flame, then stared transfixed. They'd had fire pits on the Ark so birthrighters-in-training could learn to build a blaze, but the Ark couldn't simulate anything like a glowing fire under a cold sky.

When darkness fell, Niki helped them set up the sled as a shelter. "Put Kwesi between you as you sleep. He needs to be kept warm."

After they wrapped up in their blankets, she draped the canvas tarp over them. Anastasia peeked through a crack, watching Niki take her blanket to the far side of the fire. "There's room for you in here."

"I prefer the open sky," Niki called back.

Anastasia pulled the tarp tight, then got up on her elbow so she could face her comrades. "She thinks we're mess-ups."

"We *are* mess-ups," Kwesi whispered back. "Why didn't you eat the meat she cooked for us?"

"Why didn't you?"

"I'm injured."

"You think you're high and mighty, just because you scored a little scratch."

"It's more than a scratch. You saw Niki stitch it up. It's a hand length at least."

"You're hoping for a scar, aren't you? So you can tell tales about the musk cow for years."

"Musk ox," Cooper said.

"He speaks," Kwesi said. "Amazing."

"Unlike on the Ark, when he never shut up," Anastasia said. "Any other words of wisdom, smart mouth?"

"Don't mention the you-know-what," Cooper muttered. "The place where we came from."

Anastasia put her hand over her mouth. "Zipper my lipper."

"And *high and mighty*. Don't use that."

"And I'm not allowed to use *high and mighty* because . . .?"

"That's a title of respect for the nobles who run the strongholds," Kwesi whispered. "I should have remembered."

"So let me get this straight," Anastasia said. "Kwesi is the brave one and Cooper . . . is the *smart* one?"

"I was just sayin', that's all," Cooper said.

"I put up with four years of you just sayin' too much," Anastasia shot back. "I like you better not sayin'."

Cooper rolled over in his blanket. *So why haven't you been talkin' much now, Cooper?* a true friend would have asked.

Because my voice was rubbed raw from yellin' and singin', he would have answered. *Because I passed transit awake.*

The closest anyone had gotten to asking was Niki. "You all right?" And he'd simply nodded his head. She had a way of making words stick in his throat.

He had been only ten when Niki and the other first ones left the Ark. That was one big day, a high-kickin' holiday practically. The builders were scared—no one knew if they had understood the vision right. They went ahead and did it anyway. They had wrapped Brady, Niki, Tylow, and Kendo in shroud and tossed them out of the airlock into freezing cold water, a mile under the ice. Everyone on the Ark cheered when a whale came along and swallowed the husks.

It was almost six months before the first letters came back with the first collections.

We've named our camp Horesh, they said.

It's an evil world. Far fallen from the world our ancestors knew . . .

We're ready for more birthrighters . . .

And so every few months there had been more husks, more whales, more transits. Within a couple of years new camps were established, new leaders named. But none would ever be the heroes that Niki, Brady, Tylow, and Kendo became. The *first-evers,* they were called then, and were still called on the Ark. The first day of training, the rooks saw their farewell holograms: Niki, her curls wild about her head and her blue eyes wilder. Kendo, small and dark, quick eyes and hands. Tylow, tall and thin, with long fingers and a dreamy intensity about him. Brady, ordinary, except for those strange, clear eyes that seemed friendly and scary at the same time.

Tylow had died in the past year, though the news hadn't reached the Ark until weeks afterward. Cooper remembered his parents wailing with grief. He had cried, too, after the shock wore off. Somehow, every kid in training assumed those first four would live forever.

He couldn't wait to meet the other two. What did Brady and

Kendo look like now? At twenty-two, they must be full-grown men, not scrawny like Cooper or with too-big feet like Kwesi. Niki was beautiful, though she'd probably bite Cooper's head off if he told her that. Maybe in a few years, she'd decide he was worthy to tell her such a thing.

If he were still alive. If *she* were still alive. Cooper shuddered to think about her jumping onto that musk oxen. Shuddered to think if she hadn't.

Niki might be beautiful, but she was also deadly. And Cooper wasn't about to forget that anytime soon.

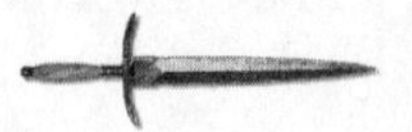

Fighting mogs was all in a day's work. Babysitting rooks required superhuman patience.

Niki had tipped the sled onto its side so the three rooks could sleep under it, with Kwesi in the middle. The dogs had returned, but kept a watchful distance from the oxen carcasses. Niki gave them most of the meat, wrapping only enough for herself since the rooks refused to eat it.

"Mogged meat won't hurt you," she had sworn to them. "We're all inoculated against the viruses. Besides, cooking destroys them."

But Kwesi had held his side, his big eyes soulful, and Anastasia had turned away. Cooper had tried, but then he'd vomited yet again. Brady would never forgive her if she brought back three rooks who looked like skeletons, so she'd let them eat more of the soy paste.

Niki settled into her own blanket on the far side of the fire, preferring to sleep under the open sky. But questions chasing in her mind drove out any hope of rest. What were mogs doing this far north? Why did that wolf dare to take on a blood-crazed mog? Did this have anything to do with Arabah? What of Horesh—was her home still safe?

And when had she begun thinking of Horesh as home instead of the Ark?

She gazed up, willing herself to enjoy this sparkling night. The sky was a regal shade of deep blue. The air was brisk and the tundra glazed over with frost, like the lace on her mother's bridal veil. What was her mother doing now?

Niki sat up and felt for the packet of letters she had bound to her ribs. Brady always waited to read his personal letters until he was back at Horesh. He said it wasn't fair that he should receive a blessing before his comrades, that they should read their letters together so they could share their joy or, if need be, comfort sorrows.

This wasn't Brady's transit. It was hers. And she had already waited nearly a week.

Niki found four letters marked with her code. One letter was from her brother, Rian, another from her godmother, Bethliza, and one from each of her parents. Rian was getting married! In her mind, she saw her little brother as twelve, his age when she left the Ark. She deciphered the name of his intended—Audree. That name meant nothing to Niki, though Rian said that they had all played together as children. As time passed, her memories of the Ark and its people became more distant. When Taryan made the transit four years ago, Niki had known her immediately. Two years ago, she had vaguely recognized Timothy. Though they claimed to remember her quite well, Kwesi, Anastasia, and Cooper simply did not register in her memory.

Bethliza sent a rare gift, a miniature painting on vellum of Rian and Audree. Her brother's hair was as curly as Niki's and almost as long. Audree's eyes were blue, her hair blonde. Bethliza had painted a plain background that would give no clue to the materials aboard the Ark that didn't exist in this world, at least not anymore. Rian's eyes were hopeful, his smile innocent—or at least Bethliza painted him that way. The builders received letters and updates, but the builders who had helped prepare the Ark and sink it under the ice had long since died—which meant that no one still on the Ark could really know what it was like out here in the world. Niki was glad that Rian hadn't been called into training, that someone she loved lived in peace.

In his letter, Father shared his passion for the latest revealed science but gave no specifics. He understood that the need-to-knows transmitted by the latest birthrighters would clarify his veiled references and took every care not to reveal anything in writing that might compromise the Ark.

The same circumspection was required of birthrighters themselves, especially in regard to camp location or activities. The code sometimes got so complex, Niki wondered if anyone understood what they were trying to report. Sent with each collection, their letters to their friends and family were not allowed to breach the isolation of the Ark, but had to be read in a glovebox. They remained in quarantine along with the collections.

Niki had saved her mother's letter for last.

> *Dear child—*
>
> *They tell me you are tall, taller even than most of your comrades. They tell me you are strong and smart, and they tell me you are beautiful. Dear one, they—*

They, Niki thought. Her campmates and their families on the Ark. They talked too much, especially about her. They should be writing about their own business, not what she was doing.

> *—they speak of your exploits, though you do not. We are not surprised, and we are proud, so proud. But sweet pea,—*

Niki put the paper to her face. Mother hadn't called her sweet pea since she was still small enough to crawl into her lap. She leaned closer to the fire, the fading embers providing little light for reading now.

> *—we have heard that you fear nothing, and that you will stop at nothing. But I know you well, and I know that has always*

been your gift and your pitfall. I long to tell you to be careful, but I cannot. I can only ask you to be faithful to your call and to the One who has called you.

Niki's face flushed. Hadn't she given her heart and body to her call? Yet that day in the smithy, she had heard the disappointment in Brady's voice. It had been tempered by a meager hope that if he sent her on transit, she would come back with a touch from God, a word to redirect her path to—to where?

What would she be, if not an outrider? The notion was too foreign to even consider. Yet when she pressed him for his reasoning, Brady had simply squeezed her hand and said, "Listen well, Nik."

Niki read on.

As the solitary has relayed to your leader, it is clear that the urgency of our mission has increased. Even so, the elders are giving each of our working groups a new directive in response to your leader's query. We have the blessing of family life to ease the strain for us. We know now that we should allow the same blessing to you who are on the front lines of this struggle. You were so young when you left us, but now you are grown women and men. Allowing you this comfort will help you endure. I will not say any more—it is for your leader to explain.

Daughter, know that I pray for you every day, sometimes every moment of every day. Feel my arms around you now, dear one, because they are always just a blessing away.

Go in peace and, though the world be troubled, take heart always.

With all my love, Mother

Niki pressed her fists to her eyes. She would not cry. She had learned long ago that this hard world allowed no weakness.

When she finally looked up, the fire had dwindled to coals. One of the rooks snored daintily, like a baby might. Niki thought of the little ones they had rescued over the years, children whose parents had died trying to save them from strong-arms and sorcerers.

Niki had risked her life for those children, though they were not her own. How much more would she give for a child of her own, a little girl who would climb into her lap and play with her curls just as she had played with Mother's curls? What would it be like to have her own baby in her arms, listening to a son breathe noisily, smelling the milk on his breath, feeling the softness of his cheek and knowing his very life was a gift from her body?

A gift of love, given between husband and wife.

What would that be like, to be in the arms of a man who was brave and strong and who loved you with all his heart?

Where was this all coming from? Perhaps she had sunstroke from the sun reflecting off the snow. Back at Horesh, spring must be in full bloom. Birds would be feverishly making nests or dancing merrily in the air currents. The heady scent of new grass and fresh buds would be giving the promise of creation, the hope that still bloomed in the remnant of this world that had managed to survive the wars and the strongholds.

"Stop it," Niki muttered. To think like this was to lose focus. To lose focus was to die. She needed to get her mind back on Birthright.

What query had Brady made of the elders, and what was the directive they had issued in response? Niki rustled through the letter packet, finding the ones marked with his personal code. At the bottom of his stack was a handful of sheets for the camp leader.

The first set of pages was all in code, specifying the next series of collections and the coordinates where Dakota had indicated certain species might be found. Dakota was Horesh's scout, a lean, dark-eyed man whose sole function was to ride the territories in a thousand-league radius of Horesh, alert for endangered species. Because of safety issues, Dakota did not know the exact location of the camp for which he was responsible. His signal to Horesh was a hawk; when needed, Brady met him out on the plains.

The scouts reported back to the builders, who determined which camp would track what species, based on location and also the talents of the trackers. The rooks would also have memorized these lists, just in case.

At the end of the directive, there was plain language. Mostly encouragement and praise, a couple of warnings, including one about depending too much on devices. *Kendo would not like to hear that*, Niki thought. He spent all his free time creating gadgets to use in camp life or for defense.

Then, at the end:

> *We have given much thought and prayer to your query. Though the urgency of the mission increases, so has the duration. As there are now many grown men and women among you, we cannot expect you to live in an unnatural state any longer. After much prayer, we do authorize you to marry. Our only stipulations are these: that you yoke with other believers; that only those of you with senior status—*

Senior status. That meant those who had been out of the Ark for a minimum of two years. Birthrighters became camp elders when they were out in the world for four.

> *—be allowed to court and wed and that, if a child is born, one parent must stay out of danger for the good of that child. Please proceed with this permission very carefully lest the younger among you fall into a frenzy and lose focus.*
>
> *Otherwise, we send our blessing and look forward to hearing your specific news as you indicate you have someone on your heart.*

Niki looked up from the letter, shocked to see the stars so bright and to hear the wind moving like music through her hair.

One parent must stay out of danger.

She let her fingers dance over the hilt of her sword, so familiar now that it was almost an extension of her, just as her comrades were. Especially Brady. That day in the smithy, his eyes had been filled with concern and worry. But there was no mistaking the love as well.

Would you give up being an outrider . . . ?

Of course, she had answered, not meaning it one bit.

But on a night like this, *yes*. "Yes," she said to the snow and the sky and the stars.

Of course she could put her sword aside in an instant to raise a child with eyes the color of a forest stream and a smile that came sudden and sweet.

TEN

AT THE FIRST LIGHT OF DAY, TIMOTHY SHOOK BRADY awake. They had spent what was left of the night sleeping in a goat stall that housed only mice and bats.

"Leave off, mate. I need my rest," Brady muttered.

"Don't you think it's time we get going?"

"And do what?"

"Go after Ajoba, of course. Bring her back to Horesh."

Brady rolled over, his back to Timothy. "Didn't we already go over this? She's got a dandy lead on us."

"We can catch her."

"Oh? So you think you can find her?"

"If I can track elk and panthers and moles, I can track a comrade."

"Ajoba knows how to cover her tracks."

Timothy brushed the straw out of his hair and the dirt from his pants. "I can uncover them."

Brady stretched and yawned. "So you know your way around the Bashans, do you?"

Timothy fell silent.

"This predicament is why we choose a course and stick to it. We need to find whether Alrod has found his gargants. And where they are."

"What about Ajoba?" Timothy said.

"One must weigh priorities. Right now, the safety of Horesh takes precedence over Ajoba's safety."

"It's not Ajoba I'm worried about," Timothy said, exasperated. "The spindle, man. She's got the spindle."

"That's what you're worried about?"

"Aye."

"Then that is a shame, mate. A real shame." Brady stood, stretching until his elbows hit the roof of the stall. His eyes widened at what looked like a ball of paper hanging in the corner. "Ah, an opportunity presents itself."

Timothy shook his head. "White-faced wasps. We collected those long ago."

"Never know when you might need them again, Tim." Brady wrapped a length of shroud carefully around the hive, out-of-time side facing inward. He flattened the fabric, then bound it around his waist like a sash.

Timothy combed out his hair. They would wait until they were closer to the marketplace to dress in their silks. "I take it those wasps are also a plan?" *For disaster*, he was tempted to add, hoping Brady had sealed the seams carefully.

"You know me, Tim. *Everything*'s a plan. Let's get a move on. We need to buy a herd of cattle."

"A herd of—" Timothy shut his mouth. He'd had enough of Brady's lecturing for one day, and the sun had only just come up.

The night hadn't gone badly.

Ajoba was warm and dry, though exceedingly stiff. What time of day was it? She couldn't seem to open her eyes. She tried to raise her hand to brush the sleep away, but her arms felt like porridge. She leaned sideways, struggling to shake her limbs into movement.

Nothing.

Was she still asleep, and this a dream? She fluttered the tiny muscles in her eyelids, trying to push them up. Something sticky rasped on her face . . . and not just on her face, but also on her hands, her legs, her chest and throat, binding her like—

The spider! Horror seized her as she remembered the webs she'd seen last night. The cave had been so dark, and she had been too focused on finding the gargant to even look for the glow of a mog. She could see it now, tiny tendrils of green trickling through her eyelashes.

The spider had wrapped her into its web and injected its numbing venom so she wouldn't feel pain or struggle. The spider would infuse digestive juices into her skin and munch through her for days. She wouldn't feel pain, but she would feel the pressure of its jaws and of her own blind pride in thinking she could trek into the mountains by herself, without Taryan's permission and without a plan from Brady.

"Friend?"

"Demas?" she mumbled.

"Little. Sister. I am not. He."

The gargant. "Help me. Please help me."

She heard a harsh rip and prayed it was the web coming apart and not the body she could not feel. The gargant's fingers brushed her face, rough textured but gentle as he tore the web from her face. Her eyes resisted opening, so the gargant tugged on her eyelids until she could see.

The gargant's face was lumpy and misshapen, his nose far too large. His eyes were off the center line but shone with awareness and concern. Too often, full-body transmogrifications left humans as unthinking shells, but this was a man for whom sense had somehow remained. How great his pain must be.

He worked at the web, ripping the strands with his hands or, when needed, cutting them with his teeth. Life returned to Ajoba's body, a rush of aching pain in her back where she had lain all night on the icy ground. She moaned, and the gargant's eyes blinked in surprise. "Be. Still."

"Yes, I'll try."

When her upper torso was free, the gargant helped her sit. He worked at freeing her legs. Something moved overhead—the spider! The size of a cat, but its mouth was mighty, its pincers gleaming razor sharp as it glided sideways along the wall.

"Behind—" she struggled to say. Before the words were out, the gargant's hand crushed the creature as if it were no more than a pesky mosquito.

He helped her up, holding Ajoba's hand like a toddler's so she could stagger out into the morning sun. He led her to a sunny spot sheltered from the wind. She leaned gratefully back against a rock, letting the warmth ease her pain.

"My pack," she said.

The gargant ripped it out of the tangle of web. She gave him the pile of flatbread and yams she had taken from Magosha's ovens. He fell on the food hungrily.

When he finished, he leaned on the rock next to her. Sitting by his side, her head only came up to where his heart would be. "My name is Ajoba, friend. I thank you for saving my life."

"No. Thanks. Needed."

"Would you honor me by telling me your name?"

He fixed his gaze on the horizon. "My name is Jasper. I once. Made shoes."

The sun was already well past the meridian by the time Timothy and Brady lied and bribed their way into Alrod's palace courtyard. A throng of people waited to be admitted to the palace proper, where they would beg for Alrod's attention.

Though Brady had been to stronghold courts many times, the various transmogrifications he saw here made him queasy. Women had flowing hair in varying shades and textures—the shining black of a panther, the rich orange of fox, even glossy peacock feathers. Some had pouting lips so large they looked to be stuffed with cherries. Others had gaudily painted claws instead of fingernails. One woman had a neck so long that her head swayed as she walked.

The men were as vain as the woman. One man towered over the crowd, his skull mogged with six inches of added bone to form a natural battering ram. Another had shoulders the width of Brady's arm span.

Brady leaned into Timothy. "If we get separated, head home. You can leave the stronghold out the main gate—no one checks citizenship on the way out, just on the way in."

"Are you expecting trouble?"

"Aren't you?"

Timothy stiffened. "I find it better to dread trouble than expect it."

Brady had to laugh at that. "You got me there. Listen, mate, and listen well. If I'm not able to return, I want you to gather whatever outriders you've got in camp. I'll leave it on your shoulders to come up with a plan. Assign someone to find our teacher and bring her—and our spindle—back to camp."

The doors to court opened. The crowd remained in place, with no one making a move to enter.

"What's this about?" Timothy said. "They're all gaudy and grand, but no one's going in."

"No one wants to be the first to encounter Alrod. He's likely to be in a foul mood after being trampled by his own gargants."

"And by some fool outrider who doesn't know his place. Alrod will be thirsty for revenge. Take care, comrade."

Brady smiled. "I always do, don't I?"

"If you define flying on the baron's back as taking care, I would scarce want to know what your notion of risk is. Be grateful you were masked and he won't recognize you."

"He might, Tim. Alrod is observant and crafty. We'll need to be the same."

A courtier dressed in the brash gold that specified the house of Alrod commanded people to enter. Brady and Timothy shuffled in behind the nobles and favor seekers.

Brady had to pause and simply consider the entirety—and irony—of what he beheld. He had seen some of the grandest corners of this continent, formed by the hand of God and the forces of nature: multihued canyons that stretched for leagues, deep forests with trees reaching up so high he had to bend backward to see their tops, a glistening ocean that roared against the sand, making and breaking continents in its path.

Brady had also seen the worst of man's corruption: huge tracts of land rendered toxic by war and pollution; transmogrifications so profane as to be unthinkable; sordid neighborhoods where children and fish were sold side by side; sorcerers gathering in the night to share mogging potions and techniques, and to experiment on slaves and babies.

Alrod's palace combined both the grand and profane. The outside featured the customary ivy-laced stone, with barred windows and fortified walls. The inside wall of the antechamber sparkled from diamond and topaz dust flowing in a continuous stream of air. Filigreed-gold chandeliers dangled from the high-arched ceiling, each lit with a hundred candles. The floor was gray granite stippled with gold and polished to a high sheen. The middle of the chamber was terraced in alternating black and gold steps that led to a pool of about twenty paces in diameter. Fish of all sizes and shape swam there, all mogged with bioluminescence. The effect was startling and lovely.

But deceptive, Brady reminded himself. *Beauty is fleeting.*

He glanced around the hall, noting the flower-laced bowers that lined the walls to provide privacy for business meetings and romantic encounters. Brady recognized the motion and form of the tiny birds flitting through each bower. *Hummingbirds.* His favorite. But the colors were all wrong—anything from stark white to lustrous black, with bright blues and startling pinks.

"Is nothing sacred?" he muttered.

Timothy's hand clamped hard on his forearm. "Steady."

"You're right, mate. But it gets to me still."

Each bower trailed a line of people waiting for an audience.

Brady scanned the area until he found the one he wanted. "That's the baron's provisioner, the man with the real power here."

Through the flowered branches, they could see a man with a long nose and pointy chin. The provisioner wore the colors of a Traxx strong-arm, but instead of a scabbard or quiver, his leather harness bulged with scrolls, styli, and coins. As they waited in line, Brady tried to resist the sensory assault: sweet smells of creams and perfumes; the sounds of laughter and debate; the flash of silks and satins; the constant bubble of water.

He forced his mind to focus instead on the wild rush of water that was the Grand, the gentle and varied delight of his friends, the birds. And on his comrades—the gift of song that was Timothy, the strength of purpose that was Niki, the quickness of hand that was Kendo, the grace of form that was Taryan. He fingered his braid, imagining he could feel the tawny strands of her hair plaited in among his own.

After almost an hour, they reached the front of the line. The provisioner looked Timothy up and down. "A fine drudge. But I can't give top dollar. He's a bit thin for the baroness's taste."

Brady slapped the table. "You insult a son of Finway? My friend is a noble prince of the lineage of David, not some lowly drudge to be bought and sold."

The long-nosed man barely blinked. "My apologies. I did not recognize his colors."

"An honest mistake." Brady gave him the smile of one reluctant to let personal affront stand in the way of a lucrative deal. "Finwayans seldom visit here," he added. "Unless they have urgent business, of course."

The man's eyebrows lifted a fraction. "And the nature of this . . . business?"

"We have a fine herd of cattle to sell."

Brady had spent most of the morning in a frenzy of bargaining to procure that particular herd. A gold coin had bought a dented sword, which, when he brought it to the weapons shop, was suddenly straight and gleaming. He'd traded that for a dull-faced but sturdy shield of bronze, which, after a visit to the smithy's barn, turned out to be edged with gold. Then on and on—from shield to copper cooking pans to rare silks to gleaming gold jewelry—until Brady had a bag of gold coins. Finally, in the holding pens outside Alrod's palace, Brady had made a deal with an impatient landowner for his herd of fat cattle, then hired some off-duty strong-arms to guard them.

Now he spoke quickly with the provisioner, detailing the number, breed, and size of the stock. "Mogged to be fat, juicy, and tender, my herd will go far in feeding many. A small army even, though the Traxx army is anything but small."

Brady was testing the man. Traxx had lost hundreds of troops when the gargants stormed back on them.

The provisioner refused to rise to the bait. Instead he leaned back in his chair. "Sorry. Our army is well provisioned. And the baron and his court do not eat mogged food. Ever."

Brady leaned close to the provisioner. "I heard that the baron might have pressing need to feed . . . shall we say . . . a different type of army?"

The provisioner's narrow eyes darted left and right. "I wouldn't speak of that too loudly," he growled.

Brady suppressed a grunt of satisfaction. So some gargants had been captured. Now he just had to find out where the baron was holding them.

He pressed even closer. "We both know an army of that size eats vast quantities. Why else would you be buying up all the grain in the near villages?"

The provisioner's cheek twitched. "Step aside while I have your herd examined." He sent a lackey out to the holding pens. The lackey came back within a few minutes and whispered something in the provisioner's ear.

The provisioner waved Brady back. "Can you offer transport as well? Our need is not here in Traxx, but elsewhere."

"Perhaps, though our time here is limited. Can you tell me where we would need to drive the herd?"

The provisioner scratched something on his slate and pushed it across the table. Brady read it and frowned. "Tough place to get to. I'm not much of an outdoors type."

Timothy covered his laughter with a sneezing fit.

The provisioner frowned at Brady's elaborate braids and his fine silks. "You'll have to pay for someone to do it, then."

"Can you commission that service for me?"

"Me?" The provisioner sounded shocked.

"I'm sure you could arrange it," Brady said. "For a fee, of course . . ."

The provisioner pretended to think that through. "I imagine I could," he finally said. "Though it would take some doing. My time would need to be compensated."

"Oh, absolutely. Please deduct whatever you think is necessary from the sale price. My Finwayan friend and I are eager to be rid of those cows and on to greater delights." After a few more minutes of negotiation, Brady signed his writ of ownership over to the provisioner, took a small bag of gold, and stepped aside.

They were almost to the door when the provisioner rushed after them. He motioned Brady to him, whispered for a good minute, then returned to his table.

"What was that about?" Timothy said.

"He asked if I would consider selling you, even though you're supposedly a noble. Said I should tell your people you got in with bandits or something and disappeared."

"And you said . . . ?"

"That it was a tempting offer."

"Thanks a lot."

Brady grinned. "That's all right, mate. I still said no."

"Glad to hear it."

"But we've got a slight complication. The lackey told a porter about you, who told a serving girl, who . . . well, it took about two minutes to get to the baroness, and now she's demanding to see the golden-haired stranger."

A strong-arm came behind Timothy and grabbed his shoulders. He tried to yank away.

Brady put his hand gently on the strong-arm's hand. "Good sir, we do not have to be manhandled. If you would be so kind as to serve as our honor guard, we would be most grateful."

The strong-arm closed his fingers over the coins Brady had slipped into his hand.

"You first," the Traxx growled.

Brady put his hand on Timothy's shoulder and walked with him to the throne room.

The fifteenth baron and baroness of Traxx sat on thrones higher than Dawnray's head, but Dawnray didn't look up. She kept her head down as she slowly climbed the dais, feeling the heat of a hundred pairs of eyes on her.

"Where ever did he find her?" someone whispered from below.

"She's nigh perfect," someone else said.

Reaching the top, Dawnray took in the throne room, barely comprehending all of what she saw. The floor seemed to be paved with fine gems; the walls burnished gold. Cream satin embroidered with shining threads lined the high ceiling. Lights flared in sconces, positioned perfectly so not one shadow was cast. Benches lined the walls, but the highest of nobles lounged in brocade chairs or sofas. Maids in gray silk dresses with gold sashes brought trays of treats, while clean-shaven men in black trousers, gray shirts, and gold cummerbunds poured wine and other libations.

People mingled everywhere except right in front of the dais. Dawnray leaned forward but could see no reason why that space remained cleared.

"Go ahead. Look." Merrihana shoved her forward with such force she almost tripped off the dais. Below her, directly in front of the dais, was a large marble slab, stained brown and crimson by blood.

Horrified, Dawnray turned to flee. But the baroness laced her fingers into her hair and wrenched her head around. "This is the reality of my life, you little piece of sow lip. You will look, and if I decide you should lick that table clean, you will do that as well."

Dawnray's knees buckled. Alrod wrapped his arm around her waist and pulled her away from Merrihana, positioning her between his throne and his wife's. "Don't worry, sweet one. I am not going to do that to you."

He turned away to give Sado detailed instructions on whom he would see when.

Merrihana leaned over the arm of her throne. "Perhaps he will not. But I just may."

"Merrihana won't keep you," Brady whispered. "The baron has little use for his wife, but he does not like competition for her attention. Listen well, now, mate. If somehow Alrod recognizes me as his outrider, you must play dumb. Strike me down and offer him my head, if you must. Remember your training."

As they were escorted into the throne room, Timothy took in the position of the strong-arms, spying instantly the guards who were dressed either as servers or guests or, in one case, as a woman. He glanced at the windows—all too high for an exit except for one that overlooked a slanting rooftop. He knew which strong-arm he could take a sword from and what his next four moves after that would be.

He also knew to stay clear of Alrod. The man was a fine fighter and no coward.

Alrod turned from his discussion to acknowledge their presence. "Ah, more young men to see my wife. She has quite the following. Well deserved, of course."

Brady bowed deeply. Timothy imitated him.

"It is a rare privilege to be asked into her presence, high and mighty, and rarer still to come before you." Brady's tone was high, his words cloudy to disguise his voice. He kept his gaze on the floor—not from humility but to keep Alrod from recognizing his eyes. The baron would not know Brady's face, because he had worn his mask when they grappled on that mogged bat. But the mask had not hidden his eyes, and they were quite recognizable.

"Yes. Well, you have about ten seconds to bring her some amusement before she orders your heads taken off."

The strong-arm at Alrod's side unsheathed a scimitar.

"I'd like to offer a song, if I may," Timothy ventured. Even as he spoke, the music came into his head, a lilting tune with a trail of mystery woven through it. He reached deep for words that would match the music. A love song, perhaps. He began.

Whispers on the water echo on the hills.
None is found that's sweeter than your face.

He fixed his eyes on Merrihana as he sang, watching for her reaction. The trick would be to impress her enough to live but not enough that she would want to possess him.

Mysteries and melodies are riding on the wind;
Those whispers in the air can never take your place.

His voice caught when he saw the girl—no, a woman. Standing between the two thrones, she was more beautiful than the sun setting behind the Bashans or a hawk soaring on the winter wind. Her hair was thick, auburn shaded, with a lustrous sheen. Her skin was creamy and her cheeks high with color. Her body was graceful, her neck long. Her eyes were the color of sapphires.

Though she wore a moss-green gown, a gold ribbon on her wrist marked her as Alrod's drudge. It took everything within Timothy to keep from leaping onto the dais and stealing her away. But he would die in an instant, and she would die in the next.

She looked his way and somehow, in an instant so fleeting

and so profound, she seized Timothy's heart. Her lips parted, and her hand went to her throat, as if she could not breathe. Time resumed, but his eyes could not leave her—not until her mouth formed a clear warning: *No*.

He forced himself to look away. If the baroness saw him staring at the girl, she would have her killed, perhaps right here on this hideous marble slab.

He shifted his gaze to Merrihana. The baroness had been examining him from the toes up and missed the exchange. Timothy sang on, turning his head to take in the baron and others in the room, remembering to rest his gaze much longer on Merrihana, but taking in the girl with his glance.

Sing to me. Move my heart.
Sing of beauty the eye may never see.
Sing of forever . . .

Was it the spark of love that made his heart thud? Or was this more deception, just as the wall of thorns had deceived him? No one falls in love at first sight, his father had told him. But what did the heart know of wisdom when beauty captured it? She felt it too; he could tell by the line of color moving up her neck.

Timothy's breath failed him and he stopped singing. The baron leaned toward his wife. "Was that amusing for you?" he asked.

"Passably."

"And how about you, Dawnray?"

Dawnray. The first light of day, shy but full of promise. It fit her perfectly.

"Anything that amuses the baron and baroness delights me."

The baroness leaned close to Alrod, whispering over Dawnray's head. The girl's eyes widened. The lift of her brow and the flick of her eye toward the door told Timothy to *go now*.

Alrod motioned to his strong-arm. The guard leaned over the dais.

Go, the girl mouthed clearly. *Now.*

Timothy moved toward the nearest strong-arm, intent on wresting away his sword.

"No," Brady whispered. "I'll take this one." He pulled at his sash as if making a simple adjustment.

A hefty woman with leopard-spotted skin screamed. Her escort slapped at her arms, then his own. The crowd became frantic, beating off the wasps that Brady had unleashed, managing to smack each other as they did so. A strong-arm swung his sword as if that could possibly help. Alrod and Merrihana vacated their thrones, leaving Dawnray alone for a precious moment in which Timothy could have taken her arm and pulled her away. But years of training made him follow his leader, even as he left his heart with the auburn-haired girl abandoned between the thrones of Traxx.

Brady swerved left down a long corridor, elbowed a guard in the jaw before he could raise his sword. Timothy heard him counting windows aloud as he ran, taking a blind dive through the fifth one, which mercifully was not barred.

Timothy followed blindly, falling for an infinite moment until he mashed into a vat of sweet butter. Brady swung over the side and raced for the rear of the compound. Timothy followed him, his lungs about to burst, his heart still in the throne room, praying that no one saw the girl cue them to escape.

They ended up in the feed bins behind the stable where they had stashed their swords, daggers, and packs. Brady sliced off his braids, cutting his hair down to the scalp. Timothy hacked his hair until it stood up in ragged spikes. Brady cut his beard as close as a sharp dagger and no water would allow.

Timothy followed Brady to the manure piles in the far corner of the corral. "No," he said, but Brady was already rolling in the muck. When he stood, he was hunched over, looking every bit like an insignificant drudge and not a strapping outrider. Timothy did the same, gasping back waves of nausea. While the strong-arms searched the antechamber and front courtyard, they climbed over the back wall and headed for the drudge sector.

"Well, Tim," Brady told him, "we certainly got what we came for."

I got more than we came for, Timothy wanted to say, but he was not inclined to share a confidence—especially that of his heart—with Brady. "Which way is the gate?"

Brady slapped his back. "Come on, mate. You don't really think the stronghold gate will still be open, with us on the loose?"

They trudged back through the thorns, their feet mired in slime and their eyes fixed on the slung. But as Timothy sang, it was Dawnray's face he saw.

The girl with the deep-blue eyes.

Eleven

BRADY AND TIMOTHY PICKED UP THEIR HORSES AND rode hard, arriving back at Horesh in the middle of the night.

"When are we leaving?" Timothy asked as they unsaddled their horses.

"I'm leaving tomorrow."

"Tomorrow? Why not now? We should get our weapons and—"

"Whoa. Slow down there, Tim," Brady said. "First things first."

"It's a three-day ride to that part of the Bashans where Alrod's got the gargants. We've lost two days at court, and there's so much ground to cover. I don't understand what is more pressing than getting that spindle back."

"Rest," Brady said gently. "We need our rest."

Timothy unsaddled Ranger, his displeasure clear in his stilted movements. He reached for the brush to rub down the horse.

Brady stayed his hand. "I'll do it."

"Why?"

"Go to bed, Timothy."

Timothy stomped out of the stable. Brady brushed Ranger and fed her while Thunderhoof stood patiently by. Their stable took up most of the east riverbank, backed partway into one of the higher caves for the protection of the livestock. Goats, cows, a donkey, and chickens all slumbered in the straw, though all the other horses were gone except for Taryan's and Ajoba's. Apparently Ajoba had ridden her pony to the Bashan foothills, then set it loose, trusting it to wander home.

While he worked, Brady prayed briefly for every outrider and tracker out on mission, for the scouts that wandered the world with no benefit of a comradeship, for all the camps, and for their families back on the Ark. Then, when he finished, he rewarded both horses with a stick of sweet cane.

Thunderhoof nuzzled him, nickering softly for more cane, and he breathed a quick thanks for this horse he had found wandering six years ago on their way south from transit. Kendo and Niki had already found mounts that fit them well, but Brady had been still afoot. He'd known why when the little band of wild horses flew through their campsite, pursued by a pack of wolves. They were scruffy and thin, like most of the feral animals that eked out a life on the plains, and a few showed signs of toxic exposure. But one stood out among them as an animal of breeding, escaped perhaps from a stronghold or village. She had spirit and strength, a fine animal with a pure black coat except for patches of white on the hindquarters and a flowing white tail. Her hooves that were so big that Kendo had cried out on first sight: "Watch out for those thundering hooves."

Catching the mare had taken the better part of two days. Taming and training her had been the work of a season—the two of them learning together. But now she was his friend and his partner, as surely as Niki was. A true gift—one among so many. Another reminder that God had not deserted even this corrupt world.

After bedding the horses down, Brady wandered about Horesh. The camp took up both sides of the river, claiming what precious little land there was between the Grand and the Blunt cliffs, especially this time of year, when the river ran high. They had chosen the site well, despite the near miss with the gargants. The Blunts cast long shadows; the covering shroud and Kendo's noisemakers protected them well. Here, on a quiet night, it was almost possible to forget the corruption that lurked upground.

Almost. Brady sniffed. Even under a layer of manure and perspiration, the distinctive smell of the stronghold—a cloying mix of flowers and decay—still lingered on him. He was tempted to strip off his clothes and let the Grand wash away every vestige of Traxx.

On quiet nights like these, he wondered what this world would be like if it hadn't been scarred by bombs and plagues and poison. The Endless Wars had brought the planet to near ruin. Beauty remained in lofty mountains and stark deserts and, thankfully, on the plains upground of Horesh. Some areas of devastation had even begun to regenerate. Even so, uninhabitable toxlands covered over almost one-fourth of the planet—sometimes just a patch and sometimes a quarter of a continent—and even the habitable lands bore marks of what had happened. In the most pristine mountain areas, the trackers had found frogs with extra legs, birds without eyes, violets the size of sunflowers, and grasshoppers the size of ants. Even the most remote areas exhibited some sign of blight.

What had it been like to see elephants and zebras roaming free, salmon bountiful in rushing rivers? Though a number of original species remained, most were trapped in geographical enclaves, unable to ramble freely because of radioactive ground or toxic water and still subject to the poisons borne by air currents and water. And if animal—or human—populations did find enough clean space to multiply and thrive, they eventually came to the notice of the stronghold princes. Tyrants like Alrod or Treffyn needed a steady supply of original species to feed their transmogrification labs, because mogged creatures were genetically unstable and blessedly unable to reproduce.

Ark historians taught that genetic manipulation had begun with the wonderful purpose of saving lives and restoring health. What should have been a blessing had, over the course of a few years, become a disaster, a tool of vanity and greed. And as men needed more covert weapons, they had turned from bombs to biologicals.

Why had all the other weapons technology been lost and yet the cell lines survived? Perhaps it had to do with the toxlands—or the wars that created them. The geographies taught that these regions still held poisons capable of changing the genomes of bacteria, flora, and even higher-order mammals. The laboratories where medical breakthroughs had become hideous weapons had been the bombs' first targets. As the world emerged from the gloom of the Endless Wars, some enterprising vendor or witch doctor must have found a stash of biologicals that had been strengthened by the very forces intended to eliminate them. Trial and error would have been reinforced by instruction manuals that the sorcerers misinterpreted as books of spells.

Thinking about it all made Brady's head ache. He walked on, trying to focus on this moment, this place by the river he called home.

Kendo's shop was empty, his blanket neatly folded. Although he shared a hut with Brady, he often found it easier to sleep where he worked. Next to the shop was the cabin where Manueo and Magosha lived. He smiled at the soprano rumbles wafting out the window. Their cook was a small, round woman who snored in loud bursts, something Bartoly found infinitely amusing. His crew had not yet been able to persuade him that his sleep was far more raucous than Magosha's. But Bartoly was away as well, with Jayme's crew of trackers at the Shoals. Two other crews were further out, but all were due back shortly. Brady, Timothy, Taryan, and Kendo had stayed at Horesh to fulfill their respite requirement.

Beyond the dining hut were the women's quarters. Ajoba's hut was dark. Though she was only sixteen, as teacher and spinner she was required to have her own hut. Had her isolation interfered with her learning the necessity of obedience? Or was it a deeper flaw—or gift—that had driven her to leave Horesh? Brady understood why she followed the gargant—it was she who had promised he would find hope in the mountains. But why take the spindle? Why endanger the whole camp with such a thoughtless stunt?

The anger surged then, born of long days and years of fighting against what never should be, only to come home to what never should be. He ran hard, leaping over rocks that he couldn't see in the dark, passing out from under the veil of shroud until he was under bright stars and deep sky. His skin flushed as if with fire, his muscles tightened, his fists felt like rocks, ready to smash and to hurt and—*God, hear me*—to kill. Brady wanted to bellow, but his own voice slapping back from the Blunts might alert a watcher on the cliffs. So he did the only thing he could do when his rage bucked him like a wild horse.

He fell on his stomach and plunged his face into the river.

His breath caught, and his heart stopped for the moment it took his fury to be swept downstream, eventually to the ocean, but *never, please Lord, never against your people or your Ark.*

He came up with a gasp but stayed on his knees long after the stars winked out and dawn touched the sky.

Timothy had been twelve, just entering training, when the first birthrighters left the Ark. Since that day, the names of those four had never stopped echoing in his ears. Niki was the warrior, Kendo the clever one, Tylow the teacher and the spinner. But Brady was the outrider of all outriders. Even as other camps were sent out and tales of valor relayed back to the Ark, Brady of Horesh remained the first and the best.

Had he lost his knack for leadership?

Ajoba roamed the countryside, carrying their precious spindle, but Brady had yet to mount a search party. He had ordered Timothy to bed while he wandered in the dark, following the river south. Timothy followed, finally spotting Brady on his knees by the water.

He was still there when Timothy came out of his hut in the morning.

Timothy sat upstream to enjoy the solitude, staying under the shelter of shroud. Brady, oblivious to the good sense he expected his comrades to obey, knelt beyond the outskirts of camp. He *should* be on his knees, what with camp falling apart. Ajoba's infraction was the worst, but Timothy was not unaware that there was some issue with Niki. Why else would Brady have sent her on transit?

The truth was, though a terrific fighter, Niki was completely unsuited to introduce rooks to their first taste of this world. And she was a complete joke as Horesh's second in command. She was little more than an extension of her own sword, only happy when she had someone or something to fight. Kendo hadn't the temperament to lead. He was by himself as often as was allowed, inventing contraptions.

It was clear that Horesh had become too big for Brady to oversee. Perhaps they should spawn a second camp. They would need another spindle and a teacher to spin. And a leader, of course. The younger trackers and outriders looked up to Timothy. He had a cool head and a clear intelligence. A natural leader, his teachers on the Ark had said.

"Whatever are you thinking about?" a lilting voice said. He turned to find Taryan behind him.

"Nothing," he grunted.

"That severe line between your eyes says otherwise. Whatever is the matter?"

"I'm trying to solve the puzzle that is Ajoba. Why would she sneak off like that?"

Taryan sat next to him and tossed pebbles into the water. "It's all my fault. I should have told her not to."

"That's ludicrous! She *knows* not to. No one leaves camp without permission."

"The first rule of training, first modus of every camp. But she's driven by different priorities. So young to be a teacher." Taryan turned to Timothy, her gaze steady on his face. "She doesn't always recognize authority, you know."

The blush worked up Timothy's neck. He was framing a reply when he saw her eyes shift. He turned, startled to see Brady behind him. For a big man, he moved like a snake.

Taryan was already up, taking Brady's hands in hers. "You didn't like my braids, lad? You had to hack them off?"

She hadn't even asked about Timothy's hair, cut more ragged than a peasant's.

"I adored your braids," Brady said. "But Alrod got too good a look at them, so they had to be sacrificed to the goat trough. Though not quite all, lass." Brady lay his hand against his chest.

Her voice dropped to a whisper. "Are you all right?"

"Fine." Brady squeezed her hand, then looked down at Timothy. "Walk with us, Tim."

They strolled with him toward the kitchen hut. The wind shifted, and Timothy caught the smell of crackling bacon and baking bread.

"A blue jay came down in the middle of the night," Brady said. "So hard to understand—all that proud squawking and posturing. But Kendo seems to have an affinity for them."

"Good news?" Taryan asked.

"The families are safe, well received with work and housing. Kendo is on his way back, Manueo with him."

"Praise be," Taryan breathed.

"Taryan, I want you to load up Kendo's armor with mine and ride out to meet him. He'll be on the old road that cuts behind the swamps. You'll have to bring a cart so you can bring his equipment."

"His equipment? Oh, you mean his toys?"

Brady laughed. "His fun is our gain."

"Which of the toys do you want me to bring?"

"All of them."

"I'll need four carts."

"Don't exaggerate—two will do just fine. You and he will join me up in the Bashans. I'll give you the coordinates we got at court. But if I find Ajoba elsewhere, I'll send a bird to alert you to the change of location."

She nodded.

"Pack your own armor also, as well as your quivers and bows." Brady scuffed the riverbank with his boot. "In case we need to liberate our teacher from some situation."

Timothy couldn't stand Brady's rudeness a second longer. "What about me?"

Brady turned to him, eyes narrowed.

Timothy stared back. Brady might be camp leader, but that was no excuse for him to exclude a birthrighter from conversation.

Brady glanced back to Taryan. "All set?"

"Yes. Certainly."

Timothy didn't miss the touch of hands as she brushed past Brady.

He turned back to Timothy. "What?"

"Why not I?" Timothy said.

"A birthrighter camp can never be left unattended."

"Manueo is coming back."

"But he's not here yet. And not technically a birthrighter."

"Why not Taryan?"

"Why not you, Timothy?"

"Am I not worthy to fight?"

Brady raised his eyebrows. "Who said we would be fighting?"

"You just sent Taryan for the armor."

"Doesn't mean we'll be needing it." Brady headed upstream.

Timothy grabbed his arm. "Stop treating me like a child, outrider."

"Is that what I'm doing?"

"Aren't you?"

Brady yanked his arm away. "What I am doing, *tracker,* is treating you like the next camp leader. Don't make me regret it."

Timothy opened his mouth to protest, but Brady somehow was already out of sight.

Dawnray had fallen into a fitful sleep at daybreak, just awakened now by a knock. She huddled below her blanket, fearing that Alrod was sufficiently recovered to demand her for his bed.

She was relieved when a little maid came in.

"Good day, lady. My name is Carin. Sado assigned me to serve you." Carin's face was pudgy, her hair tucked under a cap.

"You're from our village. The potter's daughter," Dawnray said.

The girl's pale eyebrows drew together in confusion. "Aye, lady. And you might be?"

"Don't you recognize me? My father, Marko, keeps—used to keep—a shop across the square. He was a silversmith, specializing in musical instruments. The shop was called Bells and Horns, remember?"

"Aye, indeed." Tears flooded Carin's face. "Are there none of us left at home? Are we all in that evil man's service?"

Dawnray hugged the girl close, stroking her back until she stopped crying. "Do you still pray, little sister? And hold to all Tylow taught us?"

Carin nodded.

"Then there is hope," Dawnray said, but her glance to the door betrayed her words.

Carin laughed and hugged her again. "Relax, neighbor. He's gone."

"For good?"

The girl laughed harder. "I wish. The baron has mounted an expedition."

"I don't understand."

Carin sighed. "Are you as dense as you are pretty?"

"What I am is scared. Dreading every heavy step by my door, fearing that it will at last be him."

"I assure you that he'll be gone for a while."

"What's he hunting?"

"It's supposed to be a secret. But here's what the staff thinks." She lowered her voice. "You were at court yesterday. Did you see the man who dropped a wasp's nest on the Countess of Kroy? Apparently the high and mighty one thinks he's an outrider."

"Outrider? Aren't they supposed to be ghosts or something?"

Carin nodded. "The baron is spooked, all right. He raged on all night about the outrider's eyes, couldn't tell if they were brown, green, grey. 'Blasted color kept changing,' he said. Did you happen to see them?"

Dawnray remembered only eyes of cornflower blue. No ghost there—the man with pale hair could only be an angel to be able to sing as he had. "I only remember brown hair, a little silver, a lot of braids. Maybe broad shoulders?"

Carin got to work, setting the table for Dawnray's breakfast.

"Don't," Dawnray said, feeling foolish. "I can do that."

Carin paled. "No. I must. If I don't, I'll be punished."

Dawnray squeezed her shoulder.

Carin bustled about, taking covers off dishes, resuming her chatter. "The baron used the sunny-haired minstrel as an excuse to get the brown-haired one before him. I daresay he wasn't disappointed, what with all the ruckus that followed."

Dawnray sat down to eat. "The ruckus I remember."

"The baroness still thinks those two men were brought in at her request."

"Weren't they?"

"Of course not. You think Alrod cares what that cow thinks? One of his spies spotted the brown-haired one. More properly, his eyes. I think the baron was looking for him ever since the last—"

There was a loud crack. Carin sprawled over the table, sending dishes flying. They had been so busy gossiping, neither had seen the baroness enter.

"Cow? You dare—" Merrihana raised her hand to strike again.

Dawnray jumped between her and Carin.

Merrihana slapped her as well. "You dare also? I'll have both your heads with my morning tea."

Carin grasped the back of Dawnray's gown, her hands trembling as she burrowed into her skirts. The baroness would not have Dawnray's head without Alrod's permission, but Carin could be dead in minutes.

Dawnray bowed deeply and searched her mind for the fawning words she needed. "Dear and lovely, high and mighty, I believe you may have misunderstood this little maid."

Merrihana slipped a silver-handled comb from her pocket. She clicked it open, revealing a sharp blade. "She will not misunderstand this."

Dawnray went to her knees, dragging Carin along with her as she pressed her face to the baroness's slippers. "Please, high and mighty, hear me out. The cow she referred to was the Duchess of Kroy. This maid was, of course, very wrong to refer to any noble in such terms and will expect to be disciplined. But certainly not anything too extreme, because, high and mighty—"

Dawnray peeked up. Merrihana was at least listening.

"High and mighty, you must admit. The woman *is* rather . . . um . . . bovine."

A corner of Merrihana's mouth quirked, though her face remained stern. A minute later she snapped the blade back into her comb and spoke over Dawnray's head to the cowering Carin. "Out of here, drudge."

Carin stood to leave. The baroness tripped her and jammed a gold-slippered foot on the back of her neck. "Crawl. Crawl until I give you permission to stand. That may be tomorrow, or it may be in twenty years. If you live that long."

Carin crept out on her hands and knees, whimpering. Merrihana yanked Dawnray up by the hair. "You must not encourage them. Even though you are no higher than that piece of muck, you still eat off the royal china. That requires some restraint on your part."

Dawnray nodded. "Thank you for correcting me. I have much to learn."

"Put these clothes on." Merrihana tossed a bag at her feet.

Dawnray picked it up and opened it. "Trousers and a jacket?"

Merrihana smiled. "You and I are going on a trip."

"May I be so bold—and please tell me if I may not—but if I may, may I ask where?"

"My very angry and still quite bruised husband is off chasing revenge. I intend to find it before he does."

"You intend to kill the brown-haired man?"

The baroness laughed. "I have no quarrel with the brown-haired man, and I doubt my husband does, though this chase will keep him busy. But I do have, shall we say, an interest in that fine-voiced young man that was with him. If Alrod finds them first, he'll kill everyone in sight." Her voice took on a suggestive edge. "And what a waste that would be."

Dawnray curtsied again to hide her excitement. Truly it would, and she would do whatever she could to prevent it from happening. Even if it meant delivering the silver-throated man into the hands of this cow.

Ajoba and Jasper had spent a full day and night on the ridge, discussing the ways of this world and the promise of the kingdom to come. As the last star faded into dawn, Jasper fell to his knees, weeping. Had he not been so big, Ajoba would have cradled him like a child. When he finally took his hands from his face, his eyes were bright and his smile broad. "You were right, little sister. There is hope."

His eyes sparkled as Ajoba drew letters in the dirt, teaching him how to recognize simple words. Eventually the rumbling of their stomachs couldn't be ignored. She'd sent the gargant off to hunt, saying he could easily find a rabbit or two, though he had laughed and said he expected to bring her a deer or even a bear.

Ajoba clambered up on a rock so she could see out to the plains. Traxx spread to the east, plains stretching to that abominable wall of flowers and thorns that enclosed the stronghold. To the west of the river, the plains of Slade edged into the deep forests. On the horizon she could see the Grand unfurl like a ribbon between the two territories. Were she able to take flight, she would be able to see down into the Narrows. The craggy cliffs bounded the river before wilderness eased into farmlands and the river broadened to a wide swath that separated the two warring strongholds.

She felt a pang of guilt at leaving Horesh as she had. But Demas had told her to go quickly and tell no one. "Take the spindle," he had instructed. Obviously, she would need it, but for what she could not guess.

"And you shouldn't."

She jumped to her feet. "I found him."

"You lie." Demas's eyes went black.

"I misspoke. He found me, and I helped him find his faith."

Demas shook his head. "Flesh and blood. As if you have any say in any of it."

Ajoba looked down, strangely ashamed of her dusty boots. "Requesting pardon, but now what do I do with him?"

Demas circled her, his head tilted. "What have you considered, child?"

"Jasper is too big to send to a sanctuary. Perhaps we need to establish one in the far outlands, but how would he get there without help? I don't know the way."

"So you're focused on ridding yourself of him?"

"No, of course not! It's just—you know mogs are not allowed in Horesh. And even if he were . . . he is so big!"

"You judge him unworthy because of his size? You are smaller than the average woman. Are you judged unworthy?"

"No."

His face darkened. "Do not judge lest ye be judged."

She knew the words, had memorized them as a child. "Forgive me."

He smiled, and his sparkle returned. "Forgiveness doesn't enter into it, child. Not where I am concerned. Allow me to help you reason this one through. You have located one gargant."

"The one I told to come north, because you—" She put her hand to her mouth. "I'm sorry, I should not have interrupted."

He touched her shoulder, his fingers hot through her tunic. Or was that biting sensation cold? His smile broadened. "No, little one. We are reasoning this together. You located one gargant. Does your responsibility end there?"

"Of course not."

"What of the others?"

The others. The day after the battle, she had ridden out over the plains. Hundreds of bodies lay there, festering in the sun. Kendo said the Traxx troops had eventually rallied and speared the gargants to death. Some, however, had survived. He had scouted a company of strong-arms following a small group of gargants into the Bashans.

Ajoba had seen their footprints on her trek north. As a trained tracker, she had found it easy to distinguish the footsteps of the lone gargant who made it to the Narrows and to keep far away from the strong-arms roaming the mountains.

"Ajoba," Demas was saying. "I asked you a question."

"They have the same need as Jasper."

"See to it." Demas disappeared into the afternoon sun.

TWELVE

AFTER A WEEK OF TRAVEL, THE ICE WAS JUST A MEMORY for Niki. When she had picked the dogs up in Chiungos almost three weeks ago, the outpost had still been knee-deep in snow, the riverbank caked with ice. Now she saw more mud than snow.

Chiungos was the ragged village on the banks of the snow-swollen Camara River that Brady and Bartoly had helped build four years ago. It was the northernmost sanctuary in Horesh's growing constellation of communities outside of stronghold reach.

Brady had an arrangement with Rebeka, the village elder. He supplied them with much-needed items like ax blades and flints, herbals and honey, tea and onions, cotton and silk. In return, the villagers kept a sled and dogs for him and furnished him with the occasional longboat. On the way back to Horesh from a transit, he would take a longboat downriver with the rooks and sell it in Kinmur to help pay for horses. By the next time he came through Chiungos, Rebeka's people would have made another longboat out of caribou skin and willow bark, ready for him to use and later sell.

Out of necessity, the seven families who lived in Chiungos had adopted the ways of the northern climes. Brady had persuaded a nomadic ice dweller to spend a full year there, helping them adjust. They lived in sod houses that they banked under blocks of ice in the winter. They trapped fish, speared seals, and hunted bear, existing almost solely on meat. They wore furs and hides with silk unders, except during the short days of summer, when they soaked up the sun in cotton tunics.

"You had better eat whatever is put in front of you," Niki said quietly as they sat under the stars, soaking up heat from the community campfire. "You will not dishonor Rebeka—and annoy me—by turning your nose up at their hospitality."

Children crowded about, exclaiming over Kwesi's dark skin and Cooper's red hair. Anastasia held a chubby toddler on her lap, her cheek pressed to his.

She's left a little brother or sister back on the Ark, Niki realized. *I haven't even bothered to ask about their families.*

With the help of her comrades, Rebeka heaped wooden trays with pungent food and proudly offered them to her guests. Anastasia pretended to be busy telling the toddler a story. Kwesi wiped his forehead but nodded up at his hostess. Cooper chewed his lip.

Mixed chunks of meat—probably caribou and seal—floated in steaming seal oil. Whole cod had been skewered with willow sticks and roasted. Small birds, stuffed with grain and liver, had been baked with what smelled like cod oil. The birds were fresh; an hour earlier Niki had seen the children luring them with snake-worms hung on caribou bones, then clubbing them.

The rooks looked at Niki with such consternation that she laughed aloud. "Thank you, Rebeka. And Jon and Tarra. Thank you for this wonderful meal. You do us great honor. Isn't that right, Kwesi?"

He nodded, his face solemn. "Thank you. You do." He tapped Anastasia's hand.

"Thank you for . . ." she suppressed a gulp. "For doing all this for us. I've never had anything like this."

Cooper nodded, still biting his lip. But after Rebeka said grace, he was the first of the three to reach for a skewer of fish. The rooks nibbled and picked, though Niki spotted Kwesi pocketing more food than he actually swallowed.

Niki ate huge quantities, feeling the rush of energy that soy and dried meat somehow couldn't provide. Rebeka, an older woman with sparkling eyes and flyaway white hair, couldn't stop singing

Brady's praises. "Such eyes—a strange color, you know, but, dearie, so clever. You know that, don't you?"

"Yes, indeed." Niki dipped a chunk of meat in the oil.

"And that hair. Does it still curl around his ears?"

"I don't think he's cut it since his last visit. It's longer now. Past his shoulders."

"Ah, yes. And how he loves his tunes. Last time he was here, he sang the gophers right out of their holes."

Niki laughed. "That would be Brady, all right."

"The little girls were always on his heels. 'Let the man rest,' I'd say. But he's so friendly, telling funny stories, giving them rides on his shoulders. If I weren't so old, I'd chase him around myself. Marry the fellow—that's what I'd do. But I expect he's spoken for. Right, dearie?"

Niki stirred her tea. "Not that I'm aware of. Brady keeps his business to himself."

The woman bit her lip. "Yes, of course. It's just—he'd been so good to us up here. My daughter's little ones and I were on the drudge cart, heading for the sorcerer's den when he—well, you remember; you were there too. Oh my, it *is* all right to speak of such things in front of these young friends of yours, isn't it?"

Niki patted her hand. "I remember, Rebeka. And yes, these three can be trusted."

"You all gave us this new life. It's cold and it's barren and, oh, how that wind howls. But free we are, and free we will stay." Rebeka leaned toward the rooks. "Your Niki here swings quite the sword. Fought off three Slade strong-arms like they were monkeys. So if she tells you to do something, you do it."

Anastasia said, "We try, ma'am. We really do."

Niki stood. "I'm glad to see you again, Rebeka. But we've had a long day, so if you wouldn't mind, we'd like to spread out our blankets, get some sleep."

"Oh, certainly. I've got the guest room swept out for you." The woman stood with a loud groan. "Old bones, don't you know? If

I were a girl like you—but I'm not. So listen, dearie. Be sure to give Brady a big kiss and squeeze the sweetness out of him for me."

Thankfully, the shadows hid the blush rushing up Niki's neck. "I will, Rebeka. He'll be pleased to know you were asking for him."

The guest room was a lean-to shelter built on the back of Rebeka's sod hut. They spread their blankets out onto pallets, and the rooks were asleep within minutes. But Niki felt restless. Despite the cold night, the lean-to was stifling. She shifted a pine slat aside to bring some fresh air in.

Looking at just the right angle, she could see the stars glittering by the thousands, the same stars shining over Horesh. She drifted to sleep, Rebeka's chatter still in her ears. *Marry the fellow—that's what I'd do.*

She woke late, the sun trickling in through the slat, the rooks staring down at her. When Anastasia saw her eyes open, she hid the packet of soy behind her back.

"Hey," Niki said, stretching. "Go ahead and eat it. I'm in a good mood."

She shooed them out so she could get cleaned up. She folded her blanket, stuffed it into her pack just as Brady had done in this same space eight times before her. It was only fair that she take on some of this duty. If she had known how annoying rooks could be, she would have volunteered to do this earlier to help out.

No, you wouldn't have, she told herself, laughing.

Niki imagined Brady sleeping on the same pallet she had. He would be packed by now, but he wouldn't have left yet, not without a moment alone to say his morning prayers. Niki wasn't as devoted as he—she wasn't made that way. Action spoke to her. Silence made her nervous, though Brady told her time and again that his prayer time only *looked* silent.

She knelt by the pallet just as she had seen him kneel so many times, whether during worship or before riding out against a threat. She imagined his profile—the little bump in his nose from the time in training when she whacked him with a wooden sword, the scar across his chin and the other under his ear. She saw his big hands clenched together and pressed to his forehead.

A tangy odor trickled in through the slat. A yellow eye blinked at Niki.

"You're back, eh?"

The wolf drew back a pace, lifting its lip and showing teeth.

"You don't need to fear me, wolf. But you'll need to leave before someone hurts you—you're not so thin that someone won't want to roast you."

He pressed close again, his eye against the slat. Perfectly silent.

"Please. Don't make me chase you away. Just go now, before someone takes an arrow to you."

She put her hands to her eyes. When she looked a minute later, the wolf was gone.

She rubbed her face, studying her ragged fingernails, tugging at her curls. She had been still for hours at a time, hiding from strong-arms or stalking mogs. But to keep still like this seemed nigh impossible.

Listen, Niki.

"What?" Niki looked around.

"Did I startle you? I am so sorry," Rebeka said. "Oh, I see you found it. I was coming in to show it to you."

"I'm sorry, I . . . I'm not following. Found what?"

Rebeka peered under the pallet. "Look, down here. See? It must have slipped back there last time Brady was here. I tried to dig it out, but I'll tell you, honey, that little scrap of cloth burned my fingers. So I left it, figured he would pick it up next time he came around. Except he is you, this time around. Can you touch it, or is it something that burns women's fingers and not men's?"

Lying on the wood chips under the pallet was a short length of shroud tied with twine. What Rebeka described as burning was simply the odd sensation of touching the out-of-time side of shroud.

"I've got it, thank you." She'd take it back, give it to Brady.

Rebeka hugged her. "Oh, thank you. I know he'll be missing that."

"Why do you say that?"

"Because . . ." Rebeka smiled, letting the word linger.

"What?" Niki hadn't meant to snap, but given the choice between coy Rebeka and that ratty wolf, the wolf might be easier to comprehend.

"It's just . . . oh, he's such a sweet boy, you know."

Niki stared, trying to will the woman into speaking clearly.

"Sometimes when he's here on those trips of his—coming by himself, coming back through with those young people—I know it's a secret, but I'm betting they're rescues too."

"Rebeka, I'm sorry, but I've got to get onto the river before the day ages any further." She grabbed her pack and went outside. The sun was already high; she had wasted the morning sleeping and daydreaming. The rooks should be at the boat, securing their packs, oiling the paddles, loading the food Rebeka insisted they take.

Niki trotted for the river, Rebeka's boots clomping after her. Moments later, the old woman linked an arm through hers. "You understand, I wasn't prying. I just like to check on my young Brady like a mother would. So before I close up at night, I usually peek in on him. See him asleep—like an angel, that one. This last time—before this past winter had set in—I saw something glittering in his fingers. That thing that you've got in your pocket."

Niki glanced down without thinking. She hadn't even been aware of putting it there.

"He was awake, but he didn't see me. I saw him, though. Saw him put that to his lips. He held it there for a long moment. I'm glad you're taking it back to him. Of course, the little girls here will be heartbroken, but I won't tell them if you won't."

"Tell them what?" Niki said, her fingers tight on the piece of shroud.

"Tell them that our Brady has himself a sweetheart."

So much water moving so fast. Cooper wasn't sure he liked rivers.

Niki sat in the back of the boat, guiding the rudder. "Do you all have your hand on a paddle?" she called out.

"Yes, aye, yea," the three of them answered. She had drilled them before letting them get in the boat: *The river will take us more quickly than we could paddle, but we need to be ready to steer. Until I call on you, sit back and enjoy what you see.*

Enjoy? How could anyone enjoy being surrounded by rushing water? They had tried to prepare them for this on the Ark by building a river in the hydroponics section. Propellers made it flow hard, and obstacles created white water. But that river had been ten feet wide, not a hundred or more like this one. And on the Ark, help was always a yell away.

Here, if they tumbled into the water, they could die, Niki warned them cheerfully. This water flowed from the northlands; though the air was warmer, the river still had a sting to it. Niki promised that three days on the river would bring them to warmer climes and to Kinmur, where they would pick up their horses. After a weeklong ride to Horesh, their real work would begin.

Kwesi and Anastasia talked nonstop, trying to impress each other with their knowledge of the environment. They identified white spruces, jack pines, pin cherry trees; the gray-tailed tattler, the short-billed dowitcher, the lesser yellowleg, even the lichen on a rock where they stopped so they could relieve themselves.

Cooper knew the names too. Any rook who couldn't keep a million facts in his or her head would not be allowed to leave the Ark. That didn't mean the ones who stayed were dumb; they simply hadn't been gifted to handle that much information without the benefit of computers and reference books. It also meant birthrighters embarked on their missions with amazing amounts of knowledge stuffed into their brains—including Cooper. But birds and animals weren't his strong suit. Cooper was more comfortable with codes and numbers. Detail oriented—that was why the builders had entrusted the solitary to him.

What had happened to Arabah? That the builders had given him the coordinates to pass on to Horesh showed the level of their concern for the missing camp. None of the camps—Horesh, Arabah, Canaan, Sinai, Salem, Galatia, Antioch, Achaia, Bethel—knew the location of any other. Isolation was the key to survival for the camps as well as the secrecy of the project. And that was the main thing—the protection of the Ark. Each birthrighter had been trained for the worst torment a sorcerer could devise to squeeze out vital information. Racks and whips were only the beginning of torture. Having your skin peeled off your face or—

Cooper leaned over the side, queasy.

"You sick?" Niki was only a few feet behind him in the boat, but she was difficult to hear over the steady rush of wind and water.

"I'm all right." He splashed cold water on his face. He needed to take his mind someplace the sorcerers did not inhabit. He clicked onto his geography lessons, let the numbers flow until he knew exactly where they were in this vast world.

"Hey!" he said.

"So you're not all right?" Niki said.

"No, I mean yes. I mean, I'm fine. It's just—I realized something."

Kwesi leaned forward to Anastasia. "Cooper rises from yet another stupor."

"Care to enlighten us?" Niki said.

"This river takes us close to Arabah. There's an offshoot about—oh, ten leagues from here. You follow that tributary up into the foothills, then hike into the Arojo ranges. Arabah is in a deep cavern, halfway up the mountain called Welz. We could go there if we wanted . . .

"Are we going to give it a roll?" Kwesi stared at Niki, his hand already on his short blade.

"Will you speak properly!" Niki said. "People hear your jangle, they'll take a second look at you. You don't want that."

"I glean it," Anastasia said.

Niki's brow furrowed.

Anastasia paled. "It was a joke."

"Get this, rook. I'm not one for jokes."

"What about Arabah?" Kwesi said. "Can we give it a—can we scout it out?"

Niki shook her head. "The kind of danger that could put a birthrighter camp out of action—maybe even destroy it—is not a danger that you three can take on, even with my help. It takes experience, lots of experience. Brady and I will do it, with our senior outriders."

"We could just go as far as the foothills, see if there was anything to see," Kwesi said. "Something we could report back to Horesh that would help in a rescue or recovery."

Recovery, Nikki thought. That meant locating the bodies of their birthrighter brothers and sisters. Send them back to the Ark wrapped in shroud, never to be opened again. She knew trainees who had gone to Arabah . . .

It wasn't all about numbers and codes or even protecting the Ark. It was about friends and family.

The river flowed swiftly, broad enough in this stretch to let the boat drift with Niki's hand on the rudder. She enjoyed the greening of the banks and the warm sun on her shoulders. Even so, she had to keep alert. Though the snow and ice were behind them, they now drew closer to the strongholds. And though four peasants in a boat would not interest the strong-arms, they would certainly question why Niki possessed so fine a sword. Renegade mogs, too, could be a danger: eels that had been mogged to ridiculous lengths to twist like weeds around the feet of an unsuspecting swimmer or horse; oversized fish with sharp teeth and a penchant for ramming boats; even amphibious bears and cougars that could live underwater, waiting for prey to float by.

There was no end to the evil of the sorcerers and their stronghold masters.

At midday, Niki steered to the bank for lunch. She withheld the last packets of soy, ordering the rooks to eat the caribou-tongue pies Rebeka had sent with them.

After eating, Kwesi leaned against a tree. Within minutes, he snored loudly. Cooper also had fallen asleep in a patch of sunlight. Anastasia started to poke him awake.

"No," Niki whispered. "You lie down and take a rest too."

"Why? The day won't last very long, not this time of year."

"Thank you for the report on the seasons—but do it."

Anastasia huffed and rolled over, her back to Niki.

"It's for your own good," Niki said.

"Thanks a bunch."

"I mean it."

"Me too," Anastasia said, her voice already drowsy.

Niki had to keep them out of the boat after eating to cut down on motion sickness. The rooks had gotten thin. No use rushing them back into the boat and having them throw up what little nourishment they had just taken in.

She found a dry bed of moss to sit on. *What was happening back at Horesh?* The tracker crews and their outriders should start arriving back at camp in the next few days. Brady, Kendo, Taryan, and Timothy had remained at Horesh on respite. Trackers and outriders were required to stay back at camp for one-quarter of the time. They were commanded to rest, to work about the camp, to learn new skills. And to pray, of course. Niki always found respite hard—she was built for action, movement, adventure.

Would you give up being an outrider?

Niki fingered the little packet of shroud. Was it a tiny collection that Brady had forgotten? Or perhaps special instructions from the last transit group? Brady had pressed it to his lips. A trinket, perhaps? Niki had no use for such things—no birthrighter did. They wore swords instead of finery and scars instead of ornamentation.

Niki glanced over at the rooks. Cooper hadn't moved. Anastasia had curled into a ball. Kwesi lay on his back now, eyes closed, sun casting a sheen on his cheeks. She opened one edge of the packet and let her fingers slip inside.

He put it to his lips—kissed it.

Inside the shroud was a lock of hair. "Oh, Brady," she whispered.

Straight, silky hair.

Niki's hair was curly, tight curls that popped out of every braid Taryan put in her head. But Taryan's hair was . . .

She flung the packet in the river, not caring that a birthrighter was never to let shroud out of her possession. If only this moment would disappear like the strands of tawny hair, swept away by the rushing water. If only she could wrap her heart in shroud and put it away forever.

God speaks clearly over the ice, all right. Niki should have listened better, though what did it matter? She didn't need God or anyone to tell her what Brady was too cowardly to.

Go away, Nik. Go away so I can be free to love Taryan.

THIRTEEN

NIKI WOKE COOPER WITH A KICK TO HIS BACKSIDE. "Get up!"

He rolled over, blinking his eyes against the sun. "Time to go?"

She was already past him, kicking at Anastasia and Kwesi.

"Youch!" Anastasia said. "You hurt me."

"Get used to it, rook," Niki snarled. "It's a painful world." Her face was stark white, the muscles in her jaw prominent.

"Are you all right, Nik?" Cooper said.

She shoved him. "Don't you ever call me that."

Tears came to his eyes. He blinked them back as quickly as he could. "I'm sorry. I was just concerned."

"No, I'm sorry. I let up when I shouldn't have. It won't help you if I'm soft on you, which is why you will address me with respect, Cooper. My name is Niki. Nothing more and never anything less. Understood?"

They all nodded.

"And none of you will ask personal questions, including how I am, unless I'm broken and bleeding at your feet. Even then, you will do so at your peril. Do you comprehend this, or do I need to jangle it so you can glean it?"

"No, ma'am. I mean, yes, ma'am, I understand you the way you are. I mean, the way you're talking," Cooper said.

"Anastasia and Kwesi. Do you understand me?"

"Yes, ma'am," Anastasia said, "But I don't get how—"

Niki grabbed her by her elbows and lifted her off the ground. "Now do you get it?"

Cooper watched in astonishment. How strong must Niki be to hold the girl in the air like that?

Anastasia nodded, her mouth shut tight. Niki opened her hands. Anastasia tumbled down.

"To the boat. Now."

Niki took off at a trot. Cooper raced after her with Anastasia and Kwesi right on his heels, all convinced she would take off without them if they didn't get there when she did. They piled into the same seats where they had been.

"Make sure your packs are lashed tightly to the boat," Niki said.

"We already—" Kwesi shut his mouth with a loud click.

"Yes, ma'am," Anastasia said.

"The next person who calls me ma'am will be dumped into the water. My name is Niki. Don't add to it or subtract from it. Now, get your paddles out."

Cooper almost laughed at the speed at which they grabbed their paddles.

"We are about to enter white water. Do you all know what white water is?"

"They simulated it on the Ark for us," Kwesi said.

Niki whapped him with her paddle. "I told you never to say that word except back at camp. All right—about the white water. I want you to remember what you learned in training. But what's most important is that you listen to what I tell you—and obey instantly. Understood?"

They all nodded warily.

"I may give you a command that seems to make no sense. Sometimes to get through white water, you need to almost give in to it. If you listen to me and do exactly as I say, we will be fine. Are we agreed?"

They nodded again. *She has beaten us into puppets in a mere ten minutes,* Cooper thought. *This isn't the same Niki we left Chiungos with. Joking and laughing, being kind to us. Well, kinder than this. We were only asleep a short time. What possibly could have happened here on the riverbank to make her like this?*

Niki took them back over some basics: how to paddle and how to drag; how to loop their feet under the gunnels when they leaned so not to fall out; if they did fall out, how to let the current carry them downstream until they could swim diagonally to the shore.

Before she pushed off, Niki lashed her sword to her back. "So I don't lose it if we go over," she told them. "I've had it since my second year at Horesh."

"Brady made it for you," Anastasia said.

"Yes. Well, that is neither here nor there. The truth is that I can lose my food and my blanket, but I cannot live without my sword. If you're smart, you'll all do the same with your short blades."

They quickly did, binding the scabbards against the outside of their thighs. Anastasia's legs were too short for that, so she bound hers onto her back as Niki had.

She had barely settled back in her seat before Niki pushed the boat off and jumped in.

They hated her now. Fine. Better hated and respected than loved and misused.

Niki turned the rudder to steer toward a smoother channel, changed her mind, shifted positions, told herself to settle down. The rooks had been silent since they pushed off. And while she didn't exactly miss their chatter, the quiet in the boat made her uneasy.

All she had ever wanted was to do her duty. This was an ugly world—why even pretend that happiness might be possible? The people on the Ark had it easy. Yes, they worked hard, and they sacrificed by letting some of their children come out into this world, never to return. But they also married, had more children, laughed and teased and sang. Even the science and technology came easy to them. Her parents meant well, but they had no idea what she endured out here, day in and day out, year in and year out. Generations had passed since the first builders entered the Ark. No one living there today had ever actually encountered a mog or a strong-arm.

Truth was, the builders lived in a cocoon, a hidden world, where everything came as a blessing. Niki had almost been trapped into thinking she could have that same kind of blessing. But she hadn't meant it about Brady, not really. The isolation of transit and the annoyance of the rooks had given her a few weak days, that's all. Brady was her friend and her comrade, just as Kendo and Dano were, just as Leiha and Jayme were.

She would never give up being an outrider. God would never ask that, because it was He who had made her like this. The logic loop was closed before she even had to open it. Why had Brady tried to put doubt in her head? Didn't he know how deadly doubt could be for an outrider? Hesitate at the wrong time, fear to jump or slash or keep still, and more than an outrider might die.

Perhaps he had been testing her in some odd way. Had she shown some hesitancy? Brady had expressed concern about that battle in Landsdown. Strong-arms had come on a collection party without warning, sweeping down from the sky on bizarre seed pods. She had shredded them, of course. Eight dead, all by her hand. Had Timothy complained? He had been splattered with blood, his sword out too late to even be of use. And that was as it should be. Timothy was bright and talented, but he was a tracker. It was her job to defend her people, and she had done just that.

Were their swords out? Brady had asked.

Yes. No. I don't know.

Are you sure they were a threat?

Strong-arms are always a threat.

He had bowed his head for a moment and then looked up at her. With eyes of love, she had thought. And there had been love—she knew that even now—but the love of a brother, a friend, a partner. And not a partner in all things, though they had been since they were twelve years old. She had been taller than him by a head when they entered training. They had left the Ark eye to eye; now she came up only to his ear.

Strong and tall, funny and sweet, smart and fierce—so Brady was and would always be. But he would never be more than brother, friend, partner. It hit her, how that seed had gotten planted, dug into her by his parting words after debriefing her on Landsdown.

You must be willing to love something—or someone—more than you love to fight. Do you know what I'm saying to you, Nik?

"Watch out!" Kwesi yelled.

White water. Just ahead the river narrowed suddenly, the smooth surface crinkled with rapids. Niki grabbed her paddle with her right hand, holding to the rudder with her left.

The rooks sat with their paddles poised over the water, waiting for her command.

"Right side," she said as they hit the rapids. "Straight on, full strength."

The rapids growled, a steady snarl broken only by Niki's commands and the crash of water against rocks. Her right arm ached already with the effort of paddling while she steered the boat with the left.

The first drop sent Anastasia flying from her seat. She yelped as she slammed down against the bottom of the boat.

"Better that than the river," Niki shouted. "Now hook your feet under the gunnels or seat like I showed you."

They rounded a curve; the river whipped into a growing frenzy by the narrowing of the banks, sudden and dramatic gradients, and numerous rock outcroppings.

A huge wave slapped the boat, turning them into an eddy that spun under a huge boulder.

"Dig left," Niki yelled.

The rooks paddled while she yanked on the rudder, using her full weight to help turn the boat. They grazed the rock, coming around to an overhang that Niki could never have anticipated. "Duck!"

They flattened against the bottom, just missed getting their heads bashed.

"Up," she shouted. "Dig left again. Left!"

Kwesi and Cooper came up with their paddles, digging hard. But Anastasia shot a panicked glance back at Niki. She had dropped her paddle into the river.

No time for recriminations now. A huge plunge loomed ahead, with a whirling current. If they didn't get clear, they'd be crushed.

"Cooper and Anastasia, lean right. Kwesi, keep paddling until I tell you."

Their weight wasn't enough to steer them from the whirlpool. "Kwesi, you too. All hold until I tell you. Don't come up."

Niki leaned right, pulling the rudder with all her might. The boat balanced on its side, slammed by the force of the water.

Another nest of boulders loomed right before them.

"Stay in position," Niki shouted. The river was a fist, punching anything that dared challenge it.

"Lean hard!" Niki hung backward, shifting continually to keep the boat from dipping too deep into the river. Her hair brushed the water, cold mist flushing the hot sweat from her cheeks.

Too far over. She eased up a bit.

Cooper saw her and did the same.

"No!" she cried out. But it was too late. The boat hit the rock, bouncing them into the worst of the white water, spinning and knocking them against a tangle of logs.

The boat flipped over.

The current seized Cooper, dashing him into the swirling pool, where he spun like flotsam.

Anastasia sputtered at the cold, grabbed first at rock and then Kwesi. "Get ashore!" Niki screamed at the two of them.

Stretching out so her feet faced downstream, Niki let the current carry her after Cooper. He had forgotten this instruction and flailed violently. If she didn't catch him soon, he'd break every bone in his scrawny body.

He disappeared under the water.

Niki waited a three-count, expecting him to bob back up. When he didn't, she dove. The current quickly carried her to where he was trapped—a place where the shallow bottom dropped suddenly into a deep hole. She saw the top of his head, red hair waving like weeds, thin arms waving desperately. His foot must have gotten trapped between two rocks—the very thing she had warned him about.

Niki wrapped her legs around his waist so she could get her head above the water and grab a breath without being carried downriver or sucked under. Cooper clawed at her, but Niki ignored him. Taking a huge breath, she went underwater and dug at whatever was holding his foot.

Not rocks.

Niki grappled with what looked like a tentacle wrapped around Cooper's leg. He thrashed and kicked, but the thing wound tighter.

She went back up, took a huge breath, then pressed her mouth against Cooper's. He clutched at her, not understanding. She held his head squarely, her mouth pressed to his, until he finally dared to open his own mouth and take in the air she was bringing him.

She went up three more times, giving him enough air to relax, then getting her own breath. She pulled out her flip-knife and hacked at the creature holding Cooper's foot. *Let it be a weed,* she prayed, though she knew better. As she slashed it, another tentacle snaked out, wrapping around her wrist.

How many tentacles did this thing have?

She jammed hard, freeing herself. She went back up for more air, bringing another breath for Cooper, keeping her own feet near the surface. Then she took a huge breath, clasped her knife in her teeth, and dived down. She offered her left arm to the tentacle. It quickly snaked around her and she let it, grasping the tentacle with her right hand and following it toward the bottom of the hole, praying it wasn't so deep that her air would run out. Her ears popped, but she kept going, pulling against the tentacle. The creature, sensing her plan, released her wrist, but she kept her own grip, pulling with two hands now, straining to see through the murk of water and waving weeds.

The tentacle widened and others came at her, whipping against her, scoring the skin on her neck. She kept pulling, and then she reached the body of the mog, not much bigger than her own. A blob of eyes and waving arms, more than any squid or octopus had—too many, all now wrapping around her legs, knowing she had come to kill it, squeezing her lower body, cutting off circulation and feeling.

She grabbed for flesh and got it—a handful of eye. The creature bucked, but she held firm, taking her knife and driving it straight into its body. Hitting something hard—surely not skull; creatures like that didn't have skulls. But yes, some fiend of a sorcerer had created one that did. She kept jabbing, causing pain but no destruction, keeping the mog occupied while she groped over its surface. All eyes, it seemed, but somewhere there had to be a socket for the nerves to feed into the brain.

Niki found it, a round depression the size of her fist. Her air was gone, but she had one thrust of her arm left. No time, no energy for the knife—just one last punch, jamming her fist into the socket, into the mog's brain, feeling it convulse and then go slack.

No breath, no energy to kick to the surface, clothes and boots holding her down, she wouldn't float. But somehow she rose, the water growing lighter and faster, and then she broke through and gasped for air.

Cooper was free of the mog but seized with panic. He clutched at her, his panic stronger than her exhausted muscles.

"Be still," she gasped, but he was beyond reasoning, panic driving him to climb up her to get out of the water. He would drown both of them.

Niki slugged him, stunning him enough that she could get her arms around his chest. She swam him into the current, kicking diagonally toward the shore until her feet found sandy bottom. She waded ashore, dragging him.

Kwesi and Anastasia ran along the riverbank until they caught up to her. Niki left Cooper at their feet. "Take care of him," she panted.

"Don't go back in there!" Kwesi called, but Niki stripped off her coat and boots and waded back into the water. She had spotted the boat a couple hundred paces downstream, caught on a downed pine. If it broke free, it would hit more white water and be lost. She let the current take her to it, calculating how much more she could endure before she lost effectiveness in the cold water. Her muscles were already spent, but perhaps she'd gain one last measure of energy as she floated to the boat.

She clutched the gunnel of the boat and ducked under it, coming up in an air pocket. She took a long breath and crouched back down under the water. She willed all her strength into her legs and heaved, raising the boat out of the water. She flipped it, then swam it across the current to get it to shore, astonished that her legs could still move.

The rooks stood on the bank, shaking. Cooper had a huge red spot on his jaw where Niki had slugged him—the beginnings of a bruise. As she neared the bank, all three waded in to help pull the boat ashore. She didn't stop them, simply let them take it while she turned toward the river one more time.

"Where are you going?" Anastasia screamed.

"Paddles," Niki gasped.

"You don't have to. There's one in the boat!" Kwesi called after her. "It got jammed under the gunnel."

She waved to let him know she had heard. If she could find one more, they might manage the rest of the trip. She hoped that their packs had stayed lashed. Their food was wrapped in shroud and should be all right. There—she spotted a paddle hung up on a tangle of brush. Her legs were numb, and some counter in her head clicked into the danger zone. She had to get out of this water. But first, just that one paddle.

Too far if she waded the whole way.

She dove headfirst into the rapid, feeling the spin, hearing her mother and Brady and Taryan and Cooper, voices braided in an odd tangle, asking, *Will you stop at nothing?* Her heart pounded back at them: *Why should I?*

She bobbed against the tangle, grabbing the paddle and using it to leverage herself against the rush of water.

A minute later, she lay facedown on the riverbank, the rooks clustered around her. "Get your clothes off," she gasped. "Down to as few unders as you need for modesty."

"It's getting dark," Anastasia shrieked. "We'll freeze!"

"You'll freeze worse if you don't do it."

She hauled herself upright, willing her legs to move, one foot at a time. She unlashed her pack from the boat, dug through until she found the flint. She blessed Kendo for waxing the box that kept it perfectly dry, even under the assault of the river.

Niki stripped off her outer layers, followed by her trousers and shirt. She wore a one-piece suit underneath; were it not for the rooks, she would have taken this off too. As they stripped down, she stumbled along the riverbank, grateful to see dry driftwood, more grateful that it hadn't rained or snowed here for some time.

She gathered tinder, struck a flint, made a fire. Within minutes, it roared fiercely. By then, she was shaking too hard to squeeze her own clothes out, but Kwesi had done it for her. "Get some long sticks so we can make drying racks," she said, her teeth chattering so hard that she feared they'd break. Her skin was a rash of cold bumps, strafed with deep bruises and cuts from the creature she had killed.

She watched numbly as the rooks carried out her orders. Even tall Kwesi was still built like a boy, his shoulder blades bony and his ribs prominent through his undershirt. Too young—they shouldn't be sending rooks out until they were eighteen at least.

Pain came with warmth. Niki curled her lips into her teeth, resisting the urge to moan. She would sooner die than show weakness in front of these three. They stood there, sticks in their hands, staring stupidly.

"Stick them in the ground, you idiots, and drape our clothes over them. Don't get them so close that they catch fire."

They worked silently. Anastasia's hair was plastered to her head, Cooper's already drying and sticking straight up. Anastasia was strong in a petite way, but Cooper was downright scrawny. Were they so low on decent candidates that they had to send out such worthless rooks? She should throw them back, like a fish that was too small.

She'd stomp her foot on the ice, breaking through with such force that the bowheads dove for the deep. She'd toss the rooks into the water, one at a time, laughing as they pleaded with her not to do it. She'd save Cooper for last, just because he had been so much trouble to bring up from under the ice in the first place.

She laughed now, couldn't stop laughing, though pain shot through her ribs.

"What?" Kwesi said.

"You don't want to know."

Anastasia glared at her. "You're right. We don't want to know."

Niki jumped to her feet, pressing her knees together to keep them from shaking. "Don't you *dare* take that tone with me, rook."

"I'll take any tone I want," Anastasia said. "I'm sick to death of your foul moods."

"Are you, now?" Niki straightened up. The agony surging through her spent leg muscles and her battered back was welcome, preferable to the pain that had gnawed her insides since opening that packet of shroud and finding the lock of Taryan's hair.

"Yes. We all are. Right, Cooper?"

He stared at his folded hands.

"Come on, Cooper," Anastasia said. "Be a man and say what you really believe."

He looked at Niki, his eyes brimming with something so incredibly offensive that she had to hold her own hand to keep from slapping him.

How dare he *pity* her?

She should throw them all back in like one might a fish that's too puny to be of any value. She laughed again, knowing she sounded addled, but why should she care about that?

"Stop laughing," Kwesi said.

Niki raised her eyebrows at him. "You must be as sick of me as the others if you're not bothering to bootshine."

"Cooper is sick of you too," Kwesi mumbled, "but he's too lame to say so."

Cooper withered under Niki's stare. "I never said that."

"All right, so you're sick of me," she said. "Understood, since I'm the one who tells you day in and day out how incompetent you are. Would you rather I lied? What good would that do you? Look at us—soaking wet, freezing, half our paddles missing. All because you don't even know to follow orders. Yet you expect to be allowed into Horesh. Well, that is not going to happen."

"What?" Anastasia said. "What are you talking about?"

These rooks needed a lesson before they got themselves killed. "All three of you are going back."

"To Chiungos?" Anastasia said.

Niki laughed. "All the way back."

Anastasia gasped.

"No, she doesn't mean it," Kwesi said. "No one ever goes back."

"No one that you *know* about," Niki said.

Cooper's tongue worked against his cheek, but he didn't have the guts to ask if she were telling the truth.

"May I ask a question?" Kwesi said.

She nodded. "If it's not insultingly stupid."

"If I understand you correctly, rooks can be sent back to that—that place from where we're sent."

"What else would we do with incompetents like you? Sell you as drudges? Even I am not that cruel, Kwesi."

"But if what you say is true—"

She grabbed his head, pushed on his forehead so his neck arched back. "Are you saying that I lie?"

He kept his gaze level with hers. "No. I am just trying to understand."

Her gut twisted. *Too far,* she could hear Brady telling her all the way from Horesh.

What do you know, Brady? You don't know what it's like to be me. You're perfect, and I am just what I have always been—incredibly furious and longing for justice in a twisted world.

"How do you do it?" Cooper said.

"I wrap you in shroud and toss you into this river. Like you were any other collection. That simple."

Cooper shook so hard that his hands bounced off his thighs.

Stop, Niki told herself. *Tell them it's a joke.* But the day pressed hard on her like an anvil, and suddenly she couldn't breathe deeply, could barely move. Shock setting in. She grabbed her clothes. Still damp, but they'd have to do.

"I need to sleep. Keep the fire going. Can you do that much?" Niki didn't wait for an answer. She just settled into her own cold arms and slept.

"She doesn't mean it," Anastasia said.

"Yes, she does." Kwesi touched his throat. "She surely does."

Cooper's insides had turned watery. "I can't go back."

"I tell you, she doesn't mean it," Anastasia said again. "The high and mighty of nasty is simply living up to her royal reputation."

Cooper slapped his hand over Anastasia's mouth. Niki slept on the other side of the fire from them. If anyone could hear over the sweep of the wind and the roar of the flames, it would be her.

"They wouldn't tell us, you know," Kwesi said. "If they did send rooks back, the builders would keep it a big secret. Otherwise no one would volunteer for training."

"I won't go back," Cooper said. "She can't make me."

"If she can take out those musk oxen—"

"Or eight strong-arms. You heard what Rebeka said," Anastasia said.

"Truly, she can make us do whatever she wants," Kwesi said.

"I can't go back. You don't know what it was like for me," Cooper said.

Anastasia tossed a stick at the fire. "Put your head back on, Coop. We did it too. We know what it was like."

"No, you don't."

"Oh, stop it. You are not top billing out here, not like you were in training. The high and mighty of getting every answer right."

"I tell you, it wasn't the same for me during transit," Cooper said.

Kwesi put his arm around Cooper's shoulder. "Hey, joe. You took some hard knocks out in the river. Take it easy."

"This isn't about the river. It's about the whale." He clutched his head, trying to stop the pounding. "I woke up. I made transit fully awake."

"You liar," Anastasia said.

Kwesi leaned into him, studying his face. "You're not lying, are you?"

Cooper shook his head.

"This is why you've been so quiet."

The tears came then, and Cooper did nothing to stop them. Anastasia did her best to dab them away with her fingers. They listened to the fire, feeling the heat but not warming up, not with the chill Niki had put into them. The sun dipped behind the trees, casting long shadows.

"What was it like?" Anastasia finally asked.

Cooper just shook his head.

Kwesi tightened his grip. "Tell us. Maybe it will help."

"It won't help me. The whole thing is pressed into me, like a second skin. But if it will help you understand why we can't let her send us back . . ."

Anastasia wrapped her arms over Kwesi's. Cooper felt warm for the first time since—

"Remember what it was like before they tranked us? Our parents were crying. Kissing us good-bye. Friends from training, all around. Sibs, grandparents."

"A party," Anastasia said. "But no one was really happy."

"They said when we woke up, we'd see sky like we couldn't imagine. And feel cold, so cold, but Brady would help us get dressed. Remember how we bragged when we found out we were going to Horesh—the first-ever camp? Thought we were top billing then."

Kwesi squeezed his shoulder.

"They gave us the shot, and it was warm."

"Warm and soft," Anastasia said. "So comfortable."

"Everything went black, right? My last thought was I was going to see a sky that never ended. Instead, I woke up and it was dark. No sky, no Brady, no cold. Just me and the inside of the husk. I felt it bouncing, even leaned sideways to try to knock against your husks. But I was just there, alone. I don't know for how long."

"Could you feel anything?" Kwesi said.

"Nothing. Except myself. I didn't like that much, being alone with myself."

Anastasia brushed the hair back from his forehead. Her eyes shone; her cheeks were damp.

"Darkness and silence that I thought would never end," Cooper said. "Maybe next time it won't. I just can't take that chance."

"So what will you do?" Kwesi said.

"All I know is I can't go back. So I guess I have to move on."

Who is weak, and I do not feel weak? Who is led into sin, and I do not inwardly burn? If I must boast, I will boast of the things that show my weakness.

2 Corinthians 11:29–30

FOURTEEN

IT HAD TAKEN AJOBA AND JASPER THREE DAYS TO FIND the other gargants.

"Alrod has them fenced like animals," Ajoba said. "That's horrid."

They hunkered behind a tangle of scrub pines, looking down on the Traxx encampment. The strong-arms had made camp on a mountain plateau, open enough on one side to prevent a blind assault, bounded on the other sides with cliffs and rockfalls.

"Shows what he. Think of us." Jasper's language had improved as he grew accustomed to his new body, but he still stuttered when gripped with emotion.

The gargants were jammed into a box canyon and barricaded behind a mogged bramble wall. The branches were green with new growth, the thorns as long as Ajoba's arm. Strong-arms with swords and spears guarded a gate cut out of the middle of the growth.

"The other gargants—they're huge. Why don't they just push through it?" Ajoba asked.

Jasper hoisted her onto his shoulder. From there she could see four dead giants lying just inside the wall, their faces bloated, their lips black. "Poison," he said. "From the thorns."

"That brute Alrod means to use them as battering rams into Slade. He already tried once. He'll try again."

"I know, little sister."

"Time is short for them. I need to get down there."

"No!" Jasper yanked her from his shoulder and set her behind him as if to block her.

"Jasper, it is my calling. Just as you were once lost, so are they."

He crouched next to her as one might a small child. "You are through. With me?"

She clutched his finger. "We are brother and sister forever. Your calling will be revealed soon. Mine has been clear for some time now."

Tears rolled down his doughy cheeks. "You will die."

"I'm small. I can slip through that bramble."

"One scratch and you will die." He wrapped his hands about her, making a prison of his fingers.

"Let me go, Jasper."

"No."

"I can show you why I won't die."

"No."

"I promise not to run. Please, let me show you."

Jasper opened his fingers. Ajoba unwrapped the spindle from the bag of shroud she had woven for it. "See."

"It's empty."

Ajoba smiled. "As you and I once were." She opened her palm to the sky. At first nothing happened. Why had Demas told her to bring the spindle if she couldn't spin outside of Horesh?

Modus forbade a birthrighter from leaving camp without permission. She had broken the most vital part of the code by bringing the spindle with her, though surely Demas's command superseded Horesh protocol.

By now Brady would know what she had done. He would be furious, she guessed, though Brady's anger ran deep and still. She had prayed he would understand the importance of Demas's guidance, the claim the gargants had on her heart. Ajoba hadn't created this passion to spin and teach and to pursue souls. It had come on her in the twinkling of glint and the authority of Brady's anointing.

Jasper stared at her as if she were mad. Indeed, she would be if the spindle did not turn.

A tiny sparkle flitted in the air, so brief that she wondered if ice crystals blew down from the heights. More came, then the tingling heat of glint, skipping over her hand and streaming onto the spindle. Her left hand became the spinning wheel, turning the spindle as it filled.

Music poured through her. She didn't realize she sang aloud until Jasper clamped two huge fingers over her mouth. She let the music go on inside, swaying her hips and tapping her feet as the glint danced and the spindle turned.

Finally the spindle was filled with thread. She looked at Jasper, triumphant.

"What is it?"

"I still have work to do." She pulled out a crochet hook. "Why don't you hunt us up some supper? This will take a while."

"No. You will go to the Traxx camp."

"I swear I won't. Not until I can prove to you that I can do so safely." She began to crochet. Though the loops were tiny, somehow her hands filled rapidly with cloth. She fell into a rhythm, not realizing she was hungry until she smelled roasting meat. She looked around. Though the sky above was still a bright blue, she sat in deep shadows.

"Here." Jasper offered her a chunk of meat. He would eat the rest of the kill, be it deer or goat. His appetite was prodigious.

After they ate, she tied off the cloth and wrapped it around herself. "See. I am now impervious to poison."

"Impossible."

"Touch my arm, Jasper."

He poked at her, then instinctively pulled away. "It's like my finger. Disappeared. I don't understand."

"It's not really here or now but somewhere else—some *when* else. We call it out-of-time, and it is a great gift that will protect me if I bump into a thorn."

He shook his lumpy head. "No. I. Forbid it."

"Do you forbid those poor souls the hope you now hold?"

He shook his head.

"Then you will not stop me. You must hide while I'm gone, Jasper. You're easy to smell and easy to hear. Take great caution."

"I'm. Not afraid. I watch."

"No, hide. Hide and pray. Can you do that?"

He sat perfectly still, barely breathing.

"Please, Jasper."

The nod was so imperceptible, she would have missed it had she not been watching his face. Ajoba folded the crocheted cloak of shroud and stuck it under her belt.

Jasper walked her to the top of the rockfall. "They'll hear you."

"No, they won't. I am trained to move like a mouse." She stood on her toes and hugged his fingers. "Stay in peace, brother."

"Go in peace, little sister."

Ajoba crept forward, her tracker training kicking in quickly. Though the rocks were loose and sharp, she moved with no disturbance, as if she were sneaking up on a cricket and not a heavily guarded Traxx encampment. She scanned the sky, alert for Alrod's hoornars, but only one circled high, watching for distant threats.

She skittered down the cliff, finding handholds more by touch than sight. Her dark skin and clothing let her blend into the dusk with ease.

Two strong-arms stood watch at the gate to the pen. One yawned; the other leaned against the gate, fighting sleep. Ajoba felt a small measure of pity for strong-arms. Yes, they executed Alrod's and his sorcerer's orders with brute force and without mercy. But, just as commoners like Jasper were kidnapped to be mogged, so were strapping young boys taken from their families and raised to kill. They enjoyed privilege, but at the cost of their freedom. And their souls.

Ajoba peered from her hiding place and studied the wall. She had heard of Baron Alrod's fondness for bramble. Usually several plant species were mixed to create something impassable. But this looked like stinging nettles, perhaps mogged with something from the rose family to produce thorns. The poison would be an ugly variant of formic acid, the danger more from the underside of the leaves than the daggerlike thorns. The bright-green branches had been cultivated in a matter of days, big enough to keep gargants contained but with enough space between that she should be able to worm her way through.

Ajoba flattened to the ground. The encroaching darkness gave her cover but also made it difficult to find a route through the tortuous branches. She stared into the thorns, trying to will herself forward as fear pressed her to the cold ground. Out of the night, a owl hooted. She heard the gargants now, heavy snores as they slept, one cursing as he dreamed. A strong-arm cursed back, and Ajoba shuddered.

She would not draw back. She must not. She gathered will more than strength and knelt to push herself into the thorns.

Someone jumped on top of her, lifting her off the ground, carrying her backward as he clamped a hand over her mouth.

Ajoba started to kick, then stopped. If she were in the clutches of a strong-arm, he'd be dragging her toward the encampment, not away. Even if this were a bandit, she didn't want Traxx soldiers coming to her rescue. She relaxed and let herself be carried back into the shelter of the rocks, surprised that the intruder made no noise either.

She felt breath on her neck and heard a whisper she didn't expect.

"That is enough of that, sister," Brady said. "Quite enough."

The first thing Brady did after apprehending Ajoba was move her and the gargant further away from the Traxx encampment. If the strong-arm guards had been alert, they would already have smelled the meat that Jasper had roasted, spotted the ruffling of brush on the ridge. They were safer in this higher location, which provided a clear view of the encampment and the approach to it. The rock overhangs gave cover from the circling hoornar and its strong-arm rider.

The second thing Brady did was send Ajoba to a shallow cave nearby to sit in silence and reflect. At least he hoped she was reflecting.

Now he and Jasper hunkered on a wide ledge under the cover of heavy brush, looking out over the valley. The gargant's massive head hung low, his shoulders slumped. "I have no place. No home."

"We will find you a place. I don't know where yet. Perhaps in the deep forests in the southern outlands," Brady said. "I'll need time to find a place that can hide you, care for you, put you to work."

"What of the others? My . . . kinspeople."

"Friend, I just don't know right now."

"The little sister says you are the leader of her village. You must be wise."

Brady smiled. "Wise enough to ask the right questions—and to know that the right answers may take some—"

He froze, a chill trickling down his spine. A sudden awareness. A dread.

His chest tightened, his muscles filled with blood. A few stars already shone through the dusk, but the darkness wrapping the cliff face was not night. Jasper seemed unaware of it.

"Jasper, can you keep watch for a minute? I need to go to Ajoba."

"I will come."

"No. Watch and keep us safe. It's important. Please."

Jasper slowly nodded.

Brady waited until he was out of Jasper's sight to unsheathe his sword. He felt the earth move, though when he looked down, not one pebble had rolled. Something deep had loosened, something beyond his reach and perhaps even his understanding. He stopped for a minute, breathing deep, gathering focus. For now, he needed to attend to the task at hand.

He moved silently toward the cave but stopped when he heard Ajoba's voice.

"I tried, but he stopped me."

The voice that answered her was thick and sweet, like molasses. "Try again."

"Brady has forbidden it."

"Am I not more than he? Have I not proven myself to be more?"

"I don't know what to do."

"Has my guidance failed you?"

"No, but . . ."

"No buts, child. You should be in that pen by now, not up here dallying."

"Would you have me go against Brady's wishes? Surely . . ."

"You already have gone against his wishes. Will you change that course now?"

Silence dangled, broken by Ajoba's tearful voice: "Can't you just leave me alone?"

"You dare speak to me like that? You are asking for discipline, child."

Brady ran into the cave, feeling a shock of bitter cold. Ajoba flinched when she saw the blade in his hand. "No, Brady. You don't need that."

The visitor stood behind the girl, his hands on her shoulders. "Ah, we meet at last. Brady of Horesh—protector of the weak, destroyer of the strong."

"Ajoba, would you please introduce me to your visitor?" Brady lowered his blade hand and kept his voice steady, not wishing to frighten her or to cue the visitor that he recognized him for what he was.

The demon was luminous, his sheen generated by the rot of skin that hung loosely off his ancient bones. The halo about his head was simply his hair smoldering. Fear wormed into Brady's spine and caused his hands to shake, birthing a dangerous hesitation that here was a foe he could not stand against.

YOU CANNOT. BUT I CAN, MY SON.

"Brady, this is Demas," Ajoba was saying. "He has been my guide, my spiritual director. Because I am so young, it was felt that I would benefit from such help."

Brady nodded. "God is good."

Demas jerked as if struck. The skin of his shoulders slid off his bones.

Brady stared, astonished to see each of his failures stacked like rings on this creature's spine. Sharp words with Timothy. Too-sweet dreams of Taryan. Resentment that he always had to think before speaking, think before striking, think before running away. Sullenness at bearing too many burdens of others while his own needs went unmet. Hatred of the strongarms he killed and the sorcerers he chased and the princes he feared. The familiar longing to ride Thunderhoof into the north and never return. The temptation to let this world sink deeper into its own darkness while he huddled in a mountain cave somewhere.

Bitter and ugly failures that bolstered the fiend, making Demas straighter and prouder and stronger until he loomed over Brady like an avenging angel.

"None of this now," Brady whispered, teeth clenched. "It's covered." He closed his eyes and let grace sweep away the shadow of that which long ago had been cast into the abyss.

Ajoba pulled on his sleeve. "He wants me to go back to the pen. I have a mission there."

"Ajoba, I believe that also. But the timing is something we need to think out." Brady held Demas's eyes as he enunciated clearly. "Something we need to pray about."

The demon shrugged, his wings peeking out from behind his skull like a crown of iron. "You do not recognize an answer when it appears before you, leader? Perhaps you are the one who needs to go to his knees."

"Brady prays," Ajoba said. "All the time. He is a righteous man."

Brady touched her shoulder, then turned back to Demas. "Not a righteous man, but one who has been ransomed. And I know the voice of He who paid the price."

Demas exploded into rubble, reconstructing in a flash so quick that Brady wasn't even sure it had happened—until a stink filled the cave, a stench Brady knew from too many failed mogs left on the plains, too many strong-arms rotting because their comrades had fled in terror, too many bodies caught in the thorns of Traxx, hung at the gates of Slade, profaned across this wide world.

This was death in its basest form. No peace, no grace, no hope.

But Demas's voice still flowed out thick and sweet. "Good man, perhaps you would benefit from my guidance as well." Demas's wings unfurled, sucking light from the rising moon and fluttering it through the cave like diamond dust. He fixed Brady with burning eyes while speaking to Ajoba: "Child, you have a mission. Attend to it now."

She reached for her cloak. "Brady, I am going back down."

"Ajoba, no. I do not ask you; I tell you. Do not go."

Demas smiled, unleashing snakes that slithered up Ajoba's legs. Her face burned with noble purpose while the serpents twined higher, slipping under her cloak, through her tunic, twisting in and out of her skin.

"He tells me I must, brother. Therefore I must."

She held Brady's gaze without wavering. He saw the chink through which this foul creature had slipped, the pride in her eyes that she had been gifted above others at Horesh. He forgave her quickly; she was young, and her gift was heavy.

"Ajoba, I tell you again that you may not."

She moved toward the entrance. Brady grabbed her arm. "Look at him, Ajoba. Tell me what you see."

Demas smiled. "Yes, dear child. Enlighten him."

She looked at Brady, her eyes wide. "Why, an angel, of course."

"He is an angel, indeed," Brady said. "One of the fallen ones."

But she was hearing only Demas's oily words. "How tragic that your leader cannot see my light. He must be looking through a veil of his own jealousy. After all, it is his pleasure to lord it over you, is it not? Giving orders that must be obeyed. Sending his people here and there, not caring about the danger. And then, when the appropriate opportunity arose, he drove the gargants back into the hands of their tormentors. What kind of man is this, child? Would you follow such a cruel and selfish leader?"

Brady tightened his grip on her arm and raised his short blade toward the demon. "I tell you to leave!"

Demas laughed. "You refuse to submit? Pride is such a sin." He leaped, his voice a roar, his breath foul, his skin colder than ice as he grabbed Brady's throat.

Brady swung with all his might, his short blade splitting on the creature's skull. Demas staggered back, laughing.

Ajoba battered Brady with her fists. "What are you doing? You can't fight an angel. Let me go before he hurts you. Let me go, Brady."

"No."

"Then I will make you let her go," Demas said. He clawed for Ajoba with one hand while he swung his sword with the other, slicing through Brady's shoulder.

No pain, no blood, no splintered bone. Only a trickle of pleasure as Brady suddenly saw Taryan bathing in the stream—the glow of her skin, the set of her shoulders, perfect in the moonlight, and all within his reach.

"In the name of . . ." He couldn't finish, ashamed that his breath came short.

Ajoba pushed herself against him, trying to shield him from Demas's sword, blocking his free hand from grabbing his own sword. "He is here at God's bequest, Brady!"

"No. You cannot see him for what he is, but I do. You must not do as he asks." Brady grappled between her body and his, trying to get to his sword, unwilling to push her away or let her go.

Demas's sword came down on him again, rocking him with delight because Taryan was in his arms, her skin like silk, her breath sweet. He bent to her, desperate to touch her lips with his while with every ounce of his being that was not caught in her embrace shouted—

"—in the name of the Lord—"

Something smacked him on the side of the head, not the demon's sword but a human hand, tearing Ajoba out of his grip and—*oh, Lord!*—out of his protection. Brady went down, too stunned to stop her from running out of the cave. All he could do was grab Demas's foot and hold him, though his fingers felt as if each cell was being slit by a razor, each tiny vessel of blood flowing with fire, even as visions of Taryan continued to reel through his mind. Brady grunted, clenched his teeth, held on. He had to endure, had to keep the foul creature from following—

His breath grew tight, new pain searing through his ribs, and Brady realized that Jasper had seized him around the middle with his mighty hands.

"Won't. Let you. Rape—" the mog sputtered with fury.

Brady felt his ribs snap one by one, his lungs compress so there was no air, only enough breath in his mouth to tell Jasper, "See, man. See the truth of what has been wrought here."

Jasper was shaking him. "Disgusting—"

"See the truth, Jasper," Brady gasped again, almost unable to bear the lie that the demon kept flashing before him.

Demas held Taryan now, undressing her with the bones of his fingers, streaking grave rot on her beautiful skin. "I'll let her go when you let me go," the demon said.

Still Brady held on, his hand almost dust, his ribs like daggers against his heart, his voice a faint whisper. "See with the eyes God gave you, Jasper."

A holy silence fell like fresh snow. Brady felt a shock of awe, a recognition that the mighty One could crush him beyond anything that Jasper could do, but—

MERCY, LAD.

This was the hand of grace that turned Brady back with an outburst of love so overwhelming that Brady could easily breathe against the mighty human hand that sought to squash him, a love so amazing that it made his ribs steel, his lungs whole, his heart strong. A love so astounding that Demas fled before it, dust cast into darkness with no claim on the light and no claim on life.

With a mighty sob, Jasper wrenched Brady from the cave and cradled him to his chest. "Oh, what have I done? What have I done?"

Brady let sweet air fill his lungs, clinging for a moment to the huge man's chest to be soothed and to also soothe. Then he struggled out of the gargant's arms but stayed at his side, stroking his hair like one might a child. "You only did what you thought was right."

"It was dark. I thought you were the threat. Then I saw that creature, and I knew . . . but it was too late . . ." Jasper shuddered, then jumped to his feet and thundered away.

Brady raced after him, every muscle in his body shrieking with pain. He leaped onto the gargant's back. "Don't even think about running off. Not while we've got work to do, friend."

Jasper slumped to his knees. "After what I did? After I . . . almost . . ."

Brady slid down. "More than ever, man. More than ever."

Jasper studied Brady's face. "You speak the truth."

Brady smiled. "I do."

"What can be done?"

"We've seen what our enemy can bring forth. Let's see what our God will do."

Fifteen

The river rushed along beside him, too fast by far. Yet his heart was strong, his legs even stronger, and his gut told him to push on. Panic crept up his spine, a mute knowledge—she was in trouble. Yet the river swept her further away, her scent long faded, the river his only way to track her. He struggled on along its bank, pacing over rocks, splashing through icy puddles.

The wind shifted from time to time and he caught her scent. He ran faster through the night with no time to hunt and feed. His blood ran thin now, but the wind blew warm, much warmer than he had ever felt.

Then he found the place with the fire, the place where her scent was strong, and he ached with a loss he knew well.

The pack had driven out the alpha yet again.

The rooks whooped and hollered as they pushed the boat ashore.

"We made it!" Kwesi said, arms high over his head.

Anastasia did a silly dance. "Was there any doubt—once we dumped our baggage?"

"Zipper that," Kwesi said. "You don't say things like that about an outrider. Even one with fangs."

"Cooper agrees. Eya, Coop? We knew we had potential, but the high and mighty of nasty held us back. Look at us now. We have proved what we can do."

"We haven't proved anything yet." Cooper handed the packs out and then motioned for his comrades to help drag the boat into the scrub pines. They had spent a day and a half on the main river, letting the current take them where it would, paddling only to keep out of what little white water remained. Cooper had kept a close watch on the position of the sun as it moved overhead and a careful count of the Arojan peaks as they rose to the east. It was past noon when he spotted the eastern branch-off. They paddled hard against the current, pushing upstream until the tributary broke into a fistful of streams pushing down from the mountains.

"We've proved we're better off without Niki than with her," Kwesi said. "True? She didn't think we had the jingle to go to Arabah, but we gave it a roll, eya?"

Cooper shrugged. This had been his idea and, with each league of river they had swept down, it had seemed more and more stupid. He had tried to get the others to stop at midday and walk back upriver. "That story about getting tossed back to the Ark had to be rank," he had argued. "Wouldn't we know it if they sent rooks back?"

"Are you saying she spun us out?" Anastasia countered.

Kwesi and Anastasia shared a long glance. Kwesi sighed. "I know you're lamed out, Coop. I would be too—we both would—if we stayed awake during transit."

"If he really did stay awake," Anastasia muttered.

"I did!"

"Really?"

"I'm not spinning out. It's the truth."

"And we believe you," Kwesi said. "Just like we believe Niki. So leave it at that."

Kwesi started for the hills with Anastasia at his side. Cooper ran to keep up. They were silent, entranced by the growing vistas revealed as they climbed higher and higher. They had come out of the ice, traveled over flat plains of snow and tundra, then dipped into a rushing river. This was the first time they had ascended to any height, the first perspective they had on how huge this world outside the Ark was, and how beautiful still, even with all that corrupted it.

Something nagged at Cooper, like a prickle on the underside of a flower. "Hey. I've got a question."

"What?" Anastasia huffed with exertion but not nearly as much as he and Kwesi did. She would be a good tracker—if they ever made it to Horesh.

"I'm not afraid." Cooper had been afraid ever since he had awakened in transit. That stitch of fear in his belly had never gone away—until they started climbing. Now it was gone.

"That's a statement."

"So here's my question—why not? We're not even two weeks out of the Ark, on our own, scouting a camp that seems to have disappeared. Shouldn't I be afraid? Shouldn't we all be afraid?"

Kwesi glanced up at Anastasia. She shrugged. "I feel . . . numb, I guess. No room for fear."

"But we've disobeyed our camp elder! Stolen a boat, abandoned her." Cooper felt the steam going out of his protest. Niki had her sword, her flint, her pack. Her courage. She didn't need the boat, and she didn't need the rooks. She could make her way back to Horesh.

"All your idea," Kwesi said.

"Eya. It was."

"So you got the call, joe. Should we keep climbing? Or go back and beg Niki not to wrap us, dump us, and send us to storage?"

Cooper chewed his lip, considering. Far below them, the river moved slowly, a silky ripple between budding trees and bright grass. To the south lay Kinmur, a trading post on the northern edge of the Brennah stronghold. It was still too far away for them to see from up here.

They had left the hills behind and now ascended the rocky slopes of a mountain that had to be Welz—it was obviously the tallest one around. The path they trod was too broad to have been formed by goats or deer; it had to be Arabah's track up the mountain. It would disappear as they approached the actual site. Birthrighter modus said that camps should have no observable approach.

Anastasia and Kwesi stood side by side, looking down the path at him. "We're giving you the call," she said.

"Keep going," Cooper said. Perhaps his stitch had disappeared because the three of them were meant to be here. If three rooks could rescue Arabah, their names would be more famous than the first-evers.

They hiked another hour, the sun hot on their backs even as it slipped toward the horizon. Hadn't they planned to turn back by now? Cooper couldn't remember. Kwesi and Anastasia didn't seem concerned. They stopped for a meal break, higher now so they could see stretches of mountains to the south, the river wandering in and out of hills and trees like a gleaming thread.

"What's that?" Anastasia pointed to the southwest. A puff of brown smoke lingered at the horizon. Somehow it made the whole sky seem dirty. They had learned early in training about the one place in this world they dare not go.

"The glow of a toxland," Cooper said. Another blessing accorded only to birthrighters. They could see the aura of mogs—that strange green glow—and they could see the stain of toxlands. Places where no one could survive and no one should go near.

"It looks . . ." Anastasia shrugged her water skin over her chest and headed up the mountain. What use was it even to comment on something so completely *foul*.

How could she ever face Brady?

The rooks had deserved it, of course. But Niki probably had too. Good thing there hadn't been someone to lie to her when she came up from the Ark, full of guts and gumption, ready to prove herself against any shadow that stepped in her way. Brady was the one who had held her back, Kendo who had sided with him. And then Tylow had sat with her, quietly talking, helping her settle out.

Soon enough she'd had to swing her sword, and to this day, she had never forgotten her first sniff of flesh and blood. She'd never admitted her shock. But Brady had shared his with the builders, and training had been modified to require the rooks actually to kill. Chickens, usually, though some arrogant youth might be asked to kill one of their older goats.

It wasn't the same as killing something rampaging toward you—an insane, hideous, snarling mog. It never could be the same as killing someone running away from you, someone you needed to chase down simply because he was a strong-arm who needed to be stopped.

Stupid rooks.

They hadn't bothered to scratch a note in a rock or in the hard-packed sand. Niki knew where they were headed, though. She had humiliated them enough, and scared them enough, that they felt they had no choice. Stupid, ignorant, foolish rooks, taking the boat down the river by themselves.

Niki followed them, running full speed along the bank, swimming as needed rather than taking the time to climb ridges as they blocked her way. The heat from her anger and her vigorous exertion made the cold water bearable.

At least they had left her pack. They'd taken all the soy; she didn't eat it anyway. She should be grateful that they wouldn't starve, though starvation would be merciful in comparison to what they might encounter. They were likely to be crushed in the river or crushed by a grizzly bear or crushed by a strong-arm.

Crushed they would be. She was sure of that.

"This is your fault!" she screamed, not sure whether she meant herself, Brady, or God. Couldn't be God—He was perfect, after all. For that matter, so was Brady, except in matters of the heart. If he had any sense, he would know Taryan wasn't right for him. She was bright and pretty. She fought well enough and she was a talented tracker. But she was mild. That was the word—*mild.*

Brady appeared placid, but Niki knew how hot he could run. How fierce he could be, without even letting a drop of sweat dampen his brow.

Taryan was *safe*. That must be her allure. Brady was tired, too busy holding hands when he should be directing missions and rescuing the oppressed.

Niki shouldn't have had to hold the rooks' hands, and she hadn't. Her one mistake was not *tying* those hands anytime she slept. She should have known they would do something incredibly stupid, ignorant, and foolish.

In a strange way, she envied them. How long had it been since she had stepped out with such abandon? It was true that she would stop at nothing, but she still moved with wisdom, knowing when to fight or when to flee.

Yet she was not nearly wise enough to lead a transit. Not wise enough to win a heart. Not wise enough to even dissuade the wolf who had once again picked up her trail. She could smell him when the wind turned just right. Had he spared her just so he could kill her? Let him try and tear her throat out.

If he failed, it would be Brady's task to tear her heart out.

Don't die, rooks! She would shout it, but she needed all her wind. Keep running; keep following the water; keep hoping that they find some sense in those stupid, ignorant, foolish heads and just sit on the side of the river and wait for her to come take care of them.

"It got dark awfully fast," Kwesi said.

"We should light a fire," Anastasia said. "If we feel along the ground, we'll find some wood."

"No!" Cooper said. "We're on the highest point in these hills. It'll be like a jam-punchin' beacon, calling all strong-arms."

"He's right," Kwesi said. "We'll just have to tough it through. It's not cold."

"It will be," Anastasia said.

"But it's not."

"But it will be."

"But it's—"

"Stop!" Cooper jumped as his voice came right back at him. It must have echoed from the rocks around them. Except they were on the highest point of this ridge, weren't they? After the path had fizzled into brush, they kept climbing, marking the trail as they had been taught so they could find their way back. With plenty of daylight left, they spent a long time scanning the side of Welz, trying to pinpoint the location of the caverns where Arabah made camp.

They had fallen asleep, lulled by the warm sun.

Kwesi had been first to awake, quickly shaking the other two. Cooper experienced a flash of panic when he couldn't see anything. "It's all right," Kwesi said. "We're right here by you."

"Stasia's right. It's not cold," Cooper said. "But it will be. So let's just move together, have something to eat. Then we can decide about a fire."

He felt Anastasia slide to his side, Kwesi to hers. They fumbled for their packs, brought out the soy packets they had stolen from Niki's pack.

"Tastes like my boot," Cooper mumbled.

"Or that gluten they made us eat on the Ark," Kwesi said. "Who ever thought we'd high-kick on caribou and seal?"

"Not me. Never me," Anastasia said.

They squeezed closer together. *Why isn't it getting colder?* Cooper worried. It should be by now. "Why isn't—" If they weren't thinking it, why dig into their heads?

They slept. Time passed and slowly, Cooper came back awake. "Kwesi, I need to relieve myself."

"Let's go."

"No!" Anastasia said. "Don't leave me."

"I took the rope," Kwesi said.

They tied it to their waists, giving Anastasia a double length. They spread out, the darkness giving them privacy.

"Here," Anastasia said. Kwesi echoed, then Cooper—*here, here, here* around and around until they were ready to come back together.

"I'm not tired," Anastasia said.

"We could sing," Kwesi said.

"No. We shouldn't even be talking," Cooper said. "Who knows how far our voices carry up here?"

"Nothing is around us," Anastasia said.

Why don't we hear anything? Cooper thought. *The wind. An owl, flying low. The river, surely.*

"Does anyone miss . . . being where we came from?" Anastasia said.

Cooper found her hand and squeezed. A second later, Kwesi's hand folded over theirs. "Let's tell the story," he said.

The story—as much a part of them as their hair or eyes or blood. Every kid on the Ark, whether in training as a birthrighter or a builder, knew it by heart.

"I'll begin," Anastasia said. Their hands stayed locked together.

"Once upon a long time ago," she intoned, "gloom came over the world. No one now remembers when it started or how long it took. This is what we do know.

"There were weapons. Burning land, burning flesh, burning hope.

"There were plagues. Sweeping through nations in a day, lingering for generations.

"There were terrors. Spewing out of men's hardened hearts, making other men beg to live—or beg to die.

"There were wars. First cities fell, then regions, then nations, then civilizations.

"Weapons, plagues, terrors, wars.

"When time and tears had swept them away, all that remained was a gloom so deep that it seemed light would never again shine. Those who survived were mind-numb and soul-spent. In bitter fear, they hunted down and killed scientists, teachers, religious leaders—anyone they could blame for the weapons and hate that had spawned the Endless Wars. Art, tradition, and religion disappeared. Generations of horror wrung hope from what once had been a sparkling world.

"What did remain were anger and greed and the lust for power. And the potions. With science long lost, people assumed the cell lines that allowed them to mutate living creatures were magic and the masters who performed such mutations were sorcerers. These sorcerers allied with stronghold princes to spawn monsters and freaks that enabled them to steal land, enslave people, and build kingdoms.

"A man named Josiah fled the strongholds to live in the icy wilderness. Unlike most of his friends, he had learned to read, for his family had carefully hidden books under their hearth. He thrilled to tales of places called Camelot and Middle Earth, though he couldn't understand the longing these stories stirred in him. He puzzled over poetry and learned the history of a world where freedom was a gift from a Maker, though his parents could not explain who this Almighty was. With his parents long dead, he took his books with him and was content to read, fish, hunt, and write his own poetry, preferring the solitude of bitter cold to the warmth of obeisance and treachery.

"One day he returned to his campsite to find a stranger named Evangel. The angel gave him a volume of ancient texts, far older than the precious books of his childhood. By his fire, under a night that lasted from the falling of leaves to their unfurling again, Josiah learned the truth. When his heart had been ripped open and his soul laid bare, Josiah received another gift—a warming in his heart, a filling that the book told him was by the Holy Spirit.

"He began to work and began to pray. And gradually, day by day, it was revealed to him that he was not alone on this dark planet. For God had preserved a remnant of those like him who remembered, who had kept and stored away the secrets of a brighter age.

"Now, as Josiah prayed, they began to gather, one by one, appearing as if by accident in Josiah's camp.

"They brought with them books and paintings and music and silicon chips, skills and methods and ideas, all carefully hidden away and preserved during the dark times. Some brought with them a knowledge of the ways of God. Others opened their hearts quickly to the hope Josiah offered them.

"The body of God's children grew, as did Josiah's comprehension of what this miracle might mean. Somehow they were being called to preserve the birthright of all humankind: God's original creation, which the years of war had corrupted. Which the strongholders and their sorcerers would eventually transmogrify out of existence.

"'Esau despised his birthright' became the rallying cry. We were—"

"We are," Kwesi said. "Not were. We *are*."

Anastasia sighed. "That's not the story."

"It is now. We are living the story, aren't we?"

"No one asked you to interrupt, Kwesi," Anastasia pushed him.

"Wait. Stop. I'll take over," Cooper said. "Just don't argue."

They both sighed and fell silent. Cooper carried on.

"We are to preserve the birthright that this creation was meant to be. But more important, we are to advance the most precious of our heritage—the gospel of Christ. For this is our lasting birthright, the gift that brings us truly into the family of God."

"Amen," Kwesi said.

Anastasia squeezed their hands as Cooper continued.

"The angel visited the group many times over long years, giving Josiah very specific instructions on how to build an ark. And more people came from every corner of the earth to help him build. Their one common characteristic was a heart for God and a calling to do this work. Some were born cobblers, blacksmiths, and weavers. Others had been trained in underground societies to be scientists, engineers, teachers, and technicians. Every need was filled—from physicist to cook to janitor to ophthalmologist to horticulturalist. And when the time was right, the angel led them to an underground facility that had been built for war but now could be used to preserve hope.

"The Ark grew and the builders multiplied. As the strongholds advanced, they moved north, then north again, destroying the sophisticated facilities they left behind so the stronghold princes would not find them. Then, after many generations, they were told to sink their headquarters under the ice—a second ark for the preservation of God's creation."

"During all this work, the builders bore generations of children who loved God and treasured their birthright." Cooper paused, took a breath. The next part of the story was newer than what had gone before—so new that even they had lived through it.

"One night, not too long ago, God sent the angel again, this time to each of the builders."

"I remember the night the angel came," Anastasia murmured. "I was only six, but the angel came to me."

"And me," Kwesi said.

"To all of us," Cooper said, continuing the story. "Our parents, grandparents, and elders emerged from their night quarters, stunned and frightened. The message had been universal, and it had been clear.

"'It is time to collect. Send your children out of the Ark.'"

"Us," Anastasia said. "Can you believe that we're actually here?"

Cooper nestled against Anastasia, his hand still clutching Kwesi's as he stared into the darkness and repeated the familiar words.

"Since that day, some of us remain to build. And some are called to leave the Ark and gather. We collect plants and animals, whatever is left from the original creation—to preserve our birthright. We gather souls, an incorruptible harvest. And we depend on God, who has given us shroud for protection and commissioned the beasts of the field, the birds of the air, and the fish of the sea to help us in our mission.

"Today if you hear this story, God is asking you to respond."

And once again they responded: "Here I am," said Kwesi. "Send me."

"Here I am," said Anastasia. "Send me."

"Here I am," Cooper whispered. "Send me."

Sixteen

It had been an ugly journey.

Alrod sorely missed Nighteye. He had begged Ghedo—even threatened to flog him—but his sorcerer said he had not the power to transmogrify a new Nighteye from her remains.

He could have ridden a hoornar into the mountains, but they were foul creatures, as apt to sting their riders as they were the foe. Besides, they made him airsick. So he had ridden this long way on a warhorse, surrounded by a battalion of fully equipped strong-arms. Two hoornars hovered overhead, their riders watching for the buzz-rats of Slade. The flying rodents were coarse creatures, not quick but razor-toothed and stubborn, holding on to prey even while stung repeatedly by the hoornars.

There were the outriders to consider as well, those blurred warriors who seemed to ride out of nowhere. Legends brewed about them—that they were avenging angels, raging demons, ghosts, mighty men of greater rank than the stronghold princes.

Ghedo swore they were mogs, perhaps from one of the powerful strongholds to the far east. Perhaps even from King Teos of Thrash, to whom all other strongholds paid tribute. But the sorcerer had backed off that claim when Alrod challenged him to create such mogs.

Did they arise from between the Blunt Cliffs, stirred from the stew of wraiths there? Hoornars and buzz-rats alike had flown down into the Narrows, never to be seen again. Alrod didn't believe in ghouls, choosing to believe the Narrows were simply impassable, at least by his armies. Gargants, on the other hand—

he still hoped that strategy would work. That sack of horse spit Treffyn knew by now of the gargants, but he'd have no time to mog a countermeasure. He would simply cower in his stronghold, powdered and rouged, quaking against the day that Alrod broke through and sliced out his bowels, one loop at a time.

And the outriders—let them come. Baron Alrod, the crown and glory of Traxx, would not let some scamp with an unadorned sword, strange eyes, and blurred face make a fool of him again. Alrod had felt the breath of the outrider as he clung to his neck. It had been faint with cinnamon and hot with exertion. Under that mask was a man, and that man would one day grace the wall of the great hall. He'd mount the outrider under Nighteye's remains, alive if possible. Alrod would drive the nails through his wrists and ankles, then watch as he died a slow death.

The baron sat in his command tent now, strong-arms tripping over each other to serve him tea or find him some choice morsel. He waved them out, each one bowing as deep as his armor would allow. He took off his boots, knowing that no other noble in Traxx or the richer strongholds would sink to take off their own boots. This was what made Alrod a force to be feared, and not some puppet master: he laced his own boots and swung his own sword.

"High and mighty, how was your journey?" In full sorcerer gear, Ghedo cut an imposing figure. His cloak was purple satin brocaded with black and gold snakes, heads posed to strike. The man under the regalia had quick hands for administering potions, sharp eyes with tremendous focus for the details of transmogrification.

"What do your assistants tell you of my new Nighteye?"

Ghedo pushed back his hood and poured himself ale, sipping as daintily as if it were nectar. "Patience is not your strong suit, Alrod. You only tire yourself by asking me every time we meet."

Alrod got up, served himself a mug of wine. He liked getting away from court, spending time among men who smelled of sweat and labor, not of perfume and intrigue. "Tell me of the gargants, then."

"The survivors are intelligent and strong. If I can get the allegiance potion to take in even a third of them, you'll have a tremendous force for personal protection. Which was why I needed you to come. Once I administer the allegiance potion, you must be the first thing they see. Then we can arm them with the weapons you've prepared, and Traxx will truly be invincible."

"This had better work."

"Not only that, I can produce more gargants with less waste, now that I've done it successfully. You'll need to get me more source material, of course."

"The villages are running thin," Alrod said.

"Why not reward the peasants for bearing children? Give them extra provisions, perhaps even a scrap of land. The women are hardy, can breed more often easily if they are kept fed."

A commotion erupted from outside the tent. Alrod instinctively grabbed his sword while Ghedo took out his dagger and pulled his hood back on.

The camp commander, a sturdy strong-arm named Willem, came in, bowing deeply. "We've captured a woman, high and mighty."

"Why should that interest me? I have no need for fleas and lice." Half-crazed peasants, seldom more than breathing skeletons, lived high in the Bashans. It was said that they subsisted on sheep dung and briar leaves.

"She's not a tramp, Baron. She's . . . unusual. Perhaps the sorcerer should examine her."

Ghedo nodded. "I'll go at once."

"No. Wait. Bring her in here," Alrod said. "I could stand a bit of entertainment. But keep a blade to her throat. I don't want any surprises."

Willem came back in with a dark-skinned woman. Her eyes were almond shaped and so brown as to be almost black. Her mouth was wide, her teeth healthy and complete, something rarely seen in peasants and never seen in the tramps. She was small enough to be mistaken for a child, but her shape under the woolen tunic showed she was indeed a woman. A misshapen knapsack hung on her shoulders, and a bulge of fabric in her waistband shimmered as if it were of royal weave.

Willem forced her head down in a bow, but her eyes never left Alrod's face.

"Let her up, commander," Alrod said. "Where did you find her?"

"She was in the pen with the gargants."

"What?" Ghedo stepped forward. "I want the heads of the gatekeepers now."

"Already been done," Willem said.

"How could you?" The woman's voice was unexpectedly full.

"Shut up, girl or I'll have *your* head on a pike," Alrod said. "What is your name?"

"Ajoba."

"Do you know who I am?"

"The man who fancies himself the jewel of the east."

Willem raised his hand to strike her.

"No," Alrod said, laughing. "Stay your hand." Her eyes were defiant but not stupid. Why could they not find women like these for court? Perhaps he could raid this woman's village. How lovely that dark skin would look in his gold silks.

"Where do you come from?" Ghedo asked.

"I have no home. I wander the villages, take shelter where it's offered."

"In Traxx?"

"I am welcome in Traxx, Slade, and beyond."

"The villages are not always friendly places," Alrod said. "What do you offer them that they feed you and clothe you?"

She smiled. "The truth."

Alrod's scalp prickled at the word, as if the single syllable were as sharp as one of Ghedo's needles. "You're a philosopher."

"No, I am not. I do not speculate or surmise. I simply tell what I know to be true."

"And what is this that you know?" Ghedo said.

She opened her mouth to speak, but Willem put his hand over it. "If I may, high and mighty, she speaks nonsense. If you allow her to start her spiel, she will not stop."

"I will accede to your advice, Commander. Ghedo, could you test her? I would like to know if she is mogged."

"I don't need to. She reeks of original." Ghedo pushed up her sleeve, kneading the muscle of her forearm and examining her palms. "She's got some strength here. You ride, girl, do you not?"

She looked down her nose at Ghedo though he towered over her. "I do ride. But I am not to be treated like livestock, pawed and inspected by the likes of you."

Ghedo raised his hand to strike her.

"Don't," Alrod said. "Tell me, woman. What exactly is the *likes* of my sorcerer?"

Ajoba remained silent.

"What happened to telling what you know to be true?"

Her eyes flared. "Your sorcerer's only magic is the ability and disgusting willingness to apply as many needles as it takes to as many good and noble species of plants or animals to produce something that pleases you. In doing this, your sorcerer is the lowest kind of scum, who knows no magic and no morality."

Ghedo remained still, but the red line at his throat belied his rage. Alrod nodded at him. "You'd like to kill her."

The sorcerer's slow smile was chilling, even to Alrod. "I'd rather punish her."

"Sorry, friend, but she amuses me. Take her tunic off."

Ghedo reached for her belt, then drew his hand back in alarm. "What is that?"

Her eyes fluttered, for the first time showing fear. "My sleeping blanket. Nothing more."

"It burned me."

"Perhaps I have caught some nettles on it. I apologize."

Alrod walked over to the girl so he could study her close up. Her skin was soft, her cheeks full. She was well nourished.

The length of fabric stuffed into her belt seemed to catch all light in one moment and no light in the next. Alrod dared to place his whole hand on it, gasping at the burn. "I know this."

"What is it?" Ghedo's eyes were on the girl, watching for any attempt on Alrod. Willem's dagger was pressed to the back of her skull, ready to drive into her spine should she give cause.

Alrod smiled, feeling his muscles come alive, his body ready to fight. "Willem, take her outside for a moment. Stand by for my orders."

Willem left with the girl. Ghedo poured another glass of ale, downed it with one gulp. "You cannot let anyone talk to me like that, Alrod."

Alrod waved him off. "You'll have your time with her. After I'm done—assuming she survives, of course."

"What is it, baron? What has caught your attention?"

"That material. I've seen something like it in the armor the outriders wear. That scrap of cloth—indeed, that scrap of a girl—will draw them to us. Ready the gargants as quickly as you can, Ghedo. We will set a trap and reel in the outrider and his troops, rid ourselves of them once and for all."

"What of the girl?"

"Tell Willem to put her back in the pen."

"She won't survive."

"Oh, I think she will. She went in there for a reason. Let's see what she does if we let her play it out."

Ajoba had brought trouble upon Horesh; she knew that now.

When Demas's sword sliced through Brady's shoulder, it had pierced her as well. She had seen herself back on the Ark, the builders and the birthrighters before her in endless rows. She stood at the podium, soaking in the adoration on their faces and praise in their voices, appropriating adulation as her own and not giving it over to the only One who was worthy.

Pride had made her thoughtless. Reckless in not insisting that

Demas meet the camp leader. Brady's wisdom would have served her well, but she had been too arrogant to seek it.

Now this—the breaking of the most solemn birthrighter modus. Shroud was divinely given, and she had exposed it to a foul noble. Alrod had it still, along with her pack and the spindle in it.

Strong-arms stood to each side of her, massive men with long swords and sharp pikes. Their mission was to keep the gargants from touching her.

Ajoba's mission was to touch all she could.

But the gargants kept their distance, their backs against the cold stone of the canyon, fearful of the bramble. Only the shortest of them, a sweet-eyed man who said his name was Martan, had tried to speak to her. A strong-arm had smacked him with the blunt end of his sword, scaring him away.

She sat still for long minutes, gathering her courage, wondering how to get through to the gargants without endangering them. Then she smiled. She had been forbidden to speak but not to sing. And what words were more powerful than those sung from the heart? The song came softly at first. But when her guards did not stop her, she lifted her head and sang out clearly: "Glorious! You are glorious . . ."

Surrounded by the sharp swords, poisonous bramble, and confused gargants—this indeed was glorious.

Ajoba was still down there. Jasper could see her from his high vantage point on the ridge. She was chained in a pen with monsters like him who could crush her without even knowing it. And if that happened, it would be Jasper's fault.

Yesterday, the man with the strange eyes—Brady, that was his name—had called a flock of geese out of the sky, interrupting them in their return north after a long winter. They had clustered around him while he spoke. When he finished, they had taken back to the sky, heading south.

"I've sent for fighters," Brady had told Jasper. He'd also told Jasper to stay put, but Jasper had crept back here where he could keep watch over her. It was his own folly that had enabled her to go down there. He had yanked her away from Brady—almost killed Brady—thinking the man was trying to harm her when he sought only to protect.

Now that he had time to think, Jasper remembered seeing Brady before. The man had ridden into Jasper's village two winters past, plainly dressed but with a well-made sword. It had been a hard winter, especially after Traxx troops raided their stores of grain. Old people had begun to die from starvation. Babies writhed with hunger, their mothers' milk too thin to nourish them. Brady had ridden in with two others—a tall woman with fierce eyes and a woman with a placid face but a confident bearing. When they were convinced the village was free of strong-arms, they brought in a cart piled high with sacks of grain and a milk cow. Before they could even be properly thanked, they had ridden back into the snow.

When there was no hope, hope had come on horseback, in the form of an outrider.

Now, Brady said, the outriders were coming again. But would they come in time? Ajoba was held captive by strong-arms, caged with men and women mogged to be monsters. It was a vast foolishness to think she would not be hurt in some way.

Jasper could not wait for Brady's plan to play out.

He needed to do something now.

Seventeen

Keeper of the manure keeper. Such a role to assign to a future camp leader.

Despite offering his finest tunes, Timothy could not get the slung to come away from the Wall of Traxx. Perhaps he wanted a new song. Timothy began the song he had created at court.

> *Sing to me. Move my heart.*
> *Sing of beauty the eye may never see.*
> *Sing of forever. Sing of a lifetime . . .*

He hadn't forgotten Dawnray, would never forget her even as he struggled to do his duty. What had her life been before Alrod stole her away? What of her life now?

The slung was back, almost tipping over as he looked up at Timothy with sad eyes. Deep inside that shell, he must know that God had created him to be upright and free.

"Thank you, but I do not want to come with you. I would like you to come with me." Timothy smiled as wide as he could without gagging.

The little guy's eyes narrowed.

Don't stop singing, the message had clearly said. The honking of the geese had been comical in relaying it, but Timothy had found Brady's instructions far from amusing. The message had also told him to wrap the slung in shroud so he would not be frightened by the outside world. *And to keep the smell down*, the goose had honked.

"Would you please come with me?" He put his best musical efforts into the request.

The tortoise man hesitated, then finally nodded, the leather of his face crinkling.

"Excellent," Timothy sang. "Let us go."

The slung turned and bashed into the thorns. He looked back, waiting for Timothy.

"You just said you'd come!" Should he drag the creature into the trees, where he had hidden his horse?

The slung moaned and banged against the thorns.

"Oh, perhaps I do understand. You need to ask permission from your leader, don't you?" he sang.

The slung nodded, his face split by a bizarre smile. Timothy forced himself not to look at those green teeth, hung with shreds of rotting meat.

Surely it would be foolish to agree. Who knew what would await him in such a place that slungs gathered? Timothy was about to back away—tell Brady he couldn't find the slung—but he saw a dust cloud rise on the horizon. Only a noble could command that many horses. They would be on him within a couple of minutes at the rate they moved.

"I would be glad to come meet your leader," Timothy sang.

The slung turned into the thorns. After slipping on his gloves, Timothy grabbed the back of his shell and followed him in, singing as he went.

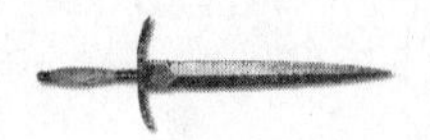

Dawnray had seen the singer's graceful form push into the thorns. Fortunately, Merrihana rode to the far side of her, whipping her poor horse in fury.

Days of riding Traxx from border to river had not uncovered the minstrel. The baroness had had to content herself with sending a strong-arm to Alrod. "Tell the baron that if he kills the singer when he kills the outrider, I will kill his new lolly. In fact, I will kill all his lollies."

The strong-arm bowed deeply. "Requesting pardon, but the baron will not take kindly to such a threat."

"And what does that matter to me?" Merrihana said. "Go!"

He bowed and took his leave. And Dawnray's heart sank.

She ran from Merrihana's side to stop him. He batted her away like a toy. "Baroness, please," she pleaded. "Tell him to stop."

Merrihana narrowed but she snapped her fingers. The strong-arm froze but did not turn. "He's afraid, high and mighty," Dawnray explained. "He knows he'll be killed for delivering such a message. So he will be inclined not to."

Merrihana considered a moment, then nodded. "None of my attendants would have dared to question my command. You may be of some use to me yet. Soldier!"

The strong-arm turned, his face flushed with embarrassment that a lolly had understood his intention.

"Tell my husband that you are to return to me alive and unharmed. If you do not, I will carry through on my threat."

"Very well, high and mighty." He bowed and left.

Merrihana had ordered her drudges to pack up the camp, and they had headed home. What odd quirk of fate had brought them by this section of the wall just as the singer was moving inside? How could he survive in there? Everyone knew the wall of Traxx was impassable, an invitation to certain and horrific death.

Dawnray kicked her horse to catch up with the baroness. "High and mighty, I feel unwell. May I stop for a short while? Perhaps a guard could stay with me so you do not have to linger."

Merrihana sighed elaborately at the interruption but snapped her fingers at a strong-arm. He escorted Dawnray off to the side of the baroness's retinue. As they approached the wall, Dawnray dismounted.

She grabbed her abdomen, knowing that the baroness would be watching to make sure she hadn't lied. She gagged until the horses disappeared around the curve of the wall. The strong-arm stared at her, his mouth half-open. He wouldn't dare touch her, not while the baron's favor rested on her.

"I need shade. Perhaps over there." She pointed to a thick patch of junipers behind them.

"Not there. We could be ambushed."

She knew that, of course. "By the wall?"

"It dangerous to get too close to it. Everyone knows that."

"I'll stay at the edge of its shade. You can see me, even if you stay here."

"The smell will make you sicker, lass. Too sweet—and it's rotten within."

"But the sun will kill me. You don't want to deliver my dead body to the baron, do you?"

"Go. But no tricks."

She lay on the ground, far enough from the wall to resist its sweet allure. Men died in there, hung on the thorns to rot—even men in armor, it was said. So what of her minstrel?

Then she heard him. Moving away, his music growing faint but so clearly, sweetly his.

Dawnray got up and moved toward the wall. If he could cross into it, why not she? The flowers were so beautiful, their perfume so entrancing. She ran her fingers over the silky petals, pressing her face to them, pushing against the wall so she could follow her minstrel.

The strong-arm jerked her away. "I warned you. You'll get us both killed."

He dragged her away, the call of the flowers already diminishing. What of the minstrel? Was he real? Or just another lure of this dreadful wall?

"That's a full battalion, mate," Kendo whispered. "And then some."

Brady scratched his chin. "Aye, Kee. It most certainly is."

"Too many for us. Unless you have a secret army to unleash on them."

"I may. Taryan, did you bring your gear?"

She nodded.

"And my equipment." Kendo rubbed his hands together.

She sighed dramatically. "You would have thought it was his birthday, the way he fell upon my carts."

"You're not worried, are you?" Brady asked her.

"What I am not is stupid," she said. "We can't take all those strong-arms on ourselves."

"Bartoly should have reached Horesh by now," Kendo said. "You've sent for him and his crew?"

"He was with one other outrider—Leiha, correct? Plus two trackers. Even if they all come"—Taryan fixed Brady with a skeptical gaze—"Lad, we have a full battalion down there."

"Do I hear an echo?" he said, laughing.

Neither Kendo nor Taryan laughed with him.

"Will you two relax? Timothy is on his way too."

Kendo flipped his dagger about twenty feet in the air and caught it by the blade. "That's the least relaxing news I've heard today. Apart from the battalion, that is."

"What I'm wondering," Taryan said, "is why the Traxx locked Ajoba up in that pen with all those gargants."

"Because they're smarter than I am," Brady said. "If I had locked her up, we wouldn't be here."

Taryan glared at him, and he conceded, "Alrod wants her out in the open. Bait."

"*He's* here as well?" Taryan said.

Brady grinned. "A gathering of our favorite people, eh?"

Kendo threw his dagger again, this time catching it in his teeth.

"Will you stop that?" Taryan snapped. "You're making me nervous."

"*I* make you nervous?" He tilted his head toward Brady. "What about your lad here?"

She grabbed Brady's arm. "Kendo asked you a question."

"No, he asked *you* the question." Brady's smile faded when he felt the tremble in her fingers. "But I do have a plan that I think—or at least I pray—will succeed."

Kendo sat and traced patterns in the dirt with his dagger.

"Let's have it. We need to be ready to move when Bartoly and the rest get up here."

Brady cleared his throat. "About Bartoly. He isn't exactly coming up here."

In the full day that Ajoba had been with the gargants, they had not been fed once. Ajoba had even been taken outside the pen to eat, so concerned was Alrod that they might rush her for the food. She would have willingly given it to them. Her time with Jasper had taught her that their need was far greater than hers.

The baron was concerned as well. Outside the gate, she could hear him screaming at Willem and then turning his wrath on his sorcerer. "How could they have eaten through all the grain I sent up here?"

"Their metabolism must have sped up," Ghedo said. "I don't dare transmogrify them until they're fed again. The process is—"

"I know how demanding the process is. You should have foreseen this."

"I did. I asked you to—"

There was a sharp slap, a soft *oof*.

"You dare talk back to me? Do not presume, Ghedo. I will have your head as quickly as anyone else's."

That would be a mercy, Ajoba thought. For Traxx and beyond.

"Requesting pardon, high and mighty. But you did tell me provisions were on the way."

Alrod's voice dropped. Ajoba put her head against the wood, trying to hear through the gate. One of her guards tried to pull her back.

She shook her head, having learned that the guards threatened much but did little. Despite Alrod's orders, she had managed to talk to quite a few gargants in the past few hours.

"I am certainly not more precious in God's sight than you,"

she told the guard now, "but I am in Alrod's. So let me go, or I will tell him you had your hands on me."

"That's my job, girl."

"I will tell him that you hurt me. You damage me, the baron will certainly damage you."

He stepped away from Ajoba, palms out. "Just keep your mouth shut, drudge. Or I will indeed damage you and say the gargants did it."

"Fine." She continued listening.

"—grain coming in from the south by next week. A herd of cattle should arrive tomorrow. I gave orders that they were not to be driven too hard. I want them still fat when they reach the Bashans."

"Alrod, the gargants are deteriorating quickly. We could lose a third of them by morning."

"I could order my men out to hunt." His voice grew softer. *They must be walking away.*

"That would take too long."

"What do you suggest?"

"I've got just the thing."

Ghedo's laughter faded, and she heard no more.

Minutes later, Willem came in with several strong-arms in full armor, armed with pikes. They forced the gargants to line up so he could study them. He drew out Martan and one other. The other strong-arms wrapped an iron chain around their waists and led them from the pen. The strong-arms brandished their pikes at the other gargants, but the poor souls were too weak even to protest.

Martan looked at her as he passed. "Remember me to that father you spoke about."

Ajoba sat down and indeed prayed. But she must have eventually dozed, because the next thing she knew her guard was shaking her awake and unwinding her chains so they could open the gate again. Strong-arms came in with carts full of roasted meat and carefully passed out a chunk to each gargant. They kept careful guard of the cart while they worked. These remaining gargants had become valuable property. It would not do to have them kill each other over a piece of meat.

The gargant named Koppe glanced her way and smiled. She smiled back, pleased to see the color returning to his cheeks. He held up his meat as if to toast her. He had chewed it down to the bone.

A trained tracker, Ajoba immediately recognized what kind of bone it was.

Once she started vomiting, she couldn't stop. Willem unshackled her and led her to Ghedo. "She only now stopped spewing, O great one."

Ajoba stood tall, unconcerned with the vomit that stained her face and tunic. She would not cower before this scum. "Detestable. Unspeakable. Hideous. You are the lowest sort of slime, Ghedo. The most vile, contemptible, shameful, loathsome piece of—" The only right word was a profanity, and she would not lower herself before him. "How could you do such a thing?"

Ghedo laughed. "Just solving a problem in a practical way. Quite simple, really, when one has the power to really get things done."

"Do you not understand the consequences of your arrogance? Your evil? Surely you will burn in hell."

"I don't even know where hell is, and I don't care." He waved her away. "Take her back to the pen. And don't disturb me unless she throws up her stomach on top of her bile."

Willem dragged Ajoba out of the tent. "You will get my head separated from my shoulders yet. Can you not just be quiet?"

She stopped. "Commander, do *you* know where hell is?"

"No."

"I'll make you a deal. If I go back without giving you any more trouble, will you let me tell you where hell is?"

"Why should I care?"

"That, my dear commander, is the most intelligent question you have asked today."

EIGHTEEN

NIKI FLUNG HERSELF TO THE GROUND. TRULY, SHE COULD run no further.

Dusk crept in from the east, blanketing the river with haze. She still needed to find nourishment in what little sunlight remained.

An hour later she sat by the fire, roasting two rabbits. She took a long drink of water, grateful that the northern stretch of the Camara ran unpolluted. Sparkling and pure, it reminded her of Horesh. Even in the winter she loved to dunk her face through the ice. In the summer, Niki was one of the few who swam just for fun. She'd never think the Grand was cold again after diving through the ice after the bowhead and chasing a longboat through Camara's whitewater.

She had ranged far in her six years out of the Ark as the outrider assigned to special collections—escorting a collector to far-flung regions where a species was in immediate danger of extinction. She had trudged through the reptile-rich swamps of the southeast and the surprisingly life-laden deserts of the southwest. She had seen rivers that lazed with silt and streams that rushed with snow-melt. She had ridden across plains as wide as seven strongholds and climbed mountains that made the Bashans look like hillocks. She had tracked rattlesnakes and prairie dogs, dung beetles and bluebirds, bald eagles and grizzly bears. She had taken seed from corn and cauliflower, bluegrass and millet, daisies and ferns.

Niki had seen stretches of creation that sorcerers and stronghold princes didn't dare imagine, even in their most ambitious dreams.

Lakes as big as any stronghold, canyons so flamed with color they made gold and gems pale; secluded glens and sparkling springs and velvet moss.

But she had also seen wastelands where living soil had been blown into crushed stone. She had spied toxlands that simmered with radioactive poison and spawned monsters beyond comprehension. Even more tragic, she'd seen traces of the toxins even in relatively untouched areas. Creatures with stunted limbs—or extras. Life forms whose grotesque alterations had nothing to do with mogging. She had even heard of men and women, exposed to contamination, who gave birth to . . . monsters.

So much had been damaged, so much lost. During training, they had studied the histories preserved by the early builders. Niki had learned of nations where people had the freedom to determine the course of their lives, where they chose their own leaders and made their own laws. She also knew of brutal tyrannies that never escaped the dark ages and rich countries that blasted each other back there. She had seen holovids of concrete and glass cities, machines that flew across oceans and to the planets, equipment that washed dishes and dried clothing and built other equipment. She understood about devices that sent instant communication from one end of the world to the other.

This world was their ancestry and their heritage—a world destroyed by entertainment and excess, pride and heresy, rage and bitterness, judgment and hate. Every birthrighter knew about the Endless Wars whose bombs and guns and plagues and conflagrations had swallowed up the earth, leaving creation to groan for what once had been, leaving a faithful remnant to pray for what had once been promised.

It was that promise that Niki had sworn to uphold and preserve.

But for all that she had learned, for all she had served, for that duty which she had done with all her heart and mind and body, she had been brought to this—sent away by the one she loved best, rejected by the ones she esteemed the least.

A lonely girl sitting by a lonely fire.

A twig cracked behind her. She hadn't lost all then. "I know you're there, wolf."

Silence.

"I've had a fix on your scent for hours now. You might consider a dip in the river, if you don't mind my saying."

The brush rustled. Niki pulled the smaller rabbit off the fire, hacked some meat off for herself, and tossed the carcass across the campsite. The wolf snatched it and fled back to the brush. A crunch of bones followed immediately.

She pulled the second rabbit off the fire, cut as much meat off as she could, and wrapped it in a piece of shroud. The rooks would be hungry when she found them. If she found them—but no, she couldn't think like that. She had to find them.

She tossed the carcass on the other side of the fire. It was a good minute before the wolf crept out, his eyes on her the whole time.

He nosed the rabbit, then locked his jaws on it. He slowly chewed, his eyes still fixed on hers, the flicker of flames reflecting in his yellow eyes.

"It's just you and me now, wolf."

He dragged the carcass into the brush. Niki heard digging—saving the bones for later. He inched back out a minute later, closer to the fire this time but still opposite her. Why would she even want him to come closer? He stank, and he was dangerous. But so was she. "I admire you, you know."

He curled into his paws, his gaze on her.

"Because of the musk oxen. Not because you saved me—thank you for that, by the way. But the thing was, you only ate the ox you killed. You honored me by leaving the others for me because they were my kills.

"You showed respect." She raised her water skin. "So here's to you, wolf."

Anastasia and Kwesi had disappeared into the night.

Cooper had the packs at his side, the rope still around his wrist. As he drew it in, he found the loops that his companions had tied around themselves. Empty.

"Kwesi. Stasia. This is not funny, not at all."

The darkness swallowed his voice just as the husk had.

They were joking with him. Served him right. He had given everyone a hard time in training. Always the mouth going, playing the jokes but untouchable because he got the highest marks. "Smart in books, dumb in the world," Kwesi would mutter.

And look where his huff-puff had gotten them. On top of a hill so black, it might as well be on the cold side of the moon. Where was the moon, anyway? Hadn't it been close to full in Chiungos? That was only two days ago—it should have risen by now. Was this some sort of tremendous cloud cover that had come upon them?

"Cooper."

He jerked around but made no answer.

"Cooper, I know you're there."

Not Anastasia's high-pitched squeal, Niki's rasp, or Kwesi's baritone. A silvery voice. Who else knew his name in this wide world? Cooper tried to scrunch into himself as if he could be his own hiding place. He covered his face with his arms so no flesh would be visible.

"I've been sent to help you."

Light flooded around him now, as if someone had turned on a spotlight. Cooper could see the ground around him, the rope and the packs. Nearby was the shadow of a figure, but it was reversed, a form of light cut out of the darkness.

He tried to stand, but a hand held him in place. "Don't. You're tired. I'll sit with you, if I may?"

"Sure," he said warily. "Pull up a hunk of dirt and kick back."

The man wore a shimmering cloak. His face was so blurry, Cooper wondered if his eyesight was going bad. "So you're slippin' 'n' slidin' onesie?" the man said.

"Eya?"

"Need me to speak old? You that far gone, Coopster?"

"Uh, no. It's just . . . well, Niki told us to lose the jangle."

"Aye, then. We'll speak it old."

Cooper didn't answer, kept his face hidden in his hands. He was trying to get a glimpse at the man's feet.

In training they'd said that footwear was a better indication of status than clothing. Strong-arms never gave up their fine leather boots, even when wearing plain clothes. Peasants wore burlap; villagers, rough leather or suede; noble women, the most delicate of sandals; and high-born men, shiny shoes.

The man's feet were hidden under his cloak. His entire body was.

As if reading Cooper's mind, the man brought his hands out and folded them over his knees. His skin was smooth, his nails clean and clipped. Cooper's nails were already filthy, and he had torn two on the boat. Niki picked at hers with her knife every night after supper.

"You're not gleaning." It was statement, not a question.

Cooper shook his head. "I don't even *know* what I'm not gleaning."

The man gave no answer but just whistled a strange melody.

"Requesting pardon," Cooper ventured, "but do you know where my comrades are?"

The man turned to him with a bright smile. "Kwesi and Anastasia."

Cooper jumped up. "Where are they? Are they all right?"

"They're high kickin'. So you can just relax. Sit down, Cooper."

"I want to see them. Please."

The man opened his hand one finger at a time, and an image took form on his palm. It was Kwesi, dressed in a fine cloak. He fisted his hand and opened it again. Anastasia looked back at

Cooper. She wore a pale pink tunic, her hair pretty and loose on her shoulders.

"Now do you know where I've come from?" the man said.

Nothing in this world could make a holovid, and surely that's what the pictures had to be. Projected from the man's sleeve, perhaps. Yet Cooper had been born on the Ark, knew every inch, every face. "If you're from the—if you're from *there*, why don't I know you?"

The man smiled. "We all have secrets. Even the people we love best keep secrets."

Cooper paced in a circle. "Why did you come? Has something awful happened back there? Has the project been found out?"

The man smiled. "Cooper, please sit with me. I've come a long way, and I'm punked out. You must be ready for a kick-back yourself, eya?"

Cooper's eyes felt like sand. He rubbed them, but they seemed determined to close. He found himself curling onto his side.

"It's all right, son. Rest up now. You been doin' a lot of leg workin'. Trying to keep the high and mighty of nasty happy."

Cooper pushed up, forcing his eyes to stay open. "Who told you that?"

The man laughed and opened his hand. Anastasia waved at Cooper.

"Why are you here?" Cooper said, barely getting the words out. Had he ever been this tired?

"She lied, you know. She was very angry, made up a nasty story. But it wasn't all a lie, though she didn't know it. It *has* been decided that you may go back. And you won't have to be left in storage. Things can be like they used to be. Before you came out."

A burst of energy seized Cooper. "Really?"

"You can be the wave breaker, the top billing. That's what you want, isn't it? You want something of your own to grab and shake. You've already done that in ways you can't even comprehend."

"I don't understand."

"Like I said, you can't glean it. But trust me, it will happen. You trust me, don't you?"

Cooper was seized with a horrible thought. "Would we have to go back the way we came?"

"Why shouldn't we?"

A trembling seized him, as if he had been doused in icy water. "My transit was messed up. Guess you wouldn't know that."

"No, Coop. That one went by me. But it'll be different this time. You'll be doing it with me. And you know you can trust . . ."

Cooper felt himself drifting back to his transit. He saw the darkness, felt the bumping of his husk against those of his comrades, remembered talking to himself, talking against the fear, promising to do anything if he could just get out of this husk. The memory of his mother came to him. A double memory, he thought—when you remember a memory.

When the time comes, sing through your fear, Mum had said.

The music came to him then, as familiar as his own name. The man in silver would know the song and sing with him, for surely this was an occasion for it.

"Glorious! You are glorious . . ." Cooper began. "You know this song, right? Sing with me."

The man wasn't singing. No matter. Cooper couldn't stop now because the music filled him, warming him through and through, more sure than this man sitting next to him, more solid than the ground under him.

"You're the Lord almighty. We sing your praise in all the earth."

The man in silver doubled over, clutching his side as if someone had stabbed him. He pushed away from Cooper, fading into the darkness.

"Don't go!" Cooper tried to follow, but he felt the fingers of his mother stroke the inside of his heart and tell him to keep singing. So he did, loud and strong.

If the man was really from the Ark, he would come back.

Niki kicked dirt over what remained of the fire. A tracker would know someone had been here, but she hadn't seen anyone since leaving Chiungos.

"You coming?"

She could smell the wolf in the brush.

"I will not beg. So come along or find someone else to plead rabbit from." Niki hefted her pack to her back and strode off. Her muscles were tight, her shins aching from running on the rocky riverbank. Another day of this, and she would be lame.

Another day of this, and the rooks would be dead.

This she knew with certainty, because she knew this world, and they did not.

As soon as her muscles loosened, Niki broke into a trot. The wolf lurked nearby, skulking in the brush for cover. She'd be doing the same if she weren't in a hurry. All day yesterday she had scanned the river as she ran. She did the same now, looking for dangerous rapids, hoping not to see debris of a shattered boat.

Around midmorning, the Arojo foothills came into view. According to the coordinates Cooper had brought off the Ark, Arabah lay beyond, in a vast cavern halfway up Welz.

Niki kicked into a sprint. Her breath came hard now, but she felt the rare need to hear her own voice. "So why are you traveling solo, wolf? Was it because you were injured? Or too old? You look to be in decent shape. But so do I, and I'm old. Half the people in this world don't live to see twenty-two years. I'm no fool—I know the younger birthrighters talk about how long we senior outriders will survive. They repent later, but—"

Forget repentance. Would being sorry make her a better outrider? She wasn't perfect, but she tried to do what was right. She never balked at an assignment, no matter how dull or dangerous. During the mandated respite weeks, she sharpened swords, cleaned stalls, even cooked. She kept her mouth shut except when there was something to say. Sure, she made mistakes, but they all did that. Dwelling on them just drained her of energy she needed to do her job.

By noon she had found the branch off the river. And by early afternoon she came upon the boat, shoved into some brush. The packs were gone, but the paddles were stored under the seats. Niki turned east and headed into the foothills, following the path the rooks must have taken. The Arojo range rose before her, with Welz lofting over the hills.

Niki moved much slower now—from caution, not exertion. Something seemed . . . off. Ice sparkled in the air, though the sun was high and the air warm enough to rouse a sweat. A shadow flashed overhead. She ducked instinctively, but when she looked up, the sky was clear. She turned quickly, scanning the hills she had left behind her, the river now a distance to the west.

A chill seized her. She shrugged off her pack and dug out her coat. Even after she pulled it on, she couldn't seem to get warm. No matter—climbing would restore her body heat. She turned uphill.

But now a shadow stretched ahead of her like a wall. A division. On this side was natural day. On the other side, it seemed to be night.

From out of the brush, the wolf growled. "I agree," Niki said. "This is not good."

She stretched her hand forward, expecting to feel a curtain of ice—perhaps the reverse of shroud—but her hand slipped into the darkness with no sensation. She pulled her hand back but inched forward, slipping her foot into the shadow. She could still feel the ground under her boot. When she dug in her heel, soil and pebbles kicked back at her.

She swiveled sideways and stepped into the shadow until her arm and leg were in darkness. The wolf continued to rumble his displeasure but wouldn't show himself. Niki leaned sideways until all of her was in the shadow but one foot.

Instant night. But not natural night.

She leaped out, soaked with sweat under her coat, though the tip of her nose was icy cold. She sat down next to her pack, rubbing her face. The grass a pace downhill rustled. Niki dug into her pack for a piece of rabbit meat. She held it out.

"Stop playing shy, wolf. I believe I may need your help here."

The wolf crept into sight but kept his distance. She tossed the meat at him. He gulped it down, growling the whole time. The fur on his spine rose.

Niki got on her hands and knees and crawled toward him. He held his ground, his eyes fixed on her face. *He'll take your nose off*, she told herself, but she inched forward anyway, so close now she smelled the rabbit on his breath and the rotting meat stuck back in his molars. His fur reeked of sweat and combat. His face was scarred, his left ear torn.

He stopped growling but stayed low. She leaned close, hoping the high collar of her coat would protect her if he went for her throat. "If you can help me, come along," she told him in a low voice. "Otherwise, be off. I need to know if I can trust you. If not, just—"

She stopped, stunned at the catch in her throat. "I'd like you to stay with me. Will you do that?"

The wolf stretched his neck and sniffed her breath. She froze, thinking how insane she was and how good it was she had found a creature equally as addled. He moved around her, smelling her shoulders, her back, and her legs until he came full circle. He sat back on his haunches, his ears fully alert and his tongue hanging out.

Niki stood. "All right, wolf. I don't know what all this is, but I do know those rooks are stupid, ignorant, and foolish enough to be in the middle of it. So let's go get them out."

NINETEEN

HE KNEW BETTER.

Every beat of his heart, every tread of his foot, every bristle of his back said he knew better.

But something had overruled all instinct. Perhaps it was because, like him, she was a pack of one now. Whether he and she would form their own pack remained unclear. Yet some force stronger than the sun and the seasons kept him at her side.

And so he followed her into night.

Against all common sense, Niki walked right into the darkness. There was no transition. It was like being in one of the storage rooms on the Ark and having someone turn off the light, leaving you in the pitch black. Niki moved slowly, using her sword as a blind person might use a cane. The wolf pressed against her side, his frequent stumbling an indication he couldn't see either.

Though Niki was the outrider who would stop at nothing, she would stop at this—if the rooks weren't somewhere up that mountain. Was this darkness what had caused Arabah to lose contact with the Ark?

"Obviously," she said, her voice muffled even to her own ears.

She could turn back, send for Brady. Modus said a camp leader had to respond to a raven sent by his or her comrades. Pride would not keep her from sending one now. Fear would—the fear of seeing his face when she told him what she had done to the rooks to make them behave so badly. His eyes would droop at the corners, and he would simply ask, "Why, Nik?"

She wouldn't have to tell him why. He would read it in her face though she would struggle to hide it. *Because you chose another over me.*

"I didn't know you felt like that," he might say.

Neither did I.

"No longer," she said.

"Who's there?"

She froze for a moment, then raised her sword. "Identify yourself or I'll strike."

"Niki?"

"Cooper? Where are you?"

"I'm here. Right here."

"I can't see you."

"I can see you! I am right here, Niki. Right here!"

"Cooper, come out right now! I am furious—" *Watch your tongue,* she told herself. *Don't drive him away again.*

"I have been worried sick about you, Cooper," she said instead. "So show yourself right now. Please."

"I am right next to you. Why can't you see me?"

Niki put her hand on the wolf's back. His fur stood straight up. "Can you see anything?"

He clamped his teeth on her wrist.

"Don't you dare bite me," she said, and he didn't. Instead, he tried to tug her backward.

"Cooper. How far am I from you?"

"Three paces at the most. Look, I've got my hand out to you. See it?"

"No. It's too dark."

"Oh, of course. It is light where I am. If you come to me, you will be able to see."

She slowly raised her hand but felt nothing other than a fierce cold.

"One step, Niki, and I can grab your hand. Why won't you

come for me? I am so sorry for what we did. Would you please forgive me?"

"Forget forgiveness. Just tell me which way to come." This wasn't like Cooper to be so talkative.

"Straight ahead. Another step, and you'll be able to see me."

The wolf blocked her way. "Move, stinky."

He wouldn't budge.

"Niki? Aren't you coming?"

"Cooper, give me a minute." She crouched down. "What's wrong, wolf?"

He knocked her onto her backside and clamped his paws on her shoulders. She pressed her dagger to his throat. "Get off me, wolf."

He growled. Somehow she knew it was *for* her and not at her.

"I promise I will not move forward without your permission. Now, get off me."

He slipped to the ground beside her. She sat up and pressed her face to his fur.

"Niki?"

"I'm still here. Don't you see me anymore?"

"Oh, sure. There you are. Just reach for me now."

Why didn't he see the wolf? She stood up and clasped hands behind her back. "Cooper, I'm trying to reach you. Is my hand near yours now?"

"Just one step, Niki, and we'll touch. Oh please, I've been so scared."

She bent down. "I have to move forward. Will you go with me?"

He pressed against her leg but moved with her. She stretched out her sword, jabbing the darkness. It clanged against what sounded like another sword. Pure reflex made her swing—hard.

Niki jumped backward as her sword broke.

"You should not have done that, Niki." Not Cooper—a very deep voice. "That was very impulsive and very unwise."

She crouched, her dagger at the ready.

"That sword means a lot to you, and now you've gone and broken it."

"Show yourself right now or I will—"

"What? Slay me? You don't have the right kind of sword, outrider."

"Who said I was an outrider?"

"You tell yourself that every minute of every day."

"Who are you?"

"Isn't that the wrong question?"

"What is the right question?"

"I'm not sure you can handle the right question."

"Forget it. I do not talk philosophy with people I do not know." Niki bent down so she could follow the line her sword had made in the sand. "Let's go back," she whispered to the wolf.

"You don't talk philosophy with people you *do* know." The voice followed her. "Don't you want to know what the right question is?"

"I don't talk philosophy with anyone, remember?"

"The right question is, where are Kwesi, Anastasia, and Cooper?"

She stopped. This time the wolf sank his teeth in. "Ow! Stop it!"

"Oh, so you don't want to know?"

"I wasn't—" Surely he must know the wolf was with her. But if not, she would be a fool to give the animal's presence away.

His laugh was a grating rumble. "You are too stubborn to ask. I will show you anyway."

Light flooded behind and around her, though, strangely, she and the wolf cast no shadow. The rooks stood about ten feet away. Anastasia was crying, while Kwesi simply hung his head. Cooper's features were blurred, as if he wore a mask of shroud.

"Cooper?"

"They can't hear you, so don't bother. Listen, Niki—"

LISTEN, NIKI.

Not the stranger's voice. This was a strong, clear voice. Somehow familiar, though she had never heard it before.

The dark voice went on and on, telling her some nonsense. But Niki had stopped listening to him and started listening for—for what?

BE STILL AND KNOW.

"I'll have you know—" She stopped.

"What will you have me know, Niki?"

"Nothing. I'm sorry I interrupted."

He launched back into his spiel, but he was really saying nothing, so she found it easy to tune him out. She listened for the wind, but it was silent. She listened for the movement of the wolf, but he was still pressed to her side. *This is stupid*, she was about to say, but then she closed her mouth. She wasn't so stupid that she didn't recognize authority when she heard it. But that tone of authority was all she could hear.

Or was it?

Was that an injured animal keening in the darkness? Or perhaps a child crying. No, the voice she heard was Cooper's—the real Cooper. She started to call for him, but the wolf took her hand and tugged. She patted him, her fingers telling him she would listen.

The words came clear now, a tune a little different from the one she knew. But perhaps it had changed since she left the Ark. Or maybe it was different because Cooper's voice sounded so raw.

You're one who heals the wounded.
You can calm the storm at sea.
Glorious! You are glorious . . .

Niki saw the real rook now, though the fake one was still on display with Kwesi and Anastasia. His eyes were closed, his shoulders slumped, but he sang on. Trapped in the same darkness as she was, so she ran to him . . . and hit a wall. She battered it with her fists, feeling her skin frost over. She went at it with her feet, almost breaking her ankle.

The man in the darkness laughed.

She whirled to scream at him.

Not him. *It.* Towering over her, its skin as transparent as glass, though what was underneath was unspeakable, a fetid mixture of rot, offal, and scum. Deep in its chest was a knot that perhaps had once been a heart—but who could know, with all those tangles and warts?

"What are you?" Niki said.

"I am Azazel. Your master and soon-to-be lord, girl."

"No one is my master or my lord. And don't call me girl."

"I'll call you whatever I wish once you belong to me, *girl.*"

The creature swelled even larger, its chest rising and exhaling a flood of putrefaction.

"What did you do with them?" Niki said.

"Who?"

"My comrades?"

"You should thank me for ridding you of them."

"Let them go!"

Azazel laughed. "Who is going to make me? *You*, outrider?"

She grappled for her sword, forgetting that she had broken it with one swing.

"That's all right," said a familiar voice. "I'll make you another."

She looked to her right, startled to see Brady standing by her. "You . . . you can't be here," she said.

"No time for explanations now, Niki. We've got to get out of here."

"What about—" She pointed to where the creature had been, but a stir in the darkness was all she could see.

"All taken care of. Now, come with me." Brady reached for her with a slow smile. A knowing smile.

She stretched her fingers toward him, feeling her body come alive in a way she had never experienced. A slow and *knowing* way.

The wolf jumped past her, leaping for Brady's throat. Niki raised her dagger and slashed for the wolf's neck, turning her hand in the last split second so that she struck the animal with her fist and not her blade.

He fell limp at her feet. She sheathed her dagger and looked at Brady. Thankfully, the wolf had not drawn blood. Good enough, then—she took a moment to bend down to the wolf. The animal lay still. She drew him up against her, surprised at how heavy he was for one so scrawny. His chest was still, but she felt his heart beating through his fur—or was that her own echoing back at her?

"Niki. What are you holding?"

"The wolf. He didn't mean to jump at you like that."

"A wolf, eh? Put that bag of fleas down and come to me."

She cradled the wolf tighter to her chest as if to stop the ache in her own heart. The real Brady would know this animal was far more than a fleabag. The wolf came to in her arms, struggling to find his feet.

"Niki, I said to come to me!" Brady's voice—but no, simply an ugly counterfeit.

"Shut up, Azazel." Niki turned back to Cooper. "Cooper, can you hear me?"

Was that a shift of his gaze, a sense that something beyond himself was near?

"Hold on until I come back. I promise I *will* come back."

Niki picked up her broken sword and let the wolf lead her back toward the light.

TWENTY

OVER THE COURSE OF THE AFTERNOON, NIKI TRIED EVERY trick she had learned as an outrider to get Cooper out of the darkness. She had fastened a leash for the wolf so he could lead her in and out each time.

She cast rocks, hoping to break through that black wall. She tried to dig under, sneak around, even built a crude ladder to come from above. She tried misdirection, making a dummy from brush and sending the boat down the river with her fake self at the helm.

Nothing worked.

The rook still sang raggedly, on his knees now. "Keep singing, Cooper," she called.

The only response was the laughter of Azazel, punctuated by hideous images that scored her eyes. Even when she squeezed them shut, her eyelids burned with things she hadn't seen in her worst nightmares. For some reason, the creature didn't challenge her again. He seemed content to watch her try to splinter his dark stronghold.

Coming out this last time, Niki panicked to see the darkness had spread. But no, night had simply fallen. She huddled by the light of her fire, too spent to hunt for something to eat. The wolf disappeared into the brush and came back after a while, dragging the fresh-killed body of a wild boar.

"I don't deserve this." Something sharp scraped at the back of Niki's throat. Tears—had it been so long that she didn't even recognize the sensation? "I'm sorry I hit you, wolf. I thought you were hurting . . . my pack leader. I'm sorry."

The wolf dragged the boar onto her feet.

Niki laughed. "I'm with you. Less talk, more action. I must say, you are the fearless one."

The wolf sat patiently while she gutted the boar. She let him take the carcass while she roasted some meat for herself. She ate slowly, staring the whole time at her shattered sword. "What manner of enemy can do this, wolf?"

He rested his snout on his paws and blinked up at her.

After she had eaten, she tried to sleep. But though every muscle in Niki's body screamed with exhaustion, her eyes would not close.

Why did Cooper's singing keep the creature away? How had it snared Anastasia and Kwesi? Were they really inside that darkness, or was that another deception? There must be some way to break through to Cooper.

The wolf stared at her, the fire flickering in his eyes.

"Yes. That might do it! Come on, wolf. We've got work to do."

Cooper walked through a garden. It was not like the ones on the Ark where trees grew in rows and flowers twined around trellises. Here, flowers bloomed with full abandon. Butterflies with wings like flame fluttered about blossoms the color of sunset. Sweet cherries and tart apples hung ripe on low branches, while thornless raspberry bushes clustered by a rushing stream. The green leaves of shade trees rippled in the breeze and cooled the path. Cooper squinted up through the branches, but he couldn't find the sun, though it surely must be high in the sky to cast light this sparkling.

"Cooper." The voice was melodious, strong yet full of laughter.

Cooper shaded his eyes against the glare. Before him stood a creature—or was it a man?—somehow perfectly at peace, yet in constant motion. "You're not like the other. The one in silver."

"No. But he was once like me."

"What happened?"

"He tripped over his own pride. Had a long fall."

Cooper hung his head. He had tripped over his pride more than anyone he knew.

"I've been asked to give you a message, Cooper."

"I'm so sorry."

"I know you are. May I give you the message?"

Cooper nodded, thinking he should check the footwear, but this creature—

"Not creature. Messenger."

Cooper looked up and smiled. "Is it all over, then? Am I finally home?"

"No, Cooper. There's still more work to be done. But for now, you are in a dream."

"No! I can't sleep! If I stop singing, that man in silver—"

"Is being held off. You don't need to worry. Also, you sing quite well in your sleep."

"Oh. Well then, thank you. Is Niki going to come help us?"

"She cannot help you until you help her."

"I don't understand," Cooper said.

"You don't need to. Are you willing to help Niki?"

"What do you want me to do?"

"Will you help her?"

Cooper shivered. If an angel asked him, the task would not be easy. "Yes," he said after a hesitation. "What should I do?"

The angel touched his shoulder. "Stop singing."

"Will she save me if I do?" Cooper asked. But the angel was gone, the garden was gone, and the darkness closed around him again.

Leaving him alone with his song.

Working by the light of the moon, Niki stuffed her coat with straw and wrapped it around pine branches, binding it all tightly with twine to form a torch. She strapped her short blade to her thigh, stuck her flip-knife into her belt, and grabbed the spear she had sharpened from an aspen sapling. She looped the leash onto the wolf and tied that to her belt so her hands would be free.

"You ready?"

He growled but got up. Niki scooped embers into the clay jar that Rebeka's caribou-tongue pies had been packed in. The moonlight made the going easy, especially since Niki had beat a path from her many trips up and down the mountain that day.

Like the plunge through the ice, the darkness took her breath away and stilled her heart for an awful moment. The wolf stopped. She knelt down and rubbed his chest. "Haven't you heard, wolf? I don't stop at anything. If you won't guide me, I will get on my hands and knees and feel my way in."

The wolf shuddered but continued on.

Niki heard Cooper before she saw him. His voice was cracked and trembling; he was at the end of his endurance. As she drew near, putrefaction blew over her in waves. She ignored the stench, just as she ignored the images that flashed in the darkness. Her brother, Rian, and the girl he was to marry—Audree, that was her name, though Niki hadn't remembered how she looked until her image waved at her from out of the darkness. Not Rian and not Audree, Niki knew, just as she knew that it was not Brady holding his arms open to her.

Taryan stepped between her and Brady. "Hello, Niki."

"Go away."

"We need to talk."

"You're not Taryan."

"You're wrong, you know."

"No, I'm not. Taryan is back at Horesh, not here in this strange place."

"I meant you're wrong about Brady. It's not me. Never was. I mean, I wanted it to be but—"

"Shut up. I found the lock of hair he carried." Niki kicked the ground, furious that she had even responded.

"But that's the thing. I hid it in his pack. It mattered nothing to him, which was why he lost it so easily. When he came back from that last transit, he told me that we couldn't be. He told me he loved another."

Niki fumbled with the flint, resisting the ridiculous hope that this Taryan was real and telling the truth. "Liar."

"Dear me. Could the pot be calling the kettle black?"

"What are you talking about?" Niki muttered.

"You lie quite as easily as you accuse me of doing."

The wolf nudged her leg. "You're right, wolf. I'm a fool to talk to what isn't real."

"I'll tell you what wasn't real. The story you told to get accepted into training—what you said about your faith. One big lie, wasn't it, Nik?"

How did this thing—whatever it was—know about what had happened on the Ark? Something that no one else knew. It must be some sort of virus—that was it. A new mog that somehow burrowed into people's brains and mocked them with their own secrets.

"Are you listening, Niki?"

"You're not real."

"Neither was what you said. You lied to all those people."

"Shut up."

"Not your fault, not at all. You were only twelve years old then. But smart—you knew what the builders wanted to hear. All those theology courses."

For Niki, those courses had just been a waste of time. But she had to pretend to be interested. Otherwise, they wouldn't have let her continue training. And even if she had to pretend, she had done the work. She had tried her best. If God knew anything, He had to know that she always tried her best.

Suddenly she couldn't see Cooper or even feel the wolf. "Cooper, where are you?"

LISTEN.

That voice again—something out of the darkness as well, but not of this darkness. Unfortunately, Niki couldn't stop to discern who was friend and who was foe. She had a mission. She needed to find Cooper.

LISTEN.

She strained for his voice, finally hearing what was now not much more than a whisper.

Glorious . . . You are glorious . . .

Niki saw him, little more than a wisp in the shadows. His hair hung in sweaty clumps; his face was pasty and strained. The darkness hovered about him, winged like a thousand bats, but he was not touched by it. With each whisper of his song, the darkness—nothingness—moved faster but not closer. He shivered, chilled by the icy wind that Niki also felt.

"Cooper, if you can hear me—I'm coming!"

He tipped his head as if trying to listen. His mouth still formed the song, but his eyes widened as he finally saw her. "Niki?"

"Cooper, I'm coming! I'm almost there, I just need to—"

He closed his mouth, his lips tight together.

"Cooper, don't stop singing. Not now, not while I'm almost there."

He looked at her with eyes too sad for someone so young. "I hope this helps you, Niki."

Cooper opened his arms and let the darkness swallow him.

He wanted to stay by her, but something tugged harder than she did.

He snarled, though he recognized a force more powerful than the wind or ice or seasons. He was allowed to curl up and wait by her side. After a while, she put her face to his fur.

He circled and nudged until she stood up. He walked to the light, and she followed him. They both collapsed by her fire.

He did not sleep until he knew she did.

Twenty-One

Niki woke in the bright sunlight, the wolf curled up next to her.

Spring hung in the air, so sweet and warm that she breathed it in many times before she remembered what she had—*oh please*—perhaps just dreamed.

She sat up, stretching toward the sun. She winced as blood flowed freely into muscles that had been tested to the extreme.

Or had they?

She had heard of people experiencing dreams so complete that they seemed to have lived through a day or a week in the course of a night. If this was the case, the rooks would be at the boat, preferring to sleep under its shelter instead of the open skies.

But a dream did not explain the wolf. He sat up now, staring into the northeast, his ears flattened to his skull.

Niki turned slowly toward the southwest. *I can feel the sun on my back. It must be there, climbing into the sky. So why can't I see it?*

She stopped, thinking perhaps it was better to just continue south with the warmth to her back. The truth to her back, if it need be. She could take the boat, drift back to Kinmur, reclaim Tekk from the man who had ridden north to Chiungos with her and brought her horse back with him for safekeeping, cross the plains and cut through the Forest of Cholk, where mogs roamed but bears and elk still lived as well.

She could ride into Horesh and tell Brady the truth. The rooks were rebellious; they had stolen the boat and been lost on the river. He would believe her because she had never lied to him. Ever. And shouldn't that count for something?

Niki could walk down to the river, go home to Horesh, and not look back.

But she could not abandon her duty. And truly, Cooper, Kwesi, and Anastasia had been her duty.

She turned again, looking for the rising sun, still feeling it on her face, though all she could see was a swath of black where Welz was. Or where it had been. Because surely the world was being swallowed up, with Arabah as the first bite and the whole mountain next.

She sank back to the ground, face in the dirt, feeling the tears that hadn't flowed in these long years, not in all the pain and trials and fear. They came now—a rush, a flood, an affront to the girl who wouldn't stop at anything. Yet something had stopped her.

"What do I do? What do I do?"

Niki heard the flap of wings and the firm *phip, phip* of a large bird in flight. She rolled to her back. Overhead, a raven circled.

Brady had the true gift for talking with birds, and most of her campmates could send some semblance of a message. Niki had always struggled in this area, could never seem to distinguish all the tweets and whistles. But Brady had insisted she learn the whistle that all Horesh must learn, the one cry that would always be answered immediately—and answered by the camp leader.

Niki wiped the tears from her face and leaned on the wolf to stand. She took a deep breath, put her fingers to her mouth and whistled.

Calling for help.

TWENTY-TWO

EXPECTING BRADY TO WORK MIRACLES HAD BECOME A habit at Horesh.

A bad habit, Ajoba realized. Not even he could sweep down from the mountainside and oppose this battalion of soldiers.

Another bad habit was thinking the spindle was hers. Ajoba was the only one who could make it spin, but truly it belonged to Horesh. She had no right to take it out of camp. But she did, and now Alrod had it.

The guards had long since given up on keeping her away from the gargants. More had sparked with interest while a few looked at her with dull eyes. The one named Taumis snarled. "If God exists, He is without mercy."

"Mercy may yet come," she told him. *Please!* She prayed.

Moments later, she heard a familiar voice from outside the gate. "I come to serve the baron, not harm him."

Jasper. Whatever was he doing?

She yanked her chains so she could see through a crack in the gate.

Jasper stood in the clearing. Strong-arms surrounded him, swords and pikes pushed against his belly. His wrists and ankles were shackled, the cuffs big enough to clamp around Ajoba's waist.

Ghedo emerged from behind the towering rock slab that sheltered the encampment's command post. Alrod followed, dressing himself in full armor that had been mogged from some toughed-skin creature. Alligator, perhaps.

Jasper bowed to them all. "I present myself to your service."

"What trick is this?" Alrod turned to Willem. "Are the perimeters secure?"

Willem nodded. "We've been patrolling a league to the open side of the encampment and have sentries up on the cliffs. No sign of the outriders, high and mighty."

"Outriders!" Alrod slapped Willem. "They're a quarter of the size of a gargant. How did you miss this one?"

"He came scrambling out of a rockfall to the south. I believe he may have crawled out of a cave. He seems to be on his own."

On his own. Had Brady left? He never would have allowed this.

Ghedo circled Jasper. "A fine specimen. I've done excellent work here."

"He's not to be trusted," Alrod said.

Even from a hundred paces away, Ajoba could hear the smile in Ghedo's voice. "He can be if I inoculate him for loyalty. This one is ready for the potion—look how well nourished he is. Of proud bearing."

Alrod frowned. "Stop your blather and just do it."

The baron returned to the command post while Ghedo huddled with Willem.

Ajoba dared a whisper through the gate. "Jasper. How could you?"

"How could I not? Now, keep still."

The strong-arms marched Jasper into a large tent that bore Ghedo's insignia, black and gold snakes, heads posed to strike.

Ajoba slumped to the ground and bowed her head.

Brady followed Timothy and the slung through the bramble. Both men wore birthright armor, silk and metal laced with shroud. The slung was protected amply by his shell, and entranced by Timothy's singing. The young tracker had been repelled by the notion of putting his lips against the slung's ear so the guard wouldn't hear him singing, but it couldn't be helped. They came out in the corner of the pen, where the bramble twisted up into the canyon walls. Darkness provided a fine cover, though it was truly a miracle that nobody heard the song.

"Thank you, Tim," Brady whispered. "Be off now and get to work."

Timothy didn't move. "I think you need me here."

He was eye to eye with Brady. *When had he gotten this tall?* Brady wondered. It seemed like yesterday that he had done Timothy's transit. Two years of fine service, and he challenged Brady at every turn.

"Your time will come, brother." Brady lay his hand on Timothy's forearm. Holding his gaze, he dug the fingers in. "Now do as I tell you."

Timothy disappeared back into the thorns, his head still bent to the slung's ear. He would hide on the outside of the wall, waiting for Brady's call. The slung would travel inside the thorns as he pleased, spreading what Kendo had provided just as he had spread manure in the stronghold's wall of thorns. If the strong-arms were alarmed by the rustling, that would be to Brady's advantage, a distraction. Unless they could carry a sweet tune, they would never get the slung to come out.

The gargants clustered in the middle of the pen. Even sitting as they were, knees up and heads down, they formed a massive presence. Their thighs were thicker than Brady's body. As tall as he was, he only came up to the hips of most. They had been roughly clothed in burlap, their massive feet wrapped in goatskins. Their skin was slack, their hair matted. Poor souls—to not only have survived but to have excelled in transmogrification. The crown of Alrod's and Ghedo's glory was a profanity of the worst sort, a hideous denial of birthright.

Brady took in the rest of the pen. Four gargant corpses had been left to rot, a clear warning against escape. He crept silently to one of the bodies and took cover there. He scanned the ledges, knowing already where the guards were. They would be dealt with quickly when the time came.

Ajoba was shackled to the gate, singing to herself. He mimicked the call of a mockingbird. She took care not to react, but let her eyes circle the pen until she saw him. He put his finger to his lips and lay there, studying her guards. They were awake and alert, eyes constantly roaming over the mass of gargants. There was no way Brady could deal with both strong-arms without their sounding an alarm. Ajoba would need to help him. Could she still fight? *Would* she?

He pointed at the strong-arm furthest from him. She closed her eyes, let her song drift off, let her head drop forward. Feigning sleep—good girl. Her eyes went back to him to see if he had understood her response.

He nodded. *Yes, I understand.*

Ajoba put her hand up as if to yawn. Her palm faced outward, toward him. *Wait.*

He raised four fingers: *I'm four paces away.* Then two, meaning *I need to get closer.*

She nodded, again pretending to be drowsing.

He crept forward and rose to a crouch. Ready to spring, once she was ready.

She rolled toward the strong-arm and moaned. Instinctively the guard bent down. She sprang up, slamming the heel of her hand against his face. As the second guard turned toward Ajoba, Brady jumped on his back and twisted his head, breaking his neck. As he dragged the bodies into the shadows, the gargants watched in silence. One eyed the bodies and spat.

Ajoba wept.

"No time for that," Brady whispered. "No reason for that."

"But I killed him."

"As you were taught."

"I never—"

He pulled her to her feet. "You did what you must, as did I. Now, we need to get you out of here."

She pulled back from him. "No. I can't leave now."

The anger came in hot waves. Brady swallowed it back. There would be time for recriminations later, though *later* never seemed to come. Just another streak of silver in his hair.

He fished in the dead guards' pockets, coming up with the keys to her shackles. "You will leave," he told her as he unlocked her chains. "Timothy will come through the wall with our friend to take you out."

"No," she said. "I will not leave these men."

"Did that spirit come to you again?"

"No. This is my own judgment."

"You will not disobey me again. I can attend to these gargants better without you here."

"Not gargants," she told him stubbornly, meeting his gaze. "Men. And two women."

Another wave of anger, then his heart heard what she was telling him. "You're right. They're human beings. But you must leave them to me."

Her eyes went wide. "Will you kill them?"

"Surely you know me better than that."

She made no response other than to stare at him.

"I will offer them an opportunity to fight for their freedom."

Ajoba folded her arms. "They are frightened. Angry. They know me. They don't know you."

Brady scanned their faces, eyes shining out of the night. More anger than fear—a good thing in people who have been enslaved.

"I will take that chance."

She looked down at her feet. When she looked up at him again, her face was flooded with tears. "Brady, it is of no value to bring me out of here."

"Of course it is."

She shook her head. "Not while Alrod has the spindle."

He had once made shoes.

He had once wooed a woman, raised a son, helped a neighbor, drunk an ale, built a barn, laughed and cried and danced and loved and fought and worked and believed that someday it would all make sense.

Now Jasper was a freak, chained and gagged so he could become more of a freak.

He had been created in God's image, Ajoba had told him. Now, the sorcerer Ghedo declared, he was to be created again, formed according to Alrod's wishes.

Was there truly no mercy to be found in this life? She had said there was. He wanted to believe it. But despair rose in his throat, nearly choking him.

The sorcerer poked at him. "A fine specimen, Alrod. Better than all the others. It was fate that brought him to the encampment."

"It had better be fate and not some outrider trick."

"Your guards have seen no sign of them."

"We hold that strange girl and that piece of cloth that burns as their masks burn. The outriders will come."

Ghedo smiled. "This one shall be ready for them. And given another day and a good feed, all your gargants will rise as an army like none other."

Ghedo poured wine over the baron's fingers and then handed him a slim needle. "I will need only one drop of blood. Not from the tip, but from the meaty part. Once I have his eye prepared, we'll have less than a minute. Be ready, Alrod."

The sorcerer looped heavy leather straps about Jasper's skull, fastening them so tight that Jasper feared the blood to his scalp would stop flowing. Something sharp pierced his eyelid, making him cry out in pain. He struggled to lift his arms, but the chains held him fast.

"Hold still," the sorcerer said. "Or I'll snip it right off."

Ghedo slipped tiny hooks through the eyelid on his right eye and snapped them to the head straps. Jasper wanted desperately to blink, but could only succeed in bringing his cheek up to close his eye from the bottom. Ghedo repeated the process on the bottom lid, stretching Jasper's eye completely open.

"Are you ready, baron?"

"Aren't you going to do both eyes?"

"One should be enough. I don't want to risk compromising his eyesight."

"Tell me when."

"Now!" Ghedo commanded.

A second later, Jasper saw Alrod's bloody finger coming toward his held-open eye. He had a tremendous urge to shrink back, but they had pinned him like a moth on a wax tablet. He cried out again as the baron pressed the finger right against his eyeball.

"Excellent," Ghedo said. "Now back off just for a bit."

Through the crimson swirl of Alrod's warm blood, Jasper saw a needle coming. Ghedo ignored his pleas for mercy, moving closer until the eyeball exploded with agony. The sorcerer dipped the needle into a glass vial that contained a milky fluid—*good Lord, not a potion!*—and jabbed Jasper again. He repeated the process five times until that eye could see red, Jasper's own blood mixing with Alrod's.

Ghedo dabbed away the fluid. "Alrod, come here now, before he fixes on me."

The baron came into Jasper's field of vision. He tried to look away by moving his good eye, but Ghedo covered it with his hand. Jasper had no choice but to let Alrod fill his line of sight.

"Talk to him, Alrod," Ghedo whispered. "Say what I told you."

"Gargant, you will be loyal to me. To your dying day, with every breath you take, every action, every thought will be of how you can serve me. Know that I am the high and mighty one, the crown and glory of Traxx, the jewel of the east, the ruler above all rulers. Your lord now, gargant, whom you will love and serve even unto death."

No, never, Jasper's soul cried, but Alrod filled his vision, and something within him started calling out *yes*.

The high and mighty one, the crown and glory of Traxx, the jewel of the east, the ruler of all rulers, filled his eye with all that was glorious.

Ghedo unclamped the eye and Jasper drifted off. His last waking thought was of his now and forever master, the baron of Traxx.

Would the complications never end?

Jasper had voluntarily surrendered to Alrod. Ajoba said he had been led off by Ghedo to be mogged with an allegiance potion.

Not good, not at all. Brady knew from his experience with the slungs that there were ways around such potions. Allegiance potions were thought to be of the scarcest magic, but they simply required a cell line boosted with the proper genes, as well as the object of adoration to be available for imprinting. They couldn't really touch the heart or the soul. But it took time and patience to determine the way to a man's heart once the sorcerer had blocked the road through his mind. And though Brady had the patience, he simply didn't have the time.

He'd have to worry about Jasper later. Right now, he had thirty other gargants to deal with. He had worked hard with Kendo and Taryan all day, cutting aspens and sharpening them into spears. They should be moving into position right this moment. But that would all be for naught if he could not sway the gargants.

Ajoba, despite her disobedience, had done good work in the pen. Some had believed her teachings of hope; many were interested; most understood her good intent.

All thought her clearly stupid for coming into the pen they all wished to escape.

"Sister Ajoba has explained to you how God created you in His own image?" Brady asked them now in a low voice.

The converts nodded. The rest looked on, at least listening. Except for one—Taumis—who glared continuously. Might as well take him on straight.

"You have an objection, friend?"

The gargant spat, a gigantic foaming puddle. "We're swine," he said. "Once I was a respected village leader, but now I'm Alrod's sheep. Nothing more."

"You are a man. Transmogrification does not change that."

"Easy to say for a healthy man of normal size. Look at us. *Freaks*. Our own children would run from us in screaming horror. Woman would scorn us; men would drive us off as monsters."

"You have been terribly wronged. Does that mean you will just give up?"

Brady studied the faces of the others, seeing eyes of brown, blue, green. Hair color from white to black, with all shades in between. Some with no hair at all, some with too much hair. The faces of broken men with broken hearts.

"You were created to be free," Brady said. "Will you join me? Prove to yourselves that you have what it takes to fight for that freedom?"

"With what?" the bald one asked.

Brady smiled. "We have weapons for you."

Taumis leaned back in. "Why should we believe you? You're just a little scrap of flesh. Weak and insignificant."

"Because—" Brady smiled. "Because when I am weak, only then am I strong."

TWENTY-THREE

TIMING WAS EVERYTHING.

Brady had stacked the pieces of his plan but couldn't move them into play until the time was ripe. He sat in the shadows, speaking with the gargants. Most had been simple people from the villages, some from the southernmost border of Traxx, some from the neighboring stronghold of Nuevo. Many had been farmers. Some, like Jasper, had been craftsmen.

"I will find a place for you," Brady promised. Surely some outland village would welcome hefty men who could protect them from raiders.

"They won't welcome mogs!" a woman cried out.

"They will when I vouch for your good intention." He watched hope take hold in her eyes.

A starling fluttered out of the night. The gargant named Koppe batted at it as if it were a moth. "Don't!" whispered Brady. "That's friend, not foe."

"Sorry. It spooked me. The sorcerer has made us fear all flying things."

"So they can control you with their hoornars."

The bird sang good news. As per orders, Bartoly had purchased the cattle from the men driving them north. Brady smiled at the thought of having paid for the same livestock twice. Bartoly and his crew had driven the herd into the mountains, stopping outside the encampment where most of Alrod's battalion was quartered. There he and his crew had unloaded bags of grain and barrels of ale for the troops.

The strong-arms were too disciplined to drink the ale without having a taster test it for poison. They had not been as careful when it came to the boxes of honeycomb that just happened to tumble off Bartoly's supply wagon. Traxx strong-arms had a notorious affinity for sweets. Those who had sucked on the honeycomb had soon climbed into their blankets, longing for a nap. They would not wake for a long time.

Now the birthrighters would only be outnumbered twenty to one instead of a hundred to one. The gargants would even those odds considerably.

Bartoly was about to enter the main encampment with the cattle. With him were Leiha, the outrider, and Jayme and Dano, experienced trackers who were quite able to fight.

Brady whistled to the starling: *Wait fifteen minutes*. He touched Ajoba's shoulder. She looked up at him from her prayers, her eyes bright.

"I really need you to obey me this time. Will you?"

She nodded.

"Fine enough, then. When I leave the pen with the gar—with these people—you are to follow. Run to the cliff edge and climb back up the way you came down here. Don't wait for Timothy, because he has other matters to attend to now. Have I your sacred word that you will do this?"

She squeezed his hand. "Aye, Brady."

"Stay near the gate for now. Once I bring these folks forward, you step aside."

The guard on the ledge above the pen had been dealt with, but the others on the far ridges might catch movement. He moved into the circle of gargants, most of them still taller when seated than he was on his feet.

"If you're willing to fight with me, I need to know now. Otherwise, I will ask you to stay out of my way."

"What if we choose to fight with Alrod?" Taumis said. "One of our kind showed up earlier, volunteering to do just that."

Koppe glared at Taumis. "If that is your choice, neighbor, then you have been corrupted beyond all hope."

Taumis shook his head. "None of this is my choice. I'm sitting this out."

Brady looked at the others. "How about you others? Extend your hand if you will fight."

All the rest extended their hands, palms up in the manner of the villages.

He nodded. A smile was not appropriate when asking men and women to face death. "Keep to the middle of the pen while I gather your weapons."

"He's insane," Taumis said. "Where could he have weapons fit for our kind?"

Brady grinned. This indeed was the time to smile. "Stay right where you are and watch."

He popped a glowworm, waved it over his head, and waited.

It was a long drop, making it imperative that Kendo or Taryan have near-perfect aim. A spear thrown short would clatter against the cliff face and alert the Traxx. Too long, and it might kill someone in the pen. But the first spear flew straight and true, piercing the soft ground. Then another, and still another.

Brady prayed the whole time the giant spears rained from above.

Fire exploded in the sky.

Ajoba knew of Kendo's toys, but this was the first time she had seen the most spectacular of them in action. Though birthrighters were forbidden to take any technology off the Ark, they were allowed to use any resource that existed in this world, as well as their own ingenuity. Kendo had plenty of that, and it showed in the fireworks crashing above the encampment.

The gargants stood with Brady at the gate, silent but ready to charge. He wore the birthrighter armor Tylow had woven him and the mask and gloves he had made.

Another barrage filled the sky, shaking the pen and echoing against the rock walls. Kendo aimed high to illuminate the sentries on the far ledges. They would need to be taken out first.

Sure enough, Ajoba heard the *whisk, whisk* in the momentary silence—Taryan's arrows flying far and hard. One sentry tumbled from his post, then another. A third tried to take cover, but she was quick to reload, and he, too, went down.

Brady roared, and the gargants echoed him as they rushed out into the encampment. Once the way was clear, Ajoba was to follow. She carried a short blade but prayed not to have to use it. She had killed one strong-arm this night and hoped nothing more would be required.

"Come with me," she called back to Taumis.

"Why bother?" he muttered.

"You don't need to fight. But you do need to get out of here."

"Only one way out of this." He stretched out his arms and charged—not the gate, but at the bramble.

"No!"

Though he was a tower of a man, his body stuck to the nettles as a toy might. His face contorted as poison seized his airways and fried his nerves, killing him in the time it took Ajoba to run across the pen to him.

Timothy broke through the bramble at the back of the pen, following a little creature—or was it a man?—the size and shape of a massive tortoise. He bellowed over the constant *boom, boom* of Kendo's sky fire. "What are you doing here? You were told to be out by now!"

She pointed to the body of Taumis. "I—I didn't want to leave him."

"Get out now!" Timothy sang the whole time he dragged her toward the gate, though his sword was drawn and ready to strike. When Timothy had gotten her and the tortoise man away from the pen, he lit a torch and threw it against the thorns. The bramble exploded, and raging flames ringed the pen.

"What happened?" Ajoba cried, shielding her face from the fire. "What is that?"

"My little friend has been busy inside that wall," Timothy sang, gesturing toward the little man. "Since you didn't leave when you were told, you'll have to sit out the battle down here." He found them a pile of boulders to hide behind and motioned them to sit close together. She wrinkled her nose at the smell but helped Timothy wrap the tortoise man in shroud. "Keep him safe, or Brady will have our heads."

As Timothy ran to join the fighting, Ajoba picked up on the tune he had been singing.

Every knee will bow before you
for you have set the captives free!
Glorious! You are glorious! . . .

After a few minutes, still singing quietly to herself, Ajoba crept forward so she could see the fighting. Brady swung his sword against a strong-arm on horseback, who handily knocked it away. Rather than retreat, Brady leaped straight at the man and slammed him off his horse. Bartoly retrieved Brady's sword, then fought side by side with him in a dance beautiful only in its justice, not in its necessity. She saw the other birthrighters, their movements so familiar to her that she recognized each one behind his or her mask.

She prayed for each one of them by name.

Please keep Jasper in Your hands as well. Wherever he may be.

Alrod cursed hotly. "No one wages battles at night. It just isn't done!"

"Apparently no one has informed the outriders of that." Ghedo carefully packed his needles and potions. They were sequestered in the command post, watching the battle from a ridge to the west of the rock slab. Their horses were at the ready, corralled away from the rest of the canyon but accessible through a narrow crevasse.

Willem climbed up to their lookout point, his armor cracked, blood streaming from his side. "The gargants fight."

Ghedo smiled. "Excellent."

"They fight *with* the intruders."

Alrod cursed yet again. Ghedo merely sighed. "I suppose you'll have to order them killed, Baron."

"Do it," Alrod snarled.

Willem was breathless. "My men cannot stand against them. They wield coarse spears and a vicious anger."

"The girl must have been a plant," Alrod said. "Where is she? I will turn her inside out."

Willem shook his head. "I don't know."

"You don't know?"

"The gargants charged us, led by an outrider. I tried to get to her; I knew you would want that. But the bramble caught fire. And the arrows—it's like a storm from on high."

"This is absolutely absurd. Get out there and fight," Alrod said. "My army will not disgrace me by succumbing to those lumps of flesh."

"High and mighty, retreat might be a—"

"Shut your mouth!"

"You don't know what it's like out there. Retreat—"

Alrod ran his sword through the crack in Willem's armor. Something gurgled in the back of his throat, and he toppled.

"He had a point, Alrod," Ghedo said dryly.

"As do I." Alrod held up his sword, shining with Willem's blood. "And I intend to use it on the outrider who initiated this madness. Now, get me my gargant."

Jasper woke with a violent headache.

The clang of steel rattled his skull. The thunder of hooves and the shouts of men stirred something deep inside him, though he had never even struck another man. Through the fabric of the tent, he could see exploding lights and bizarre shadows of men twenty feet tall striking at what looked like children. Jasper knew better, knew that the small ones were vicious killers, the protectorate of the high and mighty one, the crown and glory of Traxx, the jewel of the east, the ruler above all rulers, his lord—

I AM.

Jasper craned against his shackles to see if a burning arrow had pierced his chest. His skin was whole, but the war had somehow been brought deep inside him, his mind and emotions insisting that his loyalty was to the high and mighty one, the crown and glory of Traxx, while something deep under his ribs, something unfathomable and unshakable, told him there was another lord to bend his knee to, a Lord before whom all knees would bow.

Soldiers were on Jasper now. One strong-arm unshackled him, while a second pressed the point of his sword against his neck, hard enough to draw blood. He knew he could crush them easily, but something held him back. The same something that told him they served the same master.

Baron Alrod stood before him, regal in fine armor. "Will you serve me, gargant?"

Jasper's brow furrowed, the war still waging inside him. He could make no answer.

"Have you struck him mute?" Alrod said to Ghedo.

Ghedo slammed the flat side of his sword against the left side of Jasper's face—a blow hard enough to kill a normal-sized man. "Answer, man, or we'll be done with you now."

Jasper blinked and shook his head at the jarring blow, the flesh tingling around his good left eye. Then he turned so that his right eye fixed on the crown jewel of the east, the high and mighty one. How awesome and wonderful this man—his master—was. “Aye. I will serve you, high and mighty.”

“Rise, man. Rise and defend me against all intruders.”

Jasper stood, his head brushing the top of the canvas. Someone pressed a battle-ax into his hand—an ax so mighty the strong-arm could barely heft it.

“Stand and defend,” Alrod commanded.

“I will stand and defend,” Jasper agreed.

The gargants fought nobly, the birthrighters wisely, and many strong-arms fell. But though most of the force had sampled the honeycomb and slept through this fight, they still had the advantage of numbers.

A battalion, lad.

Brady spotted Taryan high on the ledge, her bow raised, her arrows flying. He whistled for a bird even as he swung his sword, staggering as a soldier landed a blow against his arm. He parried, then thrust under and up, his sword splitting lizard-hide armor that was not nearly the protection it looked to be.

When a simple canyon wren answered Brady’s call, his heart suddenly ached for Horesh. Another ache, deeper now, as Brady remembered Niki moving at his side in battle, her sword fast and true, her loyalty unwavering, her courage unmatched. Had she been here this night, the battle might already be over. Yet this skirmish was not hers to fight, not when she had a greater one to face. Had that struggle even begun?

As Brady pushed back another strong-arm, he whistled a command to the wren: *Tell Taryan to back out of the light. She is an easy target.*

He swung his sword again, severing the strong-arm’s leg.

Brady watched the man collapse in a gush of blood and now had to beat back the longing for the day when the lion would lie down with the yearling and his outrider sword would be hammered into a plowshare.

May it be soon.

The buzz made even Alrod's skin run cold. He had ordered the hoornars to join the battle. If the gargants would not be loyal, they must be destroyed.

He and Ghedo watched from the command post, the gargant named Jasper standing between them and the field of combat, his battle-ax at the ready.

The hoornars flew into the fray, stinging everything in sight as their riders jabbed them into a frenzy. There were only three left from the original hive of nine. Hoornars were as precious as gargants, almost as difficult to transmogrify.

But they were still his best asset in battle.

A hush fell over the canyon as the gargants realized what had come upon them. Then they stampeded, shaking the earth and running over the strong-arms as if they were infants. Alrod thought grimly that this was almost a better battle strategy for the outriders than arming the gargants with those ridiculous hand-sharpened spears.

One hoornar drove them out of the enclosure while the other two stayed to take on the outriders. Alrod cursed as a flaming arrow flew through the air like a lightning bolt, striking a hoornar in the eye. The mog plunged to the ground; another precious possession laid waste at the hands of these infernal outriders.

The strong-arm riding the second hoornar flew away from the battle.

"Coward," Alrod said. "I'll rip out his heart."

"No. It's an intelligent strategy," Ghedo said. "He's using the fire in the pen as a screen."

The rider and his hoornar flew low to the ground, too close to the cliff face to take another hit from the fiery arrows. Once it cleared the brush, its rider reined it so it flew almost straight up.

"You up there!" the tall outrider called out from the enclosure. "I said to back away!"

Alrod knew that voice just as he knew the form of the man, the fool who had killed Nighteye and humiliated him. He would have the outrider's strange eyes on a plate before this night was over.

The arrows flew straight down from the ledge now. The archer had either disregarded the command or hadn't heard it.

The tall outrider streaked like a cat across the canyon, flying against the cliff as if he could scale it. He could not, of course, which was why this place had been chosen to imprison the gargants. A shadow moved higher up on the ledges. "Back down, man. I've got her," another man called.

The hoornar buzzed with fury. A woman cried out; then a man shouted.

Alrod inched out in time to see the hoornar spin from the sky, a spear through its head. The tall outrider again tried to scale the wall.

"I've got her, man," his comrade shouted from above. "She is all right."

"Don't lie."

"Attend to your business, leader. I said that I have her."

The tall outrider slumped back into the canyon.

No doubt that *business* was searching out Alrod. Let the man try. Alrod had weapons of both steel and flesh waiting for this encounter. With the gargants gone and the other outriders taking on what few troops remained, the odds were once again even—except for the loyal gargant standing between him and the outrider.

Alrod smiled.

"What's so funny?" Ghedo said.

"Perhaps this rout will all turn out for the best after all."

Twenty-Four

The sting of a hoornar carried enough venom to kill ten men. But this hoornar had stung one gargant after another. Would it have expended most of its venom before going for Taryan?

"I'm taking care of her," Kendo had shouted from the ledge. "Get on with it."

"Is she all right?"

"She's alive. Trust her to me and get on, man."

Though the battle was over for now, time was not on their side. The strong-arms they fought had either been slain or were making a fast retreat. But their unconscious comrades would wake soon unless the birthrighters ran a sword through each one of them, and no one had the stomach for that. Where was Alrod's command center? It would be unwise to charge through camp without knowing exactly where to go.

"You on the ledge!" Brady knew not to shout Kendo's name aloud.

"I said, I'm taking care of her."

"I know, mate." Brady tried to infuse his voice with confidence. "I need one more flare. In sixty seconds."

"Done."

Brady told his comrades on the ground what he wanted. Another blaze of light split the sky, with each of them looking in a different direction.

"There." Jayme pointed to the northwest, at what had seemed to be a cliff face. The light from above allowed her to spot—and

Brady now to see—the glow of transmogrification. With the gargants gone from the encampment, the odd glow was likely from Alrod's mogged horses.

If the baron were still here, he would be heavily guarded. If he had fled, hopefully he had left Ajoba's belongings behind. Her bag was simple and shabby, nothing that would interest a noble. Certainly Alrod couldn't begin to guess at the significance of the spindle.

Brady sent Leiha and Jayme to stand sentry at the entrance to the encampment. "Find some Traxx armor and put it on."

"What a disgusting notion." Leiha wrinkled her nose.

"It will give you some cover if the sleepers begin to wake."

Bartoly and Dano moved with him toward the suspected site of Alrod's command center. With little trouble and no noise, they took out the strong-arms safeguarding the entrance.

What appeared to be part of the cliff face was in reality a flat-faced slab of rock that had calved from the cliff, probably millions of years earlier. Viewed from straight on, it was indistinguishable from the actual rock wall. As they crept closer, they saw the flicker of lamplight and an increasing glow of transmogrification.

The sky overhead had grayed; dawn was less than an hour away. They needed to get this done and be on the road toward Horesh before those drugged strong-arms roused.

Brady slipped around the slab of rock and spied the command post not far up on a ridge. He motioned Bartoly and Dano to stay back. As he crept forward, he could smell a heady musk of perfume and battle, an odor he recognized as Alrod. He inched now, unsure of what stood around a hunk of rock that towered between him and the ridge.

What was behind the rock face was Jasper.

The gargant's face was swollen and bruised on the left side, and the right eye was bloody. He stood watch, a massive ax in his right hand. Before Brady could back away, Jasper spotted him.

"Stop!" Jasper pressed his huge hand to Brady's chest.

Brady held perfectly still, eying the ax. His armor would not stop a blow from such a mighty arm. "Jasper, it's me."

"And exactly who is *me*?" Alrod appeared behind Jasper, clad in full armor, sword in hand and with a gleaming dagger at his waist.

The gargant was as impassive as the rock to each side of him, with no recognition of Brady showing on his face. The sorcerer must have further transmogrified the poor soul, somehow burning out his old loyalties. Through one of Ghedo's famed allegiance potions, most likely.

"I am no one you care to know," Brady said.

"I will be the judge of that," Alrod said. "Take his mask off, Jasper."

Brady stepped away. "No, Jasper. Please, don't."

Jasper swung his ax toward Brady, about to cut him in half, when Alrod called out: "No! I must have him alive."

Confused, Jasper lowered his ax.

"Jasper! Dear brother!" Ajoba ran up, Bartoly behind her.

"I tried to stop her, leader," he said.

Brady waved him silent. If they made it out of this alive, surely Brady would have to exile her to one of the sanctuaries. But there was no time to worry about that now.

"Get back," he called, motioning frantically to Bartoly. "Way back. All the way back." *All the way*—the command for retreat back to Horesh. "I want our wounded attended to immediately. Do you hear me? Take everyone."

"Surely you don't mean everyone, leader?"

"Do it! Someone needs to do what I say!" Brady grabbed Ajoba. "You go with him, or I swear—"

Jasper slammed his fist against Brady's torso. Brady doubled over, thankful for the armor that transferred half the blow somewhere out-of-time.

"Stop it!" Ajoba screamed. "Jasper, don't do this."

"You'll do as I say." Alrod was confident the gargant was his alone to command. "Bring the baggage to me."

Jasper picked Ajoba up as one would a child and placed her beside Alrod, who gripped her arm and pulled her roughly toward him.

Brady heard a tiny swish—Bartoly crawling in to intervene. "I say do not approach me!" he called behind him. "Go all the way back. Do it now!"

He listened, satisfied by the fading rustle that Bartoly had backed off.

Alrod sheathed his sword and brandished the dagger. "Take your mask off, outrider, or this girl will feel the brunt of my wrath!"

"If that's your wish, Al, I would be happy to oblige." Brady took his mask off.

"Come into the light."

"Let go of the girl and I will," Brady said.

"Come into the light, or I will drive my dagger through her skull." Alrod held the gleaming knife poised next to Ajoba's ear.

Brady walked toward him. Jasper blocked his way.

"Let him pass, gargant." Alrod said.

Brady took his time, letting Jasper get a long look at his face. Jasper squinted down at him, wincing in pain. His left eye was nearly swollen shut. His right eye still leaked blood.

"Jasper, my brother," Brady called up as he passed. "Remember the truth you know. The hope you see. The love you hold. The love that holds you."

Whether the words had any effect, he could not tell.

"Outrider!" the baron was yelling, "The girl will suffer until I see you in the light!"

Brady rushed past Jasper. Indeed, Alrod had nicked her ear. But she had not cried out, would not cry now. Nor would she meet Brady's eyes.

Alrod moved the blade from her ear to her back. "That's better. Her loss would be a tragic waste. I need fresh talent for my private use."

Ajoba stiffened, now meeting Brady's eyes.

See, he longed to shout. *See what you have brought upon yourself and your comrades?* But this was no time for recrimination. Just more gray for his hair—if he lived to see it.

Alrod's eyes glittered with intense interest. "You are big, strong. Even look a little familiar. But I expected someone more fair of face."

"I am sorry to disappoint."

"Disappoint . . . what?"

Brady frowned. "I am sorry to disappoint you, Al."

Alrod pressed the knife against Ajoba's throat. She gasped.

Brady glared at her as he bowed low. "I am very sorry to disappoint you, high and mighty one of Traxx, the shining one who dwells among the thorns, the scourge of the strongholds, the jewel in the crown of this dark world, the great and glori—"

"That will do, outrider. I recognize sarcasm when I hear it. Take one step closer."

Brady obliged, his eyes still on Ajoba. Would she defend herself, or had the fight gone out of her? Now Jasper was behind him. Brady would need to know his location before they could make any move.

"You are young," the baron was saying. "But you have much silver on your head."

"I have many troubles. You're holding one right now."

Alrod laughed.

"Perhaps we could work a trade," Brady said. "Straight up. Me for her. I assure you, I am far less trouble."

Alrod snorted.

"I could be of service in ways your strong-arms cannot."

"An empty offer, outrider, since my gargant guarantees that I have you *and* her in my custody. Now tell me your name."

"On one condition."

"You are in no position to dictate terms."

"I could lie to you. But I swear on my honor that I will tell you my name if you bring your gargant to where I can see him. If I am to die, it would suit me to take the ax to my chest rather than my back. If you allow me this, I will tell you my name. In fact, I will tell you my full lineage."

"Is this a trick?"

"My nerves are frayed, baron. I'll speak more freely if I can see the gargant, that's all."

"Fine. Gargant, move to his side."

Brady shuffled to the left as if to shrink away from Jasper. "I'm going to back up one step," Brady said. "I want to see his face to be sure he won't strike. He seems unstable."

Alrod laughed. "Unstable he is not. I have made sure of that. Now tell me your name."

"Don't cast your pearls before this swine," Ajoba called out.

Alrod slapped her.

Jasper jolted forward and stepped back just as quickly, left eye straining to see from out of the swollen flesh.

"Be quiet, sister," Brady said.

"Yes, be quiet. The men are speaking." Alrod's voice was almost giddy. "Let's hear your name, outrider."

Brady rubbed his face, feigning despair and resignation. In truth, he wanted to distract Alrod from the shift of his feet. He needed to angle his body so Jasper would get a clear look at him out of his left eye. He bowed deeply. When he straightened, he was indeed in Jasper's full line of sight. "I am Brady of Horesh."

"I am not familiar with Horesh," Alrod said. "Where is this place?"

"We are a tiny river community. Often overlooked and quite insignificant."

"And your lineage, Brady of Horesh?"

He smiled up at Jasper. "I am a child of the King."

Alrod looked down his nose, eyes narrowed. "What king?"

Brady spoke to Jasper now, his gaze locked on the gargant's swollen left eye. "His kingdom is not of this world."

"You speak nonsense, outrider! What nature of kingdom would it be if not of this world?"

"Jasper," Brady continued. "You know this kingdom—where

the poor are blessed, where those who mourn are comforted, where the merciful receive mercy and those who make peace know peace. The kingdom where no tear will ever again fall, where the blasphemed body that this snake Alrod has thrust upon you will yet find its true glory because the Prince of Peace has promised all of this and more."

"What manner of lie is this?" Alrod roared. "Kill him, gargant, for I will not bear such talk in my high and mighty presence. Kill him!"

"No, Jasper!" Ajoba cried. "Hear me, dear brother. You are a child of the King as well!"

"I command you, gargant. Raise your ax and strike off that arrogant head. Now, gargant."

A pebble tumbled behind Brady.

"No, riders!" Brady called out. "No!"

"Are you deaf, gargant? I command that you swing that ax. Now!"

Brady raised his hand—not to the gargant, but to any possible rescuer. He could just as easily drive his shoulder into Jasper's groin before the gargant swung the ax, and Ajoba might possibly be able to extricate herself from Alrod.

But this is not about her or me, is it, blessed One?

And so Brady of Horesh knelt before Jasper and offered the gargant a clear shot at his neck.

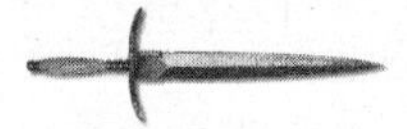

Jasper swayed, torn by confusion.

Alrod's voice echoed in his ear—the high and mighty one, the crown jewel of the east waving his sword at Jasper, telling him to swing his ax down through that frail neck. How easy that would be. And how he desired to serve and to bring forth blood, because this was a sacrifice with which he could honor the baron, his lord.

Except there was another Lord. The little sister had told him about this kingdom, too, which lay not beyond the reach of this world, but deep in the heart of those who loved the great Lord.

But oh, Jasper's heart had been fouled and ripped and would never be worthy of such a One. Would he not be wise simply to serve the one lord he could see?

He was lifting his ax, readying his strike against the neck of this frail son of man, when a mighty voice cried out—not to his ears but to his warring heart. And something deep within him cried back *yes*.

Very deliberately, Jasper dropped his ax and reached down for the baron's sword, wresting it easily from Alrod's hands.

"What are you doing?" the baron said. "I command you—"

He raged on, but Jasper was listening now to what lay deep inside him. Slowly he hefted the little blade, raised it high, then twisted it into his own right eye, amused that both Ajoba and Alrod cried in unison, "No!" The searing pain felt almost like a deliverance. If this eye of his was what caused him to follow Alrod, then he would gladly do without it.

He threw down the sword and turned for Alrod.

"I command you—"

"You command nothing," Jasper bellowed as he pulled Ajoba away from the baron.

"Back off, Jasper," Brady called. "I can take care of him."

But Jasper set the girl down and moved toward Alrod, driven now by a righteous outrage at what this piece of human refuse had dared to do to the crown of God's creation, to Jasper's brothers and sisters, their children, their world. But the blood from his right eye socket flooded his face and obscured what little vision he had from his left eye.

"Where are you?" he shrieked just as his toe caught on something. Arms windmilling, he lurched toward the ground. Jasper landed hard, lay there stunned, then pushed up with an elbow, still searching. "Where are you?" he repeated, groping with a blind hand.

"Here, fool," the baron grunted as he swung the mighty ax and let the momentum drive it deep into Jasper's heart.

TWENTY-FIVE

AS ALROD RODE INTO THE SUNRISE WITH GHEDO AT HIS side, his thoughts spun in ugly circles. This Brady of Horesh must be a wizard, and powerful indeed, far beyond Ghedo or any of the stronghold sorcerers. Who else could reverse a perfect allegiance potion? Who else would bow so confidently before the sword of a gargant and yet rise up again?

Though few in number, the outriders had struck down all of Alrod's personal guard and turned his gargants against him. Surely they were all wizards to cause such a rout of royal strong-arms. And yet this Brady had let Alrod escape, more concerned with a single dead gargant than a live noble with a talent for vengeance.

Rage filled him, and he spurred his mount. Ghedo raced to keep up, but Alrod paid him no mind. Like some fleabitten mutt, the sorcerer could find his own way home.

His powerful warhorse thundered on, and eventually Alrod felt his fury settle. There was a grim satisfaction in riding like this, no troops at his side, no hoornars flying overhead. Simply a man—though a great and glorious man—riding across the plains. True, the outriders had robbed him again and again. First his assault on Slade, then his gargants. Yet he had something of theirs as well—that strange cloth the girl had worn at her belt. Truly there was something to be gained in all of this, a knowledge that Alrod would use to his advantage.

To his advantage and his own glory.

Jasper was still alive, but barely.

Brady pushed the gargant over on his back and held the huge ax still in his chest while he bellowed at Ajoba. "Get your spindle!"

"I don't know where—"

"Find it!"

"Pull the ax out. Please, Brady, I cannot stand to see him that way."

Brady gave her such a look that she feared he would strike her, and truly she deserved no less. With no further word, she ran into Alrod's command tent and found her pack under a blanket of such fine quality that she snatched that as well.

"Is there any wine in there?" Brady called.

"Yes!"

"Bring that too."

Jasper moved under the ax, blood trickling from his chest and flowing more freely from his eye socket. "Let me die," he whispered.

The veins in Brady's arms bulged from keeping the ax in place. He had planted his feet on Jasper's shoulders, his weight barely sufficient to keep the weakened gargant from thrashing. "This is not the day for you to die, brother," Brady said with such gentleness that Ajoba wept.

When he turned his gaze back to her, his face again was hard as granite. "Get the spindle out."

She dug through the pack, breathing a sigh of relief to find it still there. "Now what?"

"Spin me some shroud—if indeed you are still allowed to."

Jasper's breath came in great gulps, fluid gurgling in the back of his throat. Brady breathed deeply to muster strength for keeping the ax still.

Ajoba raised her right palm to the air and dared hope that the glimmer she saw was not the rising sun coming off the rock but glint. And truly it was, because it flowed across her hand onto the spindle, faster than she had ever seen.

The spindle filled in a matter of three breaths. "Brady, now what?"

"We need something to serve as a needle. A sliver of bone, perhaps. Or a piece of metal."

"I have just the thing." She used Brady's dagger to sharpen the end of her crochet hook and fashion an eye in the other end. She offered it up, but he shook his head. "Thread it with the shroud."

Ajoba did as she was told. "Now what?"

"Come to my side. To my right, Jasper's left."

She did as she was bidden, first placing the soft blanket under Jasper's head. She could not bear to look at the hole he had made in his face. His head jerked as he went in and out of consciousness.

"I am about to remove the ax. You must be ready to sew the wound immediately."

She nodded, having sewn flesh before. But the ax went deeper than flesh, had surely sliced through the bone to the organ beneath. How could Brady think that stitching Jasper's chest together would save him?

Brady stepped off Jasper's shoulders and moved to his head, staring at the gargant with a fierce love. "Brother, you need to be still. It will be a mercy if you pass out, and I invite you to do that now."

Jasper's left eye burned through the purple flesh. His lips tried to form a reply, but he simply went still.

Brady looked at Ajoba. "Are you ready?"

She nodded.

"Pour the wine over my hands and yours, over your hook and thread, all the thread—"

"Not on the spindle. That wouldn't be right."

"If you cannot obey, woman, I invite you now to walk off and never—*never*—cross my path again. For surely you are begging to be counted among my enemies."

Ajoba bowed her head. "I'll do as you say."

"Pour the wine as I have said. Including over the spindle and Jasper's chest. Be sure that the thread is soaked through."

She did that. Brady waited a minute, his head bowed. When he looked up at her, his eyes were so clear they seemed bottomless. "You must stitch where I tell you. No matter what, you must stitch."

"I will."

Brady uttered a deep grunt and yanked the ax from Jasper's chest. Ajoba gasped as he reached into the widened gash and pulled the edges of bone apart, exposing Jasper's still-beating heart. With every beat, blood gushed from the organ.

Ajoba knew that there was no hope—until she saw Brady reach into Jasper's chest, seize the heart, and close the gash between his hands. "Now, Ajoba. Sew here."

She shuddered, feeling faint—but if not her, whom? She pierced Jasper's heart, drawing the hook through, and with it the thread spun from shroud. She stitched again and again.

"Closer. The stitches have to be tighter."

Ajoba felt Jasper's huge heart beat against her fingers. She gasped deeply so she would not pull away. This was insanity—to dare such a procedure out in the world. Though the Ark had superb medical facilities, it seemed foolish to try to heal a man's heart without a trained surgeon and full operating suite. Yet it was a blessing that Brady had the courage to try.

She stitched and stitched, learning quickly to pierce the tissue between beats and to draw the thread on the beat. Slowly a seam took place, and the grasp of Brady's hands became a matter of four fingers, then three, then one finger, and then, at last, a tiny hole between Brady's index fingers.

"Wait," he told her as she lifted the needle again. "Pierce my finger."

"Why?"

"You have lost the right to ask me anything, but for the sake of grace, I will tell you. Allegiance potions are blood-based; that

But he said to me, "My grace is sufficient for you, for my power is made perfect in weakness." Therefore I will boast all the more gladly about my weaknesses, so that Christ's power may rest on me. That is why, for Christ's sake, I delight in weaknesses, in insults, in hardships, in persecutions, in difficulties. For when I am weak, then I am strong.

2 CORINTHIANS 12:9–10

TWENTY-SIX

FOR MOST OF THE FIRST DAY, BRADY SLEPT, TRUSTING his horse to follow the raven. He slouched in the saddle, certain that Thunderhoof would not shake him from her lofty back.

At first his dreams were jumbled and disturbed: Taryan swept off by a hoornar, Niki throwing a raven into the wind, an ax swinging down on his neck, Kendo calling him over and over, Brady himself calling for his parents. Then they dissolved into sudden, vivid clarity, and he was reliving another first day.

The four of them were young, unbelievably young. And eager. And frightened almost out of their wits. At least Brady was, though he would not say so.

"Who will bring our husks up to the surface?" they asked their elders.

"We don't know."

"Who will open our husks once we're there?"

"We don't know."

"Why can't we bring an extra husk, one with supplies?" They knew the answer, because everyone had received exactly the same message, even the youngest children among them. But the elders answered anyway: "Because we have been told to send you with nothing except your unders."

"No weapons?" Niki asked that.

"Nothing but the spindle." Tylow pressed it against his chest. They had already discovered it turned and spun only for him.

"And your training."

"How will we live?" Kendo asked.

"*Will we live?*" Brady wanted to ask, but he didn't dare.

The dream shifted, and Brady was in his bed on the Ark, hearing his mother and father sob in each other's arms. They were afraid to let him go, and he was afraid to go. But he feared staying even more. Surely this tug in his heart that pulled him toward the surface would rip him apart if he stayed on the Ark.

Another shift, and he stood with the others near the airlock, soon to be bundled into his husk. The good-byes were endless and yet far too short. Just before their injections, Brady looked left to Kendo and Tylow, right to Niki. "See ya when I see ya, eya?"

Kendo winked. "Don't get seasick, joe-boy."

"Hey, I'm the top-boy. You watch your stomach, joe-boy."

Niki rolled her eyes, impatient as usual with their boasting. Impatient to be off.

With one last kiss from their parents, they slipped into sleep. Then Brady jolted awake, startled not to be inside his husk. Thunderhoof lumbered along gently beneath him. He scanned the sky, saw the raven still leading, then leaned on his horse's neck again.

Dozing. Dreaming he was trapped.

Brady fought to get out of his husk, a black-snouted beast chewing at his shoulder. It took him a full ten seconds to recognize the animal as a polar bear, a split-second to remember how deadly these creatures were supposed to be. Yet it padded away, leaving him to struggle out of his husk.

His comrades' husks lay nearby, but his feet were too numb to move toward them. The polar bear came back, its breath incredibly foul but very warm, thawing his feet while he turned to look for the miraculous provisions that had been promised. There—on the ice—a beat-up, bulging burlap bag. Brady yanked it open to find four complete sets of clothing: parkas, masks, mittens, boots. He scrambled to dress, knowing that everything from his hood to his boots would fit perfectly.

Under the clothing he found four short-bladed swords—or were they long-bladed daggers? He hefted each one, found the blade that fit him, and used it to open his comrades' husks.

Kendo emerged first, his arms already in motion as if planning the camp he would build, the weapons he would forge, the marvels he would bring forth using only what this fallen world—and providence—could supply. Then Tylow, quiet as usual, assessing the situation, appropriated the burlap bag to stow the spindle that made the transit with him.

Niki rose out of her husk unbowed by the cold. She opened her arms and raised her face to the brilliant sun breaking through the clouds. "Finally, brothers."

"Aye," Kendo whispered, while Tylow nodded.

"Aye and amen," Brady added. "What a world."

Brady awoke a full day later with a raging thirst and a nasty saddle rash.

Following the raven, Thunderhoof had carried him farther west than he could have imagined possible in that time. He dimly remembered drinking water, seeing that his horse was fed, checking for the raven. But mostly he had slept.

The Arojos rose before him, no more than a half-day's ride through the Forest of Cholk. He would let Thunderhoof rest until midday, ride on toward Kinmur, then camp overnight. He dismounted and found some grass for his horse.

Dust arose from the south, a brown smear against the sky.

Brady had forgotten about the toxland that bounded Slade from the plains of Brennah. It was a small patch as such went. He had seen toxlands that smoldered along a thousand leagues of seacoast, the only remnant of human existence the twisted steel towers of long-lost cities. Though he had never been able to grasp the physics, he understood full well about bombs that could chew the very essence of matter. The technology existed on the Ark to do just that—to use brutal and final force to end transmogrification and other crimes against creation.

"Why don't we make them stop? We have the weapons to do it. And if they're not enough, we have the science to make more." He had been just a child when he first posed that question to an elder.

The answer he'd received whenever he asked was always the same: "The Endless Wars solved nothing."

Now, as he gazed south toward the toxland, Brady felt an unexpected tug in his chest. His forehead furrowed at the insane idea. He couldn't take a detour that way, not when a raven had come for him. He looked skyward, expecting the bird to confirm his hesitation, but it swooped down at him, then changed its course toward the toxland.

Brady shrugged, then led Thunderhoof to a patch of scrub birch. "Stay here unless you're in danger." She shook her mane as if to say, *I've worked for days straight. Of course I'll stay here.*

Brady walked south. The raven took flight, high overhead.

An hour's hike brought him close enough to see the edge of the bomb-scarred land. The rocks were scorched black, the ground barren. The brown glow that only a birthrighter could see hung like a curtain that made his eyes ache, telling him, *This far you may go, but no further.*

Brady sat on a boulder. The tug had become a fist, holding him, and for that he was grateful. He could walk through the region and out the other side to Brennah. The damage would not be apparent until days later, when his hair fell out and his skin blistered. The vomiting of blood would only be the next sign that his body was being scorched from the inside.

He had no intention of going forward. But why had he been compelled to come here in the first place?

Something crawled toward him out of the dust. Brady went to stand, but that fist stopped him, so he went to his knees, sitting back on his heels in a nonthreatening pose. The creature inching toward him from the edge of the toxland was as grotesque and deformed as any sorcerer's work but had no mog glow. Some sort of lizard, Brady surmised, though he felt no impetus to draw his sword for defense. The creature had a hide as thick as a slung's but flexible, wrinkling as it moved. It crawled on its belly, forelegs and hind legs moving crabwise. But as the creature drew nearer, he saw fingers instead of claws and eyes that burned with awareness.

A *rad-man*. Not a myth then, though no tracker or scout had ever seen one. The villagers spun tales of humans who had taken to the toxlands in their efforts to escape the stronghold princes and their sorcerers. Most had died, but those few who survived bred children as deformed as any mog. This was their face, then.

It—he—stopped ten paces short of Brady.

"Good morning," Brady said, startled when the rad-man spoke back in a thick, slurred voice.

"Ye dare here?"

Brady smiled. "I do."

"No man dare here." He said *man* as if it was a curse.

"I misspoke. I didn't dare to come here. I was drawn here."

"By what? We no riches."

"I have no need for riches. But I always seek blessings. So when one greater than I drew me your way, I followed."

The rad-man turned a slow circle. He had a tail, studded with spikes. Brady still felt no move to his sword, though his gut clenched with cold fear and—*God help me*—a touch of revulsion.

The creature completed the circle, breathing heavily through a mouth that was three times the width of normal. His tongue looked like a slug, hulking and slimy. He had no teeth that Brady could see, and little that could be described as a face. His features were slashed into the same scaled hide that formed his body.

"One greater? How?"

"I don't understand. Do you mean how was I drawn?"

"You greater than me. And mine own."

Then Brady realized that beyond the rad-man were others like him, resting on their bellies, their tails flicking.

Brady got onto his belly and crawled forward until he was an arm's length from the rad-man. "Our skin is different. Our eyes, mouths. What we eat and how we sleep—all different. But I am not greater than any of you."

"Who, then?"

Brady smiled. "There is One who has made me and you brothers."

"No."

"Truth. Yes. You and I are brothers."

"Cannot be."

"Always has been. This One who made us so calls me and you—and yours—as His own."

The rad-mad crept backward, distrust flicking across leathery features. "Cannot be!

"The greater One does not look at appearance. Will you hear of this One if I speak?"

The rad-man spun again, his tail like a whip. Brady dug his hands into the dirt, trying not to flinch away. The others crept forward, surrounding Brady.

"We will hear," the rad-man finally said.

It was nearly nightfall before Brady finally left the place.

One day for the raven to find Brady, Niki thought. It was a long way, but ravens were hardy birds.

How long for Brady to find her?

On her way to transit, it had taken her three days to make the ride west from Horesh to Kinmur. She had not ridden hard, but surely Brady would. Kinmur was south from here, a half-day's travel downstream. The Camara flowed fast this time of year; it made no sense to force a boat north against its currents. Even so, Brady could go to Kinmur and ride Thunderhoof north along the river. The horse was a good swimmer and could cross streams as needed. Or Brady could swing the long way north to

Chiungos, borrow another boat from Rebeka, and come south on the river. That would be the easiest.

He could also move as the crow flies—or the raven—daring to cross through the Arojos. Yet if he attempted that, he might come upon Welz, not knowing the danger that lay there.

Trying to figure it all out made Niki's head split.

Brady would come. Best leave it at that.

Niki and the wolf fell into a routine. She built a campsite by the river, anticipating that Brady would come that way to get to her. She would toss in her blanket all night, lapsing into a sick sort of sleep just as the morning mist rose from the river. Then she'd wake at midday, her mouth rank. She had no appetite, though the wolf always had a fresh kill waiting for her.

He would not eat one bite until she did. She ate for his sake, and for Brady's. Niki would need all her strength when they battled . . . whatever it was they must battle. After she ate, she ran along the river until her legs burned. Then she doubled back, racing beyond pain. She would spend an hour training with what little sword she had left, vanquishing fantasy mogs and strong-arms, not daring to imagine the darkness she and Brady would have to face.

Before the cool of night set in, she swam in the river. She begged the wolf to join her—he truly reeked—but he would not budge from the bank, where he watched her with worried eyes. Though sun-warmed from running over the rocks, the river still ran icy in its depths. Niki dove there, summoning the memory of rescuing Cooper from the bowhead, hoping to find the same courage to rescue him again.

After her swim, she'd rebuild the fire and force herself to eat more of the wolf's provision. He seemed to have an affinity for boar, though once he brought her three gophers. Then she would roll into her blanket and try to sleep, numbering the stars that were as countless as the sand under her, and yet coming to what surely must be the end to find herself still awake. Sleep would roll in with the mist.

What could be taking Brady five days to find her, she asked the stars after yet another long day. They were silent, so she answered for them: *nothing*. There were only two reasons he had not come by now.

He was dead.

Or he had chosen not to come.

Niki could not decide which would be the worse.

On the fourth day, as Brady and Thunderhoof struggled over yet another Arojan peak, a hawk drifted overhead. Not an unusual sight—until the hawk dove for him. Brady drew his sword. Yet he saw no glow, no sign that the bird was anything other than the wonder it had been created to be.

Brady extended his arm. The hawk honored him by taking it as a perch. It squawked in quite comprehensible tones a message of joy from Kendo. Taryan lived, and now lived well. The hawk went on, something about Ajoba being confined to her hut and the gargant still unconscious. The message concluded with a question: *Do you need help? Shall we come?*

Of course he would need help, but—after glancing up at the circling raven—he knew this was his task alone. He had sent Niki on transit for a reason known only to him. He would bring her back. And to do that, he needed to rely on what he was given, to follow the tug inside, just as he had followed the detour to the rad-men.

He whistled his reply, added a blessing, and sent the hawk to flight.

Brady climbed with renewed vigor. The raven soared this way and dove that way, sometimes choosing the route, often just keeping close. Brady would have taken the southern route to avoid these mountains, but the raven had not taken his lead when he tried to turn southwest. So they climbed on—up one mountain, down its western face, only to face another peak.

On the fifth day, Brady saw the eastern face of Welz, the tallest mountain in the Arojo range. Though the sun blazed on his shoulders with midday vigor, a strange shiver ran through him.

The raven perched and would go no further, though they had daylight left. Brady tethered Thunderhoof and scouted the location. Mountains rose on all sides, though blessedly nowhere near the heights of the Bashans. Yet the going had been slower than he expected. And now the raven had stopped.

Was Niki here?

Brady checked the brush, searched around boulders, climbed ledges, but there was no sight of her. He climbed onto Thunderhoof and urged her westward.

The raven stayed.

Brady had to turn back. He would not find Niki without the bird's guidance, so he could only conclude that there was a purpose for his delay.

He led Thunderhoof to a stream and let her drink. He unsaddled her, brushed her, and gave her some oats. He built a fire to fight the sudden chill and put some cornmeal in a small pot of water. While it cooked, he lay in the sun and sucked on some sweet cane from his pack.

The sky above was as blue as Niki's eyes and just as unreadable.

On the sixth night, Niki moved her blanket down to the river. Perhaps the rush of water would soothe her, help her sleep.

That the creature of the darkness could haunt her with its words was ludicrous. Dangerous. Yet those words swirled in her head like an eddy in the current.

You lied to all those people.

She hadn't known then and still didn't know now what it all meant. The sky above was a mighty stretch of emptiness and scattered stars. Her meager campfire could kill her with its flames.

What power could a star wield, and how tiny that when compared to what God must be?

Niki believed in God's greatness. How could she not, when she saw the miracle of creation and what the Creator had done to preserve it? She had come out of transit stunned by the beauty of the sky and entranced by the feel of crisp air. But as they traveled south into the settlements, the dreadful state of this world had become more evident, as had the miraculous nature of the Ark. And how could she not believe in God's love when she had felt it in the touch of her mother, seen it in the wisdom of her father, known it in the kindness of Tylow, the creativity of Kendo? The goodness that was Brady?

How could her confession be a lie when she knew all this? The creature in the darkness spewed one falsehood after another, and so this accusation must be. Yet it haunted her so that sleep could not come.

Would you give up being an outrider if God asked that of you?

If not an outrider, what would Niki be? Not the beloved of her beloved—she knew that, despite what the darkness claimed. Not a leader—her disastrous guardianship of the rooks had shown her that. Not a teacher, certainly. A scout, perhaps, though scouts were trained separately and wandered the world singly.

What could God ask her to be, if not an outrider?

BE MINE.

Niki sat up, looked around. The wolf's eyes were open, locked on hers.

"Did you hear something, wolf?"

He gave himself a head-to-tail shake, circled, and sat back down. Niki scratched his nose, then pulled the blanket over her head and tried to sleep.

Twenty-Seven

Niki saw the raven long before she heard the footsteps, before the wolf growled low and disappeared into the underbrush. By habit, she crouched and reached for her short blade, but knew she wouldn't need it. Instead she rushed into Brady's arms when he appeared. The tears came then, a torrent of shame and fear. He held her until the flood subsided and she could breathe without a sob in her throat.

They sat down by the fire so she could tell him what had become of the rooks. "I'm sorry, Brady. So sorry."

"Shush, gal. Sometimes things happen for a reason. Tell me again about Arabah."

She went over Cooper's solitary, then told him about Azazel. "He seems to have taken the camp captive—the rooks too. He broke my sword." The tears came again. "You worked so hard to forge it. Look. Useless."

"It may still be of use, Niki." He leaned back against his pack and closed his eyes, his hand still on hers. She let him rest, content to look at him.

Brady had changed in the time they had been apart.

His hair stuck up in scraggly patches, barely a knuckle long. His thick beard had been shaved, though it was growing back, heavy bristles lining his jaw. There were new lines about his eyes, understandable after what Ajoba had done.

Disappointment had haunted his eyes when they talked. Truly, Ajoba had let him down, but Niki's failure was far more stunning.

She took her hand from his, ashamed to make any claim on him—even that of comradeship.

"Nik."

She grunted but wouldn't look up. She didn't want to show him any more of her tears.

"Gal, on guard!" Brady had sprung into a fighter's crouch, his short blade in one hand, dagger in the other. "There is a wolf circling the campsite."

"Put your blades away." She extended her hand, and the wolf came to her side.

"What is this about?"

"The wolf and I are comrades."

"Comrades?"

"As in birthrighter. He fought at my side. When I couldn't find my way, he was by my side, leading me."

"Well, if that's how it is—I'm always happy to make the acquaintance of a good man." Brady reached for the wolf. The animal growled. "He doesn't appear to want to share you with your other comrades."

Niki ran her fingers through the animal's ruff. "Wolf, if you would follow me, you must also follow my pal."

The wolf turned a circle and came back to Niki.

Brady got on his knees and inched forward. "Old man, if you're going to be a birthrighter, we've got some business to do." The wolf hunched his shoulders but let Brady rest his hand on his head. "May the Lord bless you as you bless others."

The wolf sat up, his ears alert and his snout proud as if to say, *Of course.*

Brady had felt the chill come on long before he, Niki, and the wolf stepped from light to—*darkness* wasn't the right word. This was beyond darkness, this absolute denial of all light, and yet it had all manner of substance to it. Brady had his sword in his right hand and Niki's sword in his left.

"That's a waste," she had said.

"I'm not so sure."

Niki held her short blade in her left hand. She had tucked the wolf's leash into her belt.

"Can that old man of yours see?" Brady said.

"I don't think so. He stumbles as much as I. But he senses the way in and out, perhaps by smell."

"Perhaps," Brady said.

They had looped rope around their waists to keep connected, with a length of about twenty paces to give them room to fight if that became necessary.

"Brady! I can see you. Tell me it's the real you."

"Why? Have you seen me here before?"

She fell silent.

"Nik. Tell me."

"Yes."

"What was I doing? Because it surely wasn't me."

"You—it—was trying to make me believe something that wasn't true."

"What?"

"Something. Leave it at that."

The wolf growled.

Black fingers snaked into Brady's boot, up his legs, into his hair. Then, as he raised his sword, the assault erupted—vicious images that cut through him more sharply than any knife could. Taryan rose out of the darkness, appearing as he should not see her unless she was his wife. As she pressed her mouth to his, longing coursed through him. He denied his desire, but with each beat of his heart, it roared back.

The next assault came in the form of Timothy, watching Brady's every move, muttering, planning, plotting, waiting for him to die so he could take over the camp and claim the power.

Alrod came next, and with him every sorcerer or stronghold

tyrant Brady had ever strived against. They knelt before him, their necks on chopping blocks. A mighty sword took shape in Brady's hand. His fingers itched and his anger rose, along with a righteous pride that he could end this evil once and for all. He pulled his arm back to strike . . . but no, this judgment, while just, was not his to deliver. But lowering that sword took every ounce of his courage and every measure of strength.

And the battering continued, now a clear view of every infraction committed by every birthrighter in camp, though Brady had no right or desire to know. The vista broadened until he was back on the Ark, where he could see every sin committed by every builder, including his own parents, in such detail that he felt his skin shrivel. And this was even harder than the sword—to forgive what was his to forgive and leave the rest to the One who had paid for that forgiveness. He had to do it person by person, scene by scene, parrying and thrusting more fiercely than he ever had in battle, crying for his own forgiveness with every blow.

And then, suddenly, it was over. Brady was back in the darkness, the rope still looped around his waist. But where was Niki?

That beast of unspeakable desolation stuck his hand down Brady's throat and pulled out his heart. Niki felt everything in her come to a stop—

no breath, no blood, no life

—and she sprang to action, swinging her short blade with her left arm, slashing the creature's arm off before it could swallow Brady's heart. It flew into the darkness, carrying Brady's heart with it, and that's when she screamed and couldn't stop screaming—

Brady had his arm around her. "Nik. Shush."

"How do we fight against this?" she whispered.

"Fire."

"I don't understand. You saw the torch I made—I couldn't even light it."

"I'm not referring to a fire we can ignite."

"Then of what sort?"

"Niki. Do you truly not comprehend what I'm telling you?"

She shivered, knowing suddenly that if she could grasp what Brady was trying to say—if she could take hold of this fire—she would never again shiver, not from this kind of cold.

Apparently there was some rule about Cooper not sleeping through anything.

Anastasia and Kwesi sat next to him, their eyes closed. Their chests rose with each breath, but otherwise they were perfectly still.

This was some sort of airlock. Cooper wished he could have gone back to the garden, but somehow he and his comrades had been put in a place like the Ark to wait it out.

What *it* was, he didn't even want to imagine. Nor did he want to think about how stopping his song had helped Niki. When the last note had faded, the darkness swallowed him up, chewing him as if he were a strip of that dried walrus blubber Niki had forced him to eat. The chewing seemed to go on forever, but he had promised to stop singing, and he held to that promise. When he had been fully shredded, he'd opened his eyes to this place. Kwesi and Anastasia were already here, sleeping soundly.

Suddenly he realized he was in shroud of some sort, somehow out-of-time, and he had again failed to sleep through it.

He sat and counted the sparkles in the shroud, one shining star at a time.

An army moved in on them, creatures of razor-honed bone and iron-cored sinew, with misshapen skulls and curved horns protruding from foreheads of rock, not bone, with arms bare of flesh but somehow muscle enough to swing blazing swords.

Brady shrank in comparison to these titans. Perhaps he had gone mad, because he kept shouting, "When I am weak, then I am strong." And all Niki could think was *I am strong, but not strong enough—not for this.*

She could only parry a bit with her short blade, relying more on ducking and jumping than on swordsmanship to survive. Brady fought with confidence and vigor, though as soon as he dispatched one agent of desolation, another would come.

Where the wolf had gone, she knew not. Niki prayed he was well, vaguely aware that a fleabitten pack reject of a wolf was an odd creature with which to begin a prayer life.

The battle must end soon, because Brady's sword had begun to slow. An almost imperceptible change—but she knew Brady, and she knew his sword.

He weakened.

She had not strengthened.

The laughter started then, and that creature—*Azazel*—dared to step out from among the other assailants. He had slipped into the guise of a kind-looking man, with Kendo's dark eyes and Brady's sweet smile. Her mother's dimple was in his right cheek and the bump on his nose the same as that on her father's. His simple shirt and trousers were like any of the builders would wear.

"You expect to find strength this way, Niki?"

"Shut your mouth!"

She heard Brady shout something, but he was too far away to make out the words.

"You lay out your doubts for any and all to see, and you expect to be strong? Talk about exposing your flank. Be wise about this, fighter."

"Wise?" *No, don't speak to it. Don't listen to it. Find Brady—he's right here, by your side.*

"Right here, by your side, Niki. But he'd rather be in Horesh. You know that, don't you? Taryan needs him—she almost died. But rather than be with her, he had to come save your little lost cause."

"It's his job." *Brady, where are you? Please don't leave me.*

The man—*he's a beast, gal, not a man*—Azazel tapped his chest. "It's his job. But not his desire. You know that, don't you? For certainly he does, which is why he's fading now."

Niki looked about, choked with panic. "Brady!" she cried.

"Nik! Watch behind you!" She turned to see Azazel swinging an ax down on her head. Brady deflected the blow with his sword, but the force spun him away. Azazel smiled and swung the ax in a circle, intent on severing both their heads. Niki raised her broken sword and Brady's short blade, forming a cross. The ax split the short blade but sheared to the side, missing her by inches.

Brady leaped back in, his sword raised to block the ax. He plunged his dagger into Azazel's side but couldn't get his arm back, howling with pain as his hand disappeared. Niki grabbed him around the waist and used her weight to pull him back. Brady's arm was stripped of its skin, his muscles hissing, his face contorted in agony. Azazel swung the ax. Brady got his sword up one more time, but Azazel shattered it. And then, before Brady could duck, he slammed the blunt end of the handle into the side of Brady's head.

He went down slowly, almost as in a dance, as the light flickered from his eyes. "Take up your sword, Nik," he whispered. She grappled in his belt for her sword, knowing it was broken and useless. But if she was to answer to any authority, it must be Brady's—not this Azazel, who wanted to be her lord and master.

Azazel raised the ax again, going for Brady's neck. Niki swiped with her sword—too short, she couldn't reach—but the wolf leaped out of the darkness and bit into the creature's arm. He cursed and flung the wolf from him, the poor beast yelping as he tumbled away.

Niki moved toward Azazel, her truncated sword held before her. Maybe she could use the hilt to club him.

"You won't stop me now. Your sword is useless, outrider." The creature leered at her. "Say good-bye to your *pal*, gal."

He raised the ax.

Brady lay there, stunned and unable to move.

Azazel swung the ax in a sweep to Brady's neck.

There was only one thing she could do.

Niki leaped on Brady, covering him with her body. She heard the ax coming, felt the blade part the air on its way to her neck. She knew that this was the final blow, that the girl who wouldn't stop at anything would be stopped by this.

The ax stopped a hair from her neck.

NIKI.

What?

WILL YOU DIE FOR BRADY?

Of course I will.

WHY?

Because I love him.

AS I LOVE YOU.

I don't know how to know that.

WATCH.

And in that infinitely tiny space between the ax and her skin, a brilliant light slipped, the Light of all people, the Light of even an outrider named Niki, the Light of an astounding love, of a precious Man and amazing God.

Finally she understood all that was necessary, and it was simply this.

In an infinity that lasted only long enough for her to breathe, "Yes," her hand tingled and her sword became whole.

She pushed back against Azazel, his breath piercing her skin like a thousand sorcerer's needles and yet incapable of wresting any change from her. Niki jammed back with all her might, pushing Azazel up and off her and Brady. She kept pushing until they were on their knees and then upright, face-to-face.

Azazel cast the ax to the side and brought out a sword. He swung and she ducked. He jabbed and she pushed forward into the blade, knowing that this weapon she had been given would stand up against anything this vile beast brought against her. Niki laughed because she heard Cooper's song in her ears, singing "Glorious" as she beat this creature back into the darkness.

Suddenly her sword was too short to reach him.

She jabbed and slashed, but Azazel stood just out of her reach.

"This far you go, outrider. But no farther."

She jumped for him, but the darkness had solidified. She couldn't beat it or kick it or slash it—Azazel was safe in his dark tower, and nothing she could do would open it. Yet she wouldn't stop because she had not yet been told to stop. So Niki battered the darkness, her fists going numb, the clang of her sword sharp and sure but still unable to break through.

Brady was up now, his arms around her to pull her away. "That's enough for now."

"The rooks . . ."

"Niki, it is time to retreat."

And the girl who stopped at nothing let her camp leader pull her away.

As they walked backward, the darkness exploded outward with an ear-shattering roar. Niki felt herself sucked into an icy void, but she held tight to her sword. And to Brady.

A strange sensation—something wet. A ringing noise. That fetid smell . . .

Niki jolted awake. She lay facedown in the dirt, the wolf licking her ears.

"Brady? Brady!"

"I'm here, Niki."

He wiped the sweat from his eyes and looked over at her. She blinked against the bright sun. Not the sun—the reflection from her sword. "It's fixed," she gasped.

"Not fixed, Nik. *Forged.*"

They sat in silence, trying to catch their breath.

"Gal?"

"What?

"Your wolf stinks."

"I tell him that, but—"

"Nik?"

"What? Are you going to tell me I stink?"

"I'm going to ask if those three lumps by the water are your rooks."

"No!" she jumped up and ran.

"They aren't? Niki, wait!"

"They can't be dead. Brady, they can't be. Please, God, don't let them—"

He grabbed her arm, pulled her away from them. "Hush. They're sleeping, that's all. Let's let them rest awhile longer."

She squinted at him. "Going soft, pal? Can't deal with rooks anymore?"

"Can you?"

She laughed. "No."

They slumped onto a rock and sat side by side, watching the river flow by. After a while Niki asked: "Is it truly over?"

He wrapped his hand on her arm, gripping her like a vise. "You haven't looked back yet, have you?"

She shook her head.

He took her hand, helped her to stand.

"Let's do it together." He wrapped his arms around her waist from the back, put his cheek along hers, and turned her face to the east.

She saw blue sky, the lesser Arojan peaks, trees and hilltops. But the mountain called Welz was swathed in fog, a veil of dark haze the sun couldn't penetrate.

"What about Arabah?" she asked. "Are they lost for good?"

"I just don't know. We'll have to do something, but in this moment I don't know. Will you ride out with me against this?"

"Well, yes. If you still want—" She bowed her head. "The Lord willing," she whispered.

"Amen, Niki of Horesh. Aye and amen."

TWENTY-EIGHT

"HOW YOU GRABBIN' AND SHAKIN' WITH THAT HORSE, Kwesi?"

"Um, fine, sir."

"The name's Brady, mate."

"Yes, sir. I mean Brady."

Brady turned to Anastasia. "What are you staring at, lass?"

She gasped. "How did you know?"

Niki laughed. "Eyes. He's got them everywhere. Better get used to it."

Brady grinned. "Stasia?"

"It's just—*she* said to lose the jangle," Anastasia said.

"Then I guess I'd better lose it, eya, Nik?"

She laughed again and slapped at him. "Stop doing that. My ribs hurt when I laugh."

"I know. That's why I do it. Pain is a beautiful thing."

"You won't think it's so beautiful when I . . ."

Niki's voice drifted off as they pulled ahead of Cooper, that ratty wolf of Niki's keeping right up with them.

He had reined his horse back because he liked to ride behind all the others. Not because he didn't want to be with them, but because he wanted to take this all in. The outriders, Niki and Brady, rode tall in their saddles. His fellow rooks were a little shaky in theirs, but who was he to judge? He had fallen off his horse three times since leaving Kinmur. Since leaving . . .

No, he had left that all behind as Brady had told him to do. Kwesi and Anastasia didn't remember anything except some man who claimed to be from the Ark. Next thing they knew, Brady had been helping them get to their feet.

"But you remember, don't you, lad?" Brady had whispered in a quiet moment by the river.

Cooper couldn't meet his gaze. "It was my fault."

"This is far bigger than any of us, and far smaller than we need to worry much about."

"If you say so."

That had been a week ago. Since then, they had hiked down the mountain, floated to Kinmur, and then ridden through forests, across plains, over hills, and—all the time—under a sky so big that Cooper felt lost. And yet, somehow, he also felt found.

Brady glanced back at him, clucked, and pressed his heels to his horse's side. "Come on, lad. Ahead are the Narrows."

Cooper held on tight as his horse raced for home.

Twenty Nine

Timothy sang at the wall, knowing now how long it would take the slung to come out, how long it would take to pass through.

Kendo was too busy managing camp to question his absences. Bartoly and his crew were nursing the gargant back to health, while all Taryan could do was sit in the sun. Ajoba was confined to her hut.

Two days ago, he had learned which window belonged to Dawnray. Yesterday he had gotten her attention and drawn a smile from her.

Today he would find a way into the palace. Tomorrow he would take her hand, put it to his lips and declare his love. And then, when the time came, he would rescue her from Traxx. What choice did he have when she had taken his heart captive?

Brady would not be pleased. But this was Timothy's heart to give, not Brady's.

Soon couldn't come soon enough . . .

Glorious

Can you hear the distant thunder?
Can you feel the tremble of the earth?
Can you see His Spirit moving?
Let us sing the power of your word.

As it was in the beginning
it will be for ages yet to come.
You're The Lord Almighty.
You're the One and Only Son.

Chorus:
Glorious! You are glorious!
We sing your praise in all the earth!
Glorious! You are glorious!
We sing your praise in all the earth

People come from every nation.
Gather 'round and let your spirits rise.
Raise your hands, a mighty chorus.
Lift it up and shout it to the skies!

You're one who heals the wounded.
You can calm the storm at sea.
Every knee will bow before you
for you have set the captives free!

Words and music by Victoria James ©2004

(Victoriajamesmusic.com)

More (Timothy's Song)

Dark may rule the day. Deep may be the pain in this place.
Hide, you slip away. Still believe love remains.

Time, you can't ignore knocking are the days upon your door.
Fear, the soul is torn. Please believe I love you more.

Chorus:
More than sands of time,
More than stars of night,
More than all the tears that you've cried,
I will love you all my life

Flowers may fall and fade, memories of life, better days
Fire, there burns a flame. Still believe love remains.

Storms, emotions roar. Tempests, like the wind, batter doors.
Gone, all you adore. Please believe I love you more.

Softly Singing to Me

Whispers on the water echo on the hills,
None is found that's sweeter than your face.
Mysteries and melodies are riding on the wind;
Those whispers in the air can never take your place.

Constant is the river that's leading me to you.
There's a yearning, churning in my soul,
I hear a well-known sonnet playing soft upon my ears.
And find this gentle voice will somehow lead me home.

Chorus:
Sing to me. Move my heart.
Sing of beauty the eye may never see.
Sing of forever. Sing of a lifetime.
Softly singing to me.

When I'm at my journey's end I hear you call my name
inviting me to quench this thirsty soul.
Rest assured this tender root will somehow find the rain
And like the springs of earth, love will freely flow.

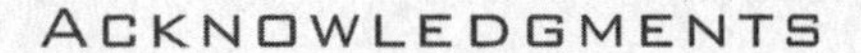

Acknowledgments

I OWE A HUGE DEBT OF GRATITUDE TO TODDI AND Kevin Norum who made their Saco retreat available whenever I asked for solitude. I'm grateful to my husband Steve who never complained when I ran off to the beach to write.

A warm thanks to colleagues who gave me a early read, including Beverly McCoy, Judy Loose, Bob Sanchez, and Lee and Max Duckett.

I am appreciative of the fine music of Steve Bell—his sharing of God's gifts goes a long way in keeping me centered. I thank the Lord for the partners He provides to help birth these stories, especially my editor, Jenny Baumgartner, and my agent, Lee Hough. I'm also grateful for Anne Buchanan who smoothed the final labor pangs of this book.

I'm also grateful for Victoria James who wrote three songs for this book and has blessed me and my readers. Go to Victoriajamesmusic.com and enjoy the rousing chorus of Glorious as well as the two love songs that the tracker Timothy 'sings' in this story.

Also look for Christian Chillers from Kathryn Mackel

The Surrogate

In the spine-tingling suspense of *The Surrogate*, desperate parents discover too late that their "perfect" surrogate mother is an impostor whose criminal ties and inner demons haunt them and their baby— even from the surrogate's coma.

Kyle and Bethany Dolan reel from years of infertility, miscarriages, and finally, a disastrous hysterectomy. They are desperate to find the perfect surrogate mother to carry their last frozen embryo. Sable Lynde, a computer genius with a dark history, is desperate to escape her own inner demons, her dark past, and a dangerous loan shark. Sable assumes the identity of a surrogacy candidate so perfect that the Dolans welcome her into their family without reservation. As the pregnancy progresses, the dangers of Sable's deception escalate until the unthinkable happens—Sable's dark demons spill out into the Dolan's lives—even as she lies in a coma. A thrill-ride of suspense and terror, this novel leads readers to a breathtaking climax. engaging characters, contemporary issues, and deep questions of faith make this story an unforgettable read.

"With a deft touch, Kathryn Mackel weaves contemporary ethical issues into an extraordinary pulse-pounding thriller that will keep readers up at night. *The Surrogate* rides like a roller-coaster and reads like a dream!"

—Angela Hunt, author of *The Debt* and *The Awakening*

Another Christian Chiller from Kathryn Mackel

The Departed

Millions of television viewers watch Joshua speaking to the dead, but none see his inner spiritual battle. Unexplained Voices. Desperate Apparitions. A Dangerous Coven of Witches. Welcome to *The Other Side.*

Joshua Lazarus and his wife, Maggie, are reeling from the overnight success of his new television show, starring Joshua as a *medium*—passing messages to the audience from their dearly departed. But when strange voices begin to haunt him without relief, and ghosts seemingly cry out to him for help, he realizes he's involved with forces he never before believed existed. As Joshua and Maggie try to make sense of the visitations, a closer, more visible force is preparing to attack. Between the killer who hunts him and the pervasive occult presence in Salem, Massachusetts, no one close to Lazarus is safe. On the brink of being consumed alive, Maggie and Joshua must fight for their lives—and their souls.

"A fabulous read! . . . *The Departed* gives riveting insight to the unsettling dangers of opening a door to the occult. I can't wait for her next endeavor!"

—Kelly Neutz, *Namesake Entertainment*